A LADY UNDER SIEGE

B.G. PRESTON

A lady under siege

A NOVEL

B.G. PRESTON

VOLATILE
BOOKS

A Lady Under Siege

© 2013 B.G. Preston

VOLATILE BOOKS
PO Box 31088
University Heights RPO
Victoria BC
Canada
V8N 6J3

Edition ISBNs
Trade Paperback: 978-0-9918618-0-4
Digital Formats: 978-0-9918618-2-8 (Epub)
              978-0-9918618-1-1 (Kindle)

First Edition 2013

This edition was prepared for printing by
The Editorial Department
7650 E. Broadway, #308, Tucson, Arizona 85710
www.editorialdepartment.com

Cover design by Kelly Leslie
Cover images © iStockphoto
Interior graphics by Vectorian
Book design by Morgana Gallaway

To Nilanjana, for all time

In a clothes chest in her bedchamber Sylvanne found the stub end of an old candle. With a shock she remembered the luxury of fire—the smell of cooking, the sensation of heat in the mouth, warming the throat all the way down to the welcoming belly. Such thoughts had once sparked angry pangs of hunger, but now her belly felt as a void, resigned and resentful of its emptiness. She brought the waxy little remnant down to the Great Hall and found a tinderbox by the fireplace. Fumbling to strike steel to flint, she teased a spark to ignite the tinder, and finally cupped the candle and its delicate wee flame in her hands.

She craved more. A broom of rough twigs leaned by the hearth. She took it, upturned it, touched its tips to the flame, and dreamily watched as a burst of purple and orange leapt from stalk to stalk. So beautiful, she thought, like a suitor's beaming face at the dance. How my suitors once beamed.

Her maidservant Mabel entered the hall and stopped short at the sight of black smoke curling up to the tall timbered ceiling, and Sylvanne holding the flaming broom like a lover. It wasn't the fire that shocked her so much as her Mistress's illuminated face. For a moment she thought she was looking upon a ghost, for it was otherworldly how Sylvanne held the broom so close— it seemed she must surely kiss the flames as they devoured the tinder-dry stalks.

"Madame, what insanity is this?"

She yanked the broom from her mistress's hands, and stamped the flames out on the floor. Sylvanne's eyes still shone with fire. "The cooking beyond the walls tempted me, it smells of unfettered gluttony. Like a great feast," she said.

"Enough of such talk," answered Mabel. "Hunger's more keenly felt when the conscience dwells upon it."

"Do you count the days, Mabel? Do you know how many days this siege has now held?"

"I wouldn't, Ma'am. I'm not accustomed to counting days."

"When my husband fell ill and stopped his own counting, I tried to number them, but it's unnatural for me. In Lent I always left track of days to the Friar." She hung her head, looking down upon the soot-smudged broom on the floor. "A single day is but a bead on a necklace, given sense only when followed by another, and another. A thousand small suns strung upon a chain of time," she said dreamily. "The seasons are my truer measure, imposing their changes upon my sisters, the fields and forests."

"Fields and forests your sisters? Don't talk strange."

"The lands beyond the ramparts belong to my husband, as

do I. That makes us equals, them and I, like siblings," Sylvanne insisted. "I rank highest among us, because he would surrender all his lands before he will surrender me."

"My Lady, I beg you, don't talk strange," Mabel repeated. It pained her heart to see her Mistress, once so widely admired for her grace and beauty, now so pallid of skin, and gaunt. The fine velvet daydress she wore, one that Mabel knew as part of her Mistress's dowry, had become shabby and dirty, and hung from her shoulders like a starveling's shroud. Her lovely hair was unwashed.

"In this season the fruits of the fields and orchards will be full and ripe, and ready for the harvest," Sylvanne continued. "I want to look upon my sisters."

At the end of the hall a staircase led to the ramparts. Sylvanne strode toward it with great purpose. Mabel, weak with hunger herself, had no will to pursue her and only enough energy to cry out after her, "You're not to do that! The enemy men keep camp there. M'Lord forbids you to look upon that rabble."

A thin fog made for a shadowless morning, but for Sylvanne, indoors all these many weeks, even this muted natural light of the outside world blinded her eyes at first. She walked unsteadily along the uneven stone ramparts of the castle. The smell of cooking fires wafting in the open air was almost too much to bear. From below she heard a voice call out.

"Dear lady, dear lady, come down! Descend and join us in some hot mint tea. We'll gladly share with you our bread and eggs, and the herbs that give savour to such humble nourishment."

She peeked down over the side through a gap in the teeth of the crenelated parapet. Back from the walls she could make out a ragged encampment, home to the two hundred men at arms laying siege to her husband's small castle. She saw a soldier wave toward her, and others turn their heads to look up at her. One held up a plate upon which fried eggs and boiled potatoes steamed. She ducked back out of sight.

"Come out my pretty, don't be shy! Grant us a glance at your lovely visage. Why the delay in revealing yourself? Our master longs to gaze upon your celebrated beauty, to possess it for himself, which stands as the sole reason for these many weeks of fruitless siege."

Sylvanne showed herself again, leaning out from behind the parapet. More soldiers had abandoned their morning tasks to gaze up at her.

"That's better," said their spokesman. "Oh, you are a beauty indeed. Pity you're imprisoned by your own choice. Double's the pity, for there's grumbling of mutiny within those flinty walls of yours, or so we hear from the deserters who've descended to surrender themselves to our mercy. Is your husband wavering at last from his stubbornness, is he finally giving way to common sense?"

"Speak you not ill of my husband," Sylvanne cried out, but she was shocked that the words sounded little more than a whisper.

"Pardon me? Didn't catch that," was the answer from below. "I am sorry, m'Lady, but your dainty voice took wing on the wind. Unpractised, is it? And by the way, my name is Kent, and I am very pleased to finally meet you."

"I said, speak you not ill of my husband," Sylvanne repeated, in the loudest voice she could muster.

"I speak ill of no one, Madame. I pity the man, is all, and I pity you too, and ask that you pity us the same—we have our homes, and a harvest to attend to—please don't keep us any longer. Our wheat and barley plead for the scythe."

Another of the soldiers piped up, "And our wives plead for the prick!" The rest laughed heartily, and muttered things Sylvanne could not make out.

"Shut it, boys," Kent shouted. They grudgingly fell silent, and he turned his attention back to the lonely figure high on the parapet.

"M'Lady, this siege has attained forty-seven days. The mind can but imagine the loveliness you must have owned when it began. Many say it was your haughty beauty that sparked our master's obsession, but now you've grown thin and pale, my dear. Your beauty is a gemstone in need of polishing. You're curling up like a worm in vinegar, desiccating like those flowers we call annuals, when autumn brings finality to their natural cycle. But we humans are not annuals, ma'am, mortal though we may be. We're meant to be hardy perennials, to survive many a season in cycle, to bloom again each spring. Before autumn capitulates entirely to winter, can you not act a sweet, benevolent Lady, and entice your husband to waver from his obstinacy? Can you not convince him to surrender you to us?"

Sylvanne felt weak, and dizzy. She summoned all her strength to answer. "We stay behind these safe walls with good reason, with righteousness as our ally and solace. We do not intend to dismiss these days, forty-seven by your count. A timid surrender now would make mock of our forbearance."

"But you look so tired, my lovely," Kent pleaded. "Won't you come down to the fire and share a morsel? We know you're eating cold sup these many nights, it's been weeks since a wisp of smoke has risen from your chimneys. Have reason, Mistress. Think of the suffering you inflict upon the loyalists locked up there with you. Is it your ambition to watch them die, merely for the sake of your own modesty, or your husband's wounded vanity?"

"I worry more for my husband's wounded heart. His love for me is what keeps him from parting with me."

"Fa! And so your husband will die a starveling, and you too, you'll all die for love, you and everyone else cooped up within. And you, Madame, could save them all. You alone are the singular source of misery within those walls, and the source of ours without. We have no quarrel with your people. We're neighbours, near enough. Look how we've spared the free men, and the villeins, the thanes and tithing men, their wives and children, all citizens of your husband's modest dominion, who we've left in peace to live on as normal, even as we encamp in their midst. That's on orders from our Lord. We've been on faultless behaviour."

Another soldier, a fat oafish fellow, interjected, "Bloody torture, it's been, too. A siege without spoils is like dinner with no meat! What point in soldiering without the rape and pillage?"

Kent swivelled about and shouted at him. "Shut it!" Turning back toward Sylvanne, he called out, "Now Madame, if you— Madame? Madame!"

But she was gone.

2

Derek was drunk again. He leaned against the rickety old picnic table in his backyard and lit a couple of dollar-store candles shoved into wine bottles. He and his bud Ken had managed to lure two college girls home from the bar, and he was trying to create a little atmosphere, hoping to bring a cozy blush to a tabletop littered with empty beer cans, bottles, paper plates and chicken bones.

"You can't beat candlelight," he crowed. "It makes you girls look straight out of some Renaissance painting. But girls, girls, girls! In the bar you said you were up for just about anything, am I right? Padding your bohemian resume by slumming with older eccentric-type guys, am I right?" He gestured to a derelict hot tub in the back corner of the yard, filled for the moment with dusty old tires. "Wish my hot tub was up and running—we'd be bobbing for panties by now! Assuming you wear panties—I should check that—"

"I do, but not into hot tubs," said the drunker of the two girls, Kaitlin by name. She made a playful little show of lifting her short skirt and pretending to wriggle out of her underwear. Derek was mesmerized by the candlelight flickering across her thighs.

"Good answer! I'm liking you more and more," he grinned. "Shit—I wish that hot tub did work. Have a drink, there's wine I think"—he rummaged around the table, shaking various bottles experimentally—"two shots of Limona here if we're lucky, half a bottle of Peppermint Schnapps if we get desperate, there's Bourbon around here somewhere, and I know there's more wine in the house—"

"Drop the voice, Derek," said Ken, busy rolling a joint on the underside of an overturned plate. "You'll wake the neighbours."

"Fuck the neighbours! Hurry up and spark that sucker, the girls are getting impatient, aren't you girls? Remind me your names again—you're both brunette and gorgeous, I'm having trouble telling you apart."

"Violetta. She's Kaitlin."

"Fantastic names—love em! Look at that beauty of a moon, you two. Matched by you! Oh Luna, Oh Isis, or Toth, or Thoth, or whatever the hell the ancient Egyptians called you, bestow us with your blessings!"

"The Egyptians had ten moon goddesses," Kaitlin said.

"Whatever!" Derek hooted. "Bloody goddess gridlock was their downfall. Monotheists kick ass, you understand? It's human nature—big eat small till one God rules all. How do you know about goddesses, anyway? You study them at that high-priced college of yours?"

"She's on full scholarship," said Violetta.

"Hurray for you! These days only an idiot would pay for an education, when you can get it for free just going to Google Books and reading the classics. Epictetus, Cicero, de Sade, Dostoevsky, all there, all free!"

"That's not exactly how it works," said Kaitlin. "In our course packs they give case studies that aren't online or anywhere. Like, I'm majoring in development—"

"Development? Of what?"

"You know. The Third World, how to help them, how to improve conditions in places where—"

"Hail Mother Teresa here! Ken, what the fuck! Spark that motherfucker and pass it around!"

"I'm not Mother Teresa," Kaitlin protested, "But I can't look at suffering and inequality—"

"Have a glass of wine, my dear. It's an old joke, but children in Africa are going to bed sober."

"Don't say that."

"Fate handed me this life, I didn't choose it, just as the starvelings of Somalia didn't choose theirs. Better luck next time."

"Next time I'm coming back as Penelope Cruz," said Violetta.

"I thought you were her," Ken said, handing her the unlit joint. "Do the honours."

"Aren't you sweet?" she purred. "But I do honestly believe in reincarnation. It's like a karma redistribution mechanism." She held her long hair back gracefully with one hand while she lit the spliff from a candle.

"Good for you," Derek applauded. "If it brings you comfort,

cling to whatever flotsam bobs along the ocean of your mind. May we all live forever among the harp-playing angels of heaven, and may the afterlife be one giant after party. For now, we're still in the *party* party, and let's all get down in the earthly, earthy, deliciously dirty *dirt* of it."

Violetta held out the joint to him. He took it from her and inhaled ferociously. The girls watched his face puff up pink as diaper rash. He held it in for an eternity, then unleashed a smoky explosion of phlegmy hacks and coughs, exaggerated for comic effect. "Smooooth," he croaked.

Then from a height, from the shadows, came a woman's voice. "Excuse me, can you be quiet? I have a ten-year-old with school tomorrow."

It took them a moment to locate her. A second story window in the townhouse next door. There she was—a face, pretty but scowling, thirtyish, blonde hair. Derek extricated his legs from under the picnic table, stretched himself unsteadily to his full height, tilted his head back and snarled, "So who asked you to procreate? The planet's overpopulated and it's your fucking fault! Get the kid some earplugs!"

For a moment there was silence. An ambulance could be heard faintly in a distant street. The woman answered, in a low, level voice, "I'd love to keep shouting, but I don't want to wake my child." She added, with a quiet, whispered fury, "You're a monster. You're not human." Then she closed the window, and was gone.

"Just ignore her," Derek said.

"New neighbour?" asked Ken.

"Yeah. Uptight bitch."

"Cute though."

Derek shouted up at the empty window, "You're cute when you're angry!" In a softer voice he muttered, "Uptight bitch."

Violetta said, "Maybe we should go."

Kaitlin made a pouty, disappointed noise.

"You wanna stay?"

She nodded.

"You don't have to win."

"What's that mean?" asked Derek.

"We had a bet—that she was going to get some tonight," Violetta said.

"Vi!" Kaitlin yelped.

"That's the spirit," Derek cried gleefully. "I'm the last man standing, and by candlelight and moonlight on this gorgeous night I could almost be mistaken for George Clooney, don't you think?"

"Maybe," Kaitlin murmured.

"George Clooney doesn't live in a junkyard," said Violetta.

"I've got grand ambitions for this night," said Derek, ignoring her. "I'm going to tip all the shit off this table, and you'll see. Before sunrise, I swear!"

"You want to do it on the table?" asked Kaitlin, giggling doubtfully.

"Oh yeah! There's something about doing it outdoors, I love it! I'll put down a blanket. Or get a sleeping bag to crawl into—ever tried it?"

She shook her head.

"Al fresco!" he hollered joyfully. "It's like hot chocolate on ice cream, only the ice cream's on the outside and the heat's all in the middle. Frozen outside, hot inside—I've never yet seen those fuckers on the Food Channel pull that one off."

"I think I'd rather be in the house," said Kaitlin, glancing up at the window, "so no one's going to start yelling down at me."

"Inside can be arranged too," Derek said. He tilted his head back and cupped his hands for one final shout toward his neighbour's darkened house. "Thought you killed the party, did you? I don't think so!"

3

Voices outside woke Meghan. She looked around uncertainly—after nearly seven weeks she still wasn't used to waking up in this bedroom, in this house. She hated this place, a drab little townhouse sardined between unkempt neighbours, just around the corner from a stretch of Queen Street East littered with greasy spoons, dollar stores, Money Marts and Laundromats. Seven weeks since she had separated from her husband, and it felt like she had traded lives along with addresses—she had left behind a leafy, upscale suburb, exchanged it for being woken up almost every night, at two, three, or even four in the morning, by *that*.

Do drunks not realize how stupid they sound to others? Of course they don't, they're drunk, she thought wearily. It's the second time tonight that idiot has woken me up. But as she came to fuller consciousness and listened more carefully, she began to realize there was more than just the usual drunken banter going on. They weren't talking. The noises made her think of the word *rutting*. Grunts and slaps and a wet sound like suction. Like animals do it, a stag and a doe. Outdoors, in nature. Oh my God, are they really doing it outside?

From her window she could see that the candles were extinguished. A giant black slug squirmed on top of the picnic table—a sleeping bag with two bodies inside. Not twenty feet away from where she watched, they were copulating.

She shrunk back discreetly to the edge of the window, peeking like a kid from behind a tree. I can't believe I'm watching this, she thought, but she didn't turn away. I have to watch, to tell people how it ends, she told herself, straining to hear the grunts and exhortations coming from below, and fighting an urge to open the window to catch more. A tingle passed through her—the unavoidable titillation in being an accidental voyeur.

The giant slug suddenly rolled off the table onto the wooden plank of the bench seat, and a female screamed, or maybe laughed, Meghan couldn't be sure, as the bag kept tumbling downward to the ground. The girl Kaitlin wriggled free from the slug's mouth, and stood naked in the moonlight. She covered her breasts with a forearm, and let her other arm dangle down, hiding her sex from the gaze of the moon Goddesses. To Meghan's eyes there was no sense of shame in that gesture, it was modest, reflexive, and beautiful. Then she saw her neighbour Derek emerge, looking like Pan, the horny old Satyr, Pan the half-goat, with an erection slapping comically against his belly as he chased his giggling nymph into the house. Meghan watched them disappear, and heard silence give way to the faint and constant electrical hum of the city. She turned away from the window and climbed back under the covers of her bed, wondering if she had really seen steam coming off their bodies. Or had she only imagined that part?

4

Gerald lay upon his bed, sickly, unconscious. Sylvanne sat on the edge beside him, holding his hand. A maidservant stood fretting beside her. Over the maidservant's shoulders a trio of menservants strained for a good look.

"He gave the appearance of such renewed vigour just this morning, ma'am," said the maidservant, a nervous young girl named Ethelwynne. "He told the valets that he intended to go out, to palaver with the enemy, to negotiate terms as it were."

Sylvanne shot a sharp sceptical look at her, then the men.

"Did he really? He said nothing of it to me. Or could it be, now that he no longer speaks for himself, others are putting their words and wishes into his mouth?"

"It's true, I swear ma'am," insisted the taller of the men, Carl by name. "You were sleeping then, he insisted we not sever your repose. It's been many hours now since he rose. He demanded his most distinguished robes be brought to him, the same princely garments as what he clothed himself in to marry you four summers ago."

"I can see that for myself," said Sylvanne, for he wore a blue tunic she had first seen on her wedding day. The blue suited his eyes, and she remembered that he had almost looked handsome in it. Almost—she had often teased him that he had the elongated face and wide-set eyes of a donkey, and now that hunger had hollowed his cheeks and stretched the skin of his face, the resemblance was even more pronounced. She loosed a button on his tunic, and undid two buttons of the white linen shirt beneath. She watched his breathing. His breast barely rose and fell.

"I say he did what's possible to look his best, ma'am," said the maidservant. "But it almost broke my heart to see him, thin as a reed and the colour of dea—" she caught herself. "The colour of a winter's sky, ma'am."

Sylvanne held her husband by the chin. His flesh felt like parchment stretched over the jaw bone. She leaned in close and whispered.

"Gerald. Gerald."

His eyes remained closed. Suddenly she slapped his face, hard. Then again, harder, then a third blow, almost vicious. Without taking her eyes from his face, she asked, "What more did he pronounce?"

"When he was dressed he looked upon himself in the mirror, and it seemed to give him a shock, ma'am," said Carl. "He faltered, as it were, and stumbled to the floor. We lifted him to the bed as one would cradle a wounded bird, so careful were we.

Then we set him in this dignified pose, and called for you. He hasn't so much as moved a digit since."

Sylvanne watched his still, silent face.

"I wish he would speak to me."

There was silence, and then Ethelwynne spoke up, timidly. "Should I fetch the Friar, ma'am?"

Sylvanne's eyes flashed angrily. "Is that what you hold? Has his condition attained that severity?"

The young maidservant lowered her eyes and said nothing. The men didn't know where to look.

Suddenly another servant rushed in the door, wildly agitated, holding before him a long pointed stick with a scrawny dead rat skewered on the end. "Here lookit what I caught, the last o' them I'm certain." He caught sight of Sylvanne. "Pardon, m'Lady, didn't know as you were present. I've brought meat I myself cornered and killed, as sustenance for my Lord."

Sylvanne surveyed the ratcatcher and his prey. The rat was truly a pathetic specimen, and the catcher for the first time seemed to recognize that sad fact. His enthusiasm faltered.

"I only wanted to help, m'Lady."

"I do admire your strength in denying your own belly satisfaction," Sylvanne told him. "But my husband would need awaken in order to eat." She turned again to look at poor Gerald's mute, ashen face. "Appetite gnaws at the rest of us," she said wearily, "but he feels none of it. Perhaps he dreams of bread and eggs. And hot mint tea."

"If I could trouble you for something of wood to burn, m'Lady, perchance a chair, or a bench from the Great Hall, I could rightly cook this creature, and the smell of hot flesh might rouse your husband."

Sylvanne was silent for a moment. Gerald coughed lightly in his sleep. "Has it come to this?" she murmured. "Eating vile rodents to stave off death?"

"It's not the first," young Ethelwynne said, with a boldness she immediately regretted.

"What do you mean?" demanded Sylvanne.

"It—well, we had no choice but to—we cooked all we could capture for m'Lord and Lady in these devilish times," she said. "Songbirds and starlings in a soup, bugs and beetles in a paste, and even mice and rats God help me, disguised and served as rabbit stew. M'Lord knew all about it, but told us to keep it as a secret of sorts from m'Lady."

Sylvanne felt herself too weak to be shocked. She let out a sad solemn breath that was almost a cry.

"But that's all past anyway," said the maidservant. "It's been many long days since even that poor meat was to be found. The best that can be said is now we all share the same burden of suffering."

Again the room fell silent. The others waited for their Lady to speak. She stared long and hard at her husband's mulish face.

"Fetch the ratcatcher a chair or stool to burn as fuel, and let him cook that thing in the fireplace here," she said at last. "But also summon our priest. I fear he'll be needed—I wouldn't want my dear husband to pass from this life without the incantations that guarantee God's protection in the next."

"I'll find him, m'Lady," said one of the menservants. A crush of people had formed in the doorway, and spilt across the threshold

into Gerald's room, pushed forward by those in back craning
for a better view. What a motley bunch, thought Sylvanne, ren-
dered as they were so gaunt and ragged by their loyalty through
the siege. She couldn't hold against them their natural human
urge to gather and gawk, to be present at the spectacle of their
Master's passing.

In short order the priest arrived, and took up his chant by the
bedside. Sylvanne found it difficult to follow the words he spoke.
She realized she felt faint and craved a sip of water, but didn't dare
interrupt to ask for it. "May Christ appear to thee with a mild
and cheerful countenance," the priest recited, "and give thee a
place among those who are to be in his presence forever. Mayest
thou be a stranger to all those who are condemned to darkness,
chastised with flames, and punished with torments. At thy approach, encompassed by angels, may the infernal spirits tremble
and retire into the confusion of eternal night..."

The priest took hold of Gerald's wrist, and after a moment
announced, "He pulsates faintly, so he lives still." He stood and
made the sign of the cross. "Should he take leave of us now, our
Lord in Heaven has assured a place for him in the firmament. His
spirit will know eternity."

"I thank you," said Sylvanne. "I must ask you a question, concerned not with his soul and spirit, but with earthly legality."

The priest nodded.

"Since we are childless, and he has no brother, am I not his
heir? And as he is now incapable of action, am I not the person
assigned to act on his behalf? Might I do what I deem necessary
to save his life?"

"This hunger has affected my mind," the priest responded. "What is your point, exactly?"

"I wish to surrender to our besiegers, those soldiers and vassals of Lord Thomas of Gastoncoe who surround our walls. I'll throw myself at the mercy of their Lord Thomas, and thereby spare my poor husband's life, for he would surely be tended to, and fed, and revived, if I were to act in time."

"But your husband has forbidden it, and this entire siege is a result of his refusal to convey you to Thomas."

"He is no longer capable of forbidding anything. It is my wifely duty above all to prevent his death, and I can do so by proceeding in his place to the enemy, so that terms might be negotiated."

"I make no moral judgement," the priest said. "Despite the promises of paradise, I myself am in no haste to leave this earth before my time, and would welcome an end to this damnable, ungodly siege."

"Then I won't let you die," said Sylvanne. "And foremost, I will not let my husband die."

She brought her hands to her lips in a praying gesture, and noticed how filthy her fingernails were. Scraping a black rind of grit from under a nail, she called out.

"Mabel!"

The maidservant pushed her way through the bottleneck of onlookers in the doorway. "Yes m'Lady."

"I have need of a bath. A proper one."

"The water will be cold, ma'am."

"The better to shake me sensate."

"Yes, ma'am."

The crowd of gawkers parted for Mabel to take her leave. Sylvanne spoke again.

"Wait. On second thought, make the bath hot, and lay out my best clothes. I'll want to look my absolute best."

"But how shall I heat the water, ma'am?"

"I don't care. Burn all the furniture in the place if you have to."

Mabel hesitated. "But how shall I decide which pieces to start with, ma'am?"

"Jesus Christ, woman!" Sylvanne cried angrily. "Have I not enough on my plate that I must attend to every detail?"

"I'm sorry ma'am," said Mabel.

"Here's a suggestion," said Sylvanne, calming herself. "Start with the chairs and tables in the rooms intended for my children. It looks very much now like those will never be needed."

The young maidservant Ethelwynne burst into tears. The priest tried to put his hand on Sylvanne's shoulder but she shuddered and pushed it away. She told herself she would not lose her composure. To the young girl she said, "Run along and help Mabel with her tasks. All of you run along. I wish to be alone with my husband."

When the room was at last cleared she locked the door, then sat on the bed and stroked his cheek gently. All was silent but for the light wheezing of his breath. She thought of her life the first time she had seen him, a mere five years ago, when she lived under the roof of her father, a respected farmer and tithing man. Sylvanne's mother had died in childbirth, giving her life, and the attending midwife, who herself had been recently made a widow, took on the task of caring for the helpless infant. Soon enough Sylvanne's father and the widowed midwife found cause to marry. They would have five more children together, but Sylvanne never felt that she was treated as anything less than a true and beloved daughter by her stepmother, whom she always called Mother, and thought of that way. As the eldest, she assumed a heavy load of responsibilities in the family, not least of which was caring for the dairy cows, and transporting their milk to market every day, in a little cart pulled by a bulldog.

One spring day in her eighteenth year, as Sylvanne brought milk as usual to barter in the bailey of this very castle, she was spotted by Gerald, son of the Squire. For him it was love at first sight, he was indeed smitten, and boldly told her at that first meeting that she would be his bride. She was not nearly so taken by him, for he was not handsome, and walked with a limp, the unfortunate result of a childhood fall from a horse. Yes, he was certainly less than perfect as a potential husband, but bold and confident none the less, and articulate too—he wooed her with extravagant phrases, all to the effect that she was the most beautiful creature he'd ever laid eyes on. She accepted his compliments with modesty, having heard similar things from the young men who worked the fields with her father, and most especially from the soldiers loitering by the castle gate, who were always enthusiastic, if more crude and less poetic in their remarks. She was known to one and all as a radiantly healthy, honest, openhearted milkmaid, and therefore had no shortage of eager suitors—farmers' sons, handsome young carpenters and broad-shouldered blacksmiths among them—although none had yet won her heart.

Gerald was the most persistent and prestigious suitor she'd yet met. When Gerald proposed, her father, keen on improving his standing, insisted she accept. If she didn't precisely love the man she was to marry, at least she could be excited at the prospect of a more adventurous life than could be hoped for as a blacksmith's or carpenter's wife.

Before any wedding could take place Gerald needed approval from his own father, who a few months previously had set off to the Holy Land to fight the Infidel. Word was sent, and after several weeks an answer was returned, but of a tragic nature: a typhoid epidemic in Sicily had killed the father en route, and suddenly Gerald, his only son and heir, was Master of his Lands and Dominion, modest though they were—an old, out-of-date motte and bailey castle in great need of repair, and a squire's rights over the peasants who worked a sliver of lands wedged between the larger holdings of the Earl of Apthwaite to the south, and a vast forest belonging to the Baron of Flechevile to the north. As well, Gerald's father had taken with him much of the best armour and the finest of his horses, along with a large retinue of servants and retainers, on God's mission to liberate the East. Left behind in the depleted castle, Gerald, a young man head over heels in love, threw all practicality to the wind in his desire to please his bride. He emptied his storehouses and granaries, and sold the stockpiles to buy his love precious stones set in gold and silver, and supply her with the kind of dowry a Lady of higher standing was expected to bring to such a marriage: rolls of damask and saraset silk to make kirtles and dresses, and gowns lined at the hem with mink and ermine. Her father, ever-practical, had mocked her the first time he had seen her clothed in that style: "You're wearing that thing upside down," he had teased her. "That's a fine fur to keep your neck warm in winter, yet you drag it through the mud like a mop."

The wedding itself was another extravagance, and Gerald had gone into debt to pay for it, borrowing heavily from the Earl of Apthwaite to throw a party for the hundreds of guests invited from far and wide. It was a three-day festival of wine, music, and every kind of cooked meat, wild and tame. Sylvanne had been overwhelmed, and although everyone was gracious to her, and praised her beauty and deportment to the heavens, still she wondered what they really thought of this simple country girl marrying into an old and noble family, especially after overhearing a notoriously opinionated Baroness describe Gerald as "a young fool without proper counsel." The grand old woman had been pontificating to a gaggle of other ladies in the coolness of the garden between dances, not realising Sylvanne had slipped out for a breath of air herself, and was listening from the shadows. "The aim of any marriage should be to solidify alliances with families of equal or greater power," the esteemed Lady had asserted. "Poor Gerald has let love's poison-tipped arrow lower his good name and water down his bloodline, mating with a mere milkmaid, however prettily clothed for the occasion." A murmur of agreement had arisen from the ladies, and not a single voice had risen in her defence.

The dutiful daughter had agreed to marry Gerald under intense pressure from her father, and after marriage she transposed that sense of obligation to her husband. She became the dutiful wife. Did she love him? She told herself she would, with time. There were reasons to love him, for he was tender with her, and kind-hearted, though he had an impetuous streak and was terribly unwise with money. She scolded him for it, but he laughed it off as none of her concern. As a year of marriage turned to two, then three and four, and they remained childless, cracks began to show in his kindness toward her, for he expected from her the son that was essential to keeping his bloodline intact. Sylvanne's mother, with her expertise as a midwife, gave her all manner of herbal concoctions to help her conceive, but to no avail. In all corners of Christendom a barren womb could only be spoken of in public as a woman's shame, but in private, in a rueful whisper so soft God might overlook it, her mother put the blame on a caprice in Gerald's bloodline. Such a failing called for discreet cures, and the remedies she concocted to make the husband more virile had to be slipped by Sylvanne into his food and drink surreptitiously. Each remedy in turn raised her hopes and expectations, only to disappoint. She remained childless.

Her marriage, forged in great expectations for happiness, had slowly begun to metamorphose into one wherein happiness grew ever more elusive, as the essential contract at its heart was neither fulfilled nor satisfied. She lived in a kind of stasis, awaiting resolution. Then one day, out of the blue, came a messenger, an envoy from Thomas of Gastoncoe, a powerful Lord with abundant lands two days ride to the east. Lord Thomas wished a private meeting with her, an unheard of thing for any man to ask of a properly married woman. The request had aroused in Gerald a horrible suspicion, and for the first time he had struck her in anger. Lord Thomas was denied, yet persisted in his demands for a meeting, and Gerald in his jealousy could not be placated. She took this as a sign that he truly loved her, and loved him a little more in return. She worked hard to regain his trust, for she had done nothing wrong, and fully supported her husband when he rudely dismissed each new entreaty from Lord Thomas.

The strange desire of this Thomas to meet with another man's wife then took on the appearance of single-minded insanity—he raised among his subjects a sizable company of soldiers, and sent them to lay siege to Gerald and Sylvanne in their little castle, with its granary still not properly replenished since the wedding, its larder nearly bare. Thomas's soldiers encamped outside the gates, and poor Gerald, "the young fool with no proper counsel," had no powerful ally to call upon. He and Sylvanne and their loyal retinue became prisoners of the worst sort, prisoners without provisions. Rationing was required almost immediately, food was scarce and poor. A few weeks later Sylvanne missed her monthly cycle, and she had rejoiced at first, and rushed to tell her husband, who was greatly pleased that she had finally conceived him a child. Shortly thereafter she came to realise that every female besieged alongside her was suffering a similar symptom, for severe hunger makes a woman cease to menstruate. When she told Gerald, it was the most painful admission of her life, and it seemed to break something inside him. An unnamed illness began to sap his will to live, his resolve to endure and prevail over his besiegers. From that day forward she never

heard him express confidence, or optimism, never saw him
smile, or even look a little healthy, for his every word and gesture spoke of fatigue and resignation. Then his very body began
to waste away, much more obviously than the rest of them, who
also suffered hunger and deprivation. And now he lay upon the
bed, unspeaking, looking as much like a corpse as a living being.
"Live for me," she whispered to him. "Please live for me." She
told herself now that she loved him, but more than that she
could not imagine life without his protection. And she could
not imagine what strange obsession could have compelled Lord
Thomas to perpetrate this siege that was killing her husband.

Young Ethelwynne poured a pitcher of lukewarm water over
Sylvanne's shoulders. She shivered as the water ran down her
naked body. Mabel, sleeves rolled up, scrubbed her skin so
harshly it hurt.

"You murder me," Sylvanne muttered.

"I'm sorry Madame, I've never seen dirt so well-entrenched."

"Concentrate on the parts of me that will show when I'm
clothed," Sylvanne said. "All that matters is my hands, fore-
arms, my face and neck, and as much of my bosom as the dress
displays."

"You've lost weight, ma'am," Mabel remarked. "The display
won't be so ample as it once was. Luckily, I'm an expert in the
artifice such an occasion calls for."

"Just get me clean, Mabel. Stop scraping at my thigh with that
course soap, and attend to the principle places."

There was a loud knocking upon the door. Ethelwynne went to investigate and came back wide eyed.

"Ma'am?"

"What is it?"

"He moves."

There was no time to get properly dressed. She ordered Mabel to wrap her body in one of the white linens used for drying, then to drape her in two finer sheets from the bed, one over each shoulder like sashes. To hold it all together they took the first belt that came to hand, meant for a lavender dress, and tied it snug under her breasts. Thus arrayed she hurried toward her husband's room, little caring that one of the sheets had slipped from her shoulder, and that her long hair hung loose instead of coiled and hidden beneath the barbette expected of a married woman. At the doorway it seemed that virtually the entire remaining populace of the castle had assembled. They parted like cattle, deferentially, but without hurry.

The room smelled of meat cooked on the flame. The ratcatcher was busy by the fireplace. At the bedside, the priest rose to give her his place. Sylvanne knelt, grasped her husband's hand, and held it to her breast. His eyes were open. He studied her with an immense weariness. He was trying to speak, she could tell, but no words came.

"Has he said anything to anyone?" she asked.

"No," said the priest. "Yet his eyes move about. He sees."

Sylvanne leaned close and kissed him on the mouth. He seemed to draw strength from it, and ever so weakly, he whispered her name.

"I hear, my love. Speak to me."

He looked up at the ceiling as though it were the sky.

"So he'll have you after all," he said finally.

"I'll die first."

His eyes met hers.

"It is I who am dying," he whispered.

"They're cooking you a rat—a mouse."

He laughed a feeble, soft cough. A faint twinkle shone in his eye.

"Likely it's as skeletal as I," he mused.

"I should have told you it's rabbit," Sylvanne attempted in a light, jaunty tone. "Apparently that's been the protocol around here for some time." But she was fighting tears.

"I've no appetite," Gerald murmured.

"Taste it first."

He shook his head. His body shuddered, and when he spoke again it was with great effort.

"Do you know your Bible?"

Sylvanne began to cry. She wiped her tears on the white linen and pretended a laugh.

"You know I never troubled with it. Many's the time you scolded me for that."

"Ask the priest how Judith slew Holofernes."

"You tell me," she said.

His eyes grew wide for a moment, as if he'd seen something beyond this earth. A faint wheeze, the soft rattle of death, issued from his mouth.

"Tell me," Sylvanne pleaded. "Tell me. Tell me!"

She took his hand, pulled it to her breast, and began to weep. The crowd in the doorway pushed closer for a better look. Mabel lifted a corner of linen and wiped her Mistress's eyes, then her own. The ratcatcher, oblivious to all but the fireplace and the skinned carcass cooking there, now turned and announced excitedly, "It's ready, Madame, it's ready!"

5

Meghan awoke and felt her face wet with tears. She stumbled downstairs to the kitchen in a trance, opened the refrigerator and squatted there, grabbing anything that came to hand— pita bread, grapes, a block of cheddar— stuffing bits from all of them into her mouth. Ravenous, she yanked the lid from a half litre of yogurt and tipped it up to her lips to suck at its runny thickness. Yogurt dribbled down her chin.

"What are you doing?"

Her daughter Betsy, in pyjamas, stood barefoot on the cold kitchen floor, taking in the sight of her mother tearing at food like a stray dog. Meghan instantly became self-conscious, thinking how strange she must look at this moment. She wiped her face and mouth with her sleeve, and put the yogurt back in the fridge without its lid.

"I—I woke up starving," she said.

Betsy picked the yogurt lid off the floor and set it on the counter. "Dreaming your dream again?"

Meghan nodded.

"What happened this time?"

Meghan tried to say it calmly: "Her husband died." She felt weak. She closed the fridge door and slumped with her back against the cabinets below the counter. "He died. Oh God. He died," she whimpered. Tears welled in her eyes. She tried—and failed—to hide them from her daughter.

"You're scaring me," Betsy said.

"Don't be scared. It's just a silly dream," she lied. It was more vivid and intensely felt than any dream she'd ever known, and the strange, painful emotions of grief and loss that gripped her now were a token of its power. But for her daughter's sake, she attempted a light tone. "As if I don't have enough going on in my life, I've got to cry over someone else's."

Betsy got herself a bowl and some cereal from the cupboard. "If the husband is dead, then the siege should be finished, right? And that's good, right?"

Drying her face with the back of her hand, Meghan said, "It would be good if I stopped dreaming."

Betsy stepped over her to get to the fridge. "I need milk." Pushing at Meghan's leg with her foot to make room for herself, she looked down at her mother, all puffy-eyed and distracted.

"Are you going crazy?" she asked.

"What? No—why? Don't think that."

"Daddy said he left because you were driving him crazy. But

maybe it was 'cause I drove him crazy. And now I'm driving you crazy."

"No, no, no," Meghan protested. She pulled herself together, stood up, rinsed yogurt and tears from her hands at the sink, then came to Betsy. She straightened a loose strand of her daughter's hair.

"Your father is full of it, which is one of many reasons he doesn't live with us anymore. I'll have to talk to him about how he's explaining things to you. And you'd better eat up quick or it'll end up being the usual sprint to school."

"Pro D day," she said.

"Shit."

"I told you."

"I forgot. I'll have to juggle." She thought for a moment. "I can get away with working here most of the day," she said. These days she actually preferred it. Working from home gave her a break from the toxicity of office gossip. She was an illustrator and graphic designer with a well-known book imprint, part of a publishing conglomerate that was by all accounts teetering on the verge of financial ruin. "I've got one meeting this morning first thing I can't cancel," she remembered. "Hopefully I'll be gone a couple of hours, max. That's the one positive thing I can say about this house—I'm so much closer to work here. But we'll still have to get someone to come be with you. Your dad, maybe."

Betsy made a face. "No fun."

"How about a play date at Brittany's?"

"Her mom is psycho."

"Good. You can help her cope."

"I'd rather stay here—I'll keep the doors locked and won't answer any phone numbers I don't know."

Meghan hesitated. "You're giving me one more thing to stress about."

"I can handle it."

"I don't know if I can. You're ten. Have you ever been alone in your life?"

"No. But I feel like I'm alone, lots of times."

Looking at her daughter's troubled face, Meghan felt herself dissolve into guilt and sympathy. "Give me a hug," she demanded. She didn't want Betsy to see it, but she was crying again.

6

Sylvanne invited the priest into a small anteroom off her husband's bedroom. She didn't close the door. She could hear and see her loyal servants, maids and men, paying their tearful respects to her dead husband laying upon his bed. She stood by a narrow gothic window, little more than a slit, through which she could also hear sounds of the besiegers below. The news had reached them, it was clear. They were shouting and whooping, in high spirits, calling on those inside the castle to surrender. "On our Lord's good word, no harm will be done you. No judgment. No reprisals. You are free to come out in peace." She had asked her servants to wait while she composed herself. She didn't want that rabble pouring in and seizing her like some living bauble. The gates would be opened soon enough, she'd told them, but on her own terms. First, there would need to be a simple, immediate funeral for her husband, done with regrettable haste but as much dignity as possible. Before that, she wanted answers from the priest.

"You heard my husband's dying words," she addressed him. "You heard me tell him that my knowledge of the Good Book is limited. He spoke of Judith. What is her story, and how might it affect me?"

"If I were you, I wouldn't make too much of such words as issue from a dying man's mouth, m'Lady," the priest answered. "In that feverish moment he may not have been in his right mind. Judith's tale barely merits inclusion in our Bible. A most inappropriate fable, really. Quite unworthy of the Prince of Peace."

"Still, I wish to hear it," said Sylvanne.

"So be it. It's like this, Madame. An Assyrian army, under the great and fearsome general Holofernes, laid a strangulating siege to the Israelites at the walled city of Bethulia. Now within those walls, the widow Judith, a Jewess of great beauty, hatching a plan, shed her widow's sackcloth, washed her body, anointed her skin with perfume, attended to her lovely hair, put on bracelets and rings, and altogether clothed herself in her finest attire. Thus adorned, she could surely captivate any man who might look upon her. She and her maid, a loyal woman named Abra, snuck out of the city, and presented themselves to Holofernes's camp.

"Now Holofernes, charmed by her, invited her to sup with him, in the tent that served as his bedchamber. Encouraged by her, he drank a great many cups of wine. He dismissed his servants, leaving himself alone with the beautiful young widow."

The priest hesitated, for effect, letting the implications of his words sink in.

"Continue," Sylvanne bade him. "I'm not such a delicate flower as that."

"Yes, m'Lady. The scripture is not exact as to what transpired between the two. It states only that after some time Holofernes, sodden with wine, lay back upon his bed. He was thus defenseless, and brave Judith took up his sword, unsheathed it from its scabbard, and raising it high, struck him on the neck. She cut off his head! Bone and flesh and gristle, all was severed by her, using his own blade against him. Then she coolly rolled that great general's head into a sheet, and gave it to loyal Abra to carry away, tucked under her arm. Together they fled from the murderous bed, and hurried through the night, back to the city of Bethulia upon the mountain. In the morning the Assyrians looked to the city, and saw the bloody head of their own supreme leader displayed to them, high upon a long pike above the walls. They fell into panic at the sight. At that moment the gates to the city burst open, and the Jews in their armor poured forth from Bethulia, and smote their confused and trembling enemy."

The priest fell silent. "There's no more," he said at last.

Sylvanne spoke in a solemn whisper. "I fear I'm not so brave, or strong. I've never used a sword. I've never tried to hurt anyone."

"The Lord gives strength where needed, m'Lady."

"Then let him hoard some, and give it all to me in that moment."

7

Meghan hurried home from her meeting to find Betsy sitting happily at the computer in the upstairs office, exactly as she had left her ninety minutes earlier.

"Did you even move a muscle?"

"No. I've been chatting the whole time, with Brittany."

"Is her mother still psycho?"

"That's exactly what we've been chatting about!" Betsy chirped excitedly. "Did you know her mom smokes pot?"

"No, but I'll definitely keep that in mind next time a sleepover is discussed."

"She goes outside to do it."

"Oh, that makes it okay then," said Meghan. Betsy looked at her quizzically. "I'm kidding, kiddo. It doesn't make it okay, but I guess there are worse things in the world."

The doorbell rang. She went back downstairs to answer it. On the front steps she found Seth, come unannounced, for a quick talk, as he put it. Seth was Meghan's husband, "my soon-to-be ex-husband," as she had taken to describing him to friends. Meghan let him in and led him through to the kitchen. "Come have a cup of whatever," she said.

"You're being very civil," said Seth. He was carrying a shopping bag, the paper kind with handles, from a sporting goods store.

"I have to be," she replied. "Betsy's upstairs, and likely to come bounding down any minute. I've gone to great pains to paint this whole business as amicable, to convince her she's got two parents who love and care for her, and even, on some level, still care for each other. You'd better be doing the same when she's with you."

"Yeah, sure. Maybe if we say it enough, it'll even come true."

"Maybe. That would be good. Living a fiction is exhausting. But then you're more practiced."

Seth made a face, exactly the kind of face she hated him making, the kind that said, that's a low blow designed to hurt my feelings, and I think less of you for it. She wanted to shout fuck you at him, but of course, as she'd already pointed out, Betsy was likely to come bounding down the stairs any moment. Betsy, in fact, chose this moment to yell from the top of the stairs.

"Mom! Who is it?"

"Your father."

Silence.

"Hi babe," yelled Seth, with an enthusiasm so achingly fake

any ten-year-old would see through it. They could hear Betsy come down the stairs, her footfalls heavy and slow.

When she came in the kitchen she said, "What are you doing here?"

"I just came by to talk to your mom."

Without sitting down, she flipped through a magazine on the kitchen table. "So talk."

"Well darling, it's kind of like, very adult talk."

"About the divorce and stuff?"

"Not exactly."

"I can handle it, Dad."

"It's just, I'd rather—look, I brought you a new soccer ball." He pulled it from the shopping bag. "The official Olympic ball."

Betsy glanced at it and went back to pretending an interest in the magazine.

"You like soccer, Bets, don't you?"

"I *play* soccer. You're the one that likes it."

"Listen, Betsy, why don't you take the ball out in the back yard and—"

"Ha. Have you seen our back yard? It's not even big enough for anything."

"Big enough to dribble a ball. See how long you can keep it in the air."

"I don't want to."

Seth's voice turned suddenly unfriendly. "Betsy. Go outside. Five minutes, I have to talk to your mother."

Betsy looked from him to Meghan, who hesitated before taking sides.

"It might be better, sweetie."

"I don't care. I'm not going."

"Betsy, give us five goddamned minutes!" Seth blurted out.

Betsy burst into tears. She strode past her father to the back door, threw it open, stepped out onto the deck, turned back and yelled at him. "Why can't I hear?"

"She'll tell you about it soon enough," said Seth. "It'll be smoother this way."

"I don't care about smoother!"

He brought the ball to her, resting it like the world in his palm, but she swatted it away. It rolled back inside into the tangle of chair legs under the kitchen table.

"Did it ever dawn on you that Mommy might like it better if she and I can talk alone for a minute? Think of mommy for a change."

"You think of mommy! You never think of mommy. You don't even love her!"

"Five minutes," Seth insisted. He took the door handle and started to close it against her.

"It's my house, mine and mommy's, and you're pushing me out! It's not your house, it's mine!"

"Yes. It's yours," Seth said sternly. "In five minutes it'll be yours again. Outside. Please."

Betsy stepped out and slammed the door shut behind her as hard as she could. The whole house seemed to shake and reverberate. Meghan opened the door.

"Darling, please. Five minutes. For me. Just to get him out of here. Then we'll do something fun together."

"Like what?"

"Whatever you want. You think of something. Take five minutes to think of something you'd really like to do."

"Anything?"

"Anything."

Meghan hated resorting to bribery, but sometimes it's whatever works. She could see the wheels begin to turn in that ten-year-old head. "Good girl," she said. "I'll be right back."

8

Betsy watched through the window of the deck door as her mom and dad moved from the kitchen into the living room.

"Make her buy you a pony."

She turned. Her neighbour, the man Derek, was in his back yard watching her.

"Don't look at me," Betsy said angrily.

"Suit yourself."

He had a wrench in his hand, but the fence prevented her from seeing what he was working on. He bent down out of sight. She could hear hammering, metal on metal, then cursing. Then more banging, and a grunting noise, the sound a man makes when he can't get a bolt to let go of its nut. "Fuck it," she heard him mutter. Then, "Good enough."

Then he appeared again, looking at her from over the top of

the six-foot fence, as if he were standing on a chair. "Come over here, would you?"

She stood still. She had an urge to run back inside the house, but even at the tender age of ten she had her pride, and didn't want to be dismissed as a child, they way her parents had just done. She wanted to stand her ground. He watched her, waiting for an answer. She stared back at him.

"Cat got your tongue? What's your name, anyway?"

She almost said it, then didn't.

"Sorry, didn't realize you were a mute," he said.

That got her back up. "I'm not supposed to talk to you," she retorted, dressing the words in a child's snobbery.

"And why's that?"

"My mother doesn't like you."

"Whatever. I'm difficult. Difficult to like, impossible to love, or so I'm told."

Betsy began to walk in tight circles on the wooden deck. Certain boards underneath her feet made different creaking sounds. She could play them like music. She stopped and looked at him.

"How come you never go to work?"

"Is that your question, or your mother's? I don't work. I don't have to."

"Everyone has to work," she told him.

"Wrong. That's what they want you to think. I have a little nest egg and I dole it out carefully. You can get by on almost nothing if you don't worry about appearances. I call it creative indolence, or shabby happiness. I'm living it."

"It sounds weird," said Betsy.

"I disagree. I think the world is weird, and I'm the sane one. I'm centered, and consistent—compared to me, most people are bipolar."

"What's that mean?"

"It's just a label. The whole world is bipolar, you see it within five minutes of turning on a TV. Two hundred people incinerate in a hideous plane crash, then zooooop, next second, you're supposed to worry about how white your smile can be! Everyone's expected to have the psychological resilience or appropriate brain chemistry to pull constant complete 180s on our emotions, well screw that, I can't do it. I stay home, quarantine myself from the craziness, right? Stay above it. Stay high, you know what I'm talking about? I'm talking about alternate states of consciousness, which is meaningless to you because you're still a child, and your consciousness is still growing, it's elastic and malleable and unformed. Someday when you're older you'll go, 'Shit, my consciousness is so fucking formed it's gone stale, I wish I had an alternate,' which is why grown-ups love alternate states of consciousness."

"You shouldn't swear."

"Sorry. What's your name again?"

"Betsy."

"That's old-fashioned. Heavens to Betsy."

"More like to hell with Betsy's all I hear," she said.

Derek laughed. "That's pretty sharp. But don't pity yourself. You're young and nimble, sweet and petite. Look at me. By comparison I'm old, slow, slovenly, and overweight. I should be complaining, not you."

"You are complaining."

"Good. Order has been restored. Now listen up. I want you to come down to the middle of your lawn, and stand just opposite me here. C'mon, you'll like it!"

She kept her arms stiffly at her sides to show her reluctance, but she did as he asked. He stepped off the chair he had been standing on, and disappeared behind the fence. She could still hear his voice.

"Are you facing the fence?"

"Yes."

"Close your eyes," he said.

"No!" She giggled nervously.

"Come on, Betsy. For the full effect you gotta close your peepers for a sec. Are they closed?"

"Yes."

"Keep 'em closed."

"They're closed."

Her ears were assaulted by a burst of unhappy metallic scrapes and squeals, and un-oiled springs stretching and straining.

"Keep 'em closed!"

"They're closed, they're closed!"

"Okay, open 'em!"

She saw the fence, and in midair above it, Derek suspended as if weightless for an instant. Then he fell to earth, or at least fell out of sight behind the fence, and the unseen springs shrieked again, and he shot back skyward to new heights, then fell again, and rose, fell, rose, and fell, again and again. For good measure with each rebound he attempted some kind of goofy pose—hands on hips, or thumbs in ears, or biceps curled like a body-builder. The whole thing was so unexpected that Betsy, entranced, giggled delightedly. Then suddenly he flew dangerously off kilter and sideways skyward, a panicked grimace on his face. "Oh shit," he muttered, and plummeted down out of sight. She heard a soft thud as he hit the earth.

Betsy rushed to the fence and tried to peek through the cracks. A knothole gave the best view—she saw a weathered trampoline, its skin stretched tight by equally aged springs, hooked to a base that might once have been painted blue.

"You like it?" Derek asked. He was back on his feet, dusting himself off, looking a bit woozy.

"I love it," she squealed. "Where did you get it?"

"It's amazing what people throw out in the trash," he replied. "It's perfectly good, except where it's broken. Not broken. Bent a little, I should say. Would you like to try?"

"I can't."

"Why?"

"My mom would freak and have a heart attack and die."

"From a little old trampoline?"

"No, from me going to your yard."

"No no, don't worry about that, my dear. The toy is for you—I brought it home specifically with you in mind, because I've seen you wandering aimlessly around your patch of perfect lawn over there. You're like some poor little waif in a children's book praying for an imaginary friend to come along. Here's my advice—keep hopping on this little number and chanting *I think I can I think I can*, next thing you know, you'll be in orbit with the space shuttle. Or at least you'll get some exercise, get the kind of colour in your cheeks all boys and girls your age and ethnicity should have. A girl like you should be ruddy-cheeked and ready to ride a balloon to the moon, right?"

"I guess so," she said. She wasn't sure what he had in mind.

"Stand back," he said. "Way, way back. In fact, go up on the deck."

She did as told, and from there she could see him work. "See these planks?" he asked. "They're two by tens, twenty-four feet long. Almost impossible to find such a thing anymore. People say my back yard is just junk, well I say look again." He took the two planks and leaned them against the fence on a sloping angle, so that their midpoint was on top of the fence, like the midpoint of a teeter-totter. Grunting and cursing from brute effort, he slid the base of the trampoline onto the planks, then up the planks— with more grunting—until the whole thing teetered atop the fence. Then with a last Herculean push the planks tottered over, and the trampoline lumbered down them onto Betsy's side, crash-landing in a flowerbed of yellow Lion's Bane and purple Foxglove.

"Don't wreck the flowers!" Betsy screamed.

"Too late for that," he muttered. He climbed the stepladder against the fence and looked over to examine the damage. "It's barely touched them," he said proudly. "No harm, no foul—and more importantly, the brilliant part is, the thing looks absolutely level, perfectly placed for you to test it out. Climb aboard!"

9

Having banished Betsy to the deck, Seth and Meghan moved to the living room for their talk. "I hate having to raise my voice to her like that," he said as he settled onto the couch. "But it's the only thing that gets her attention. I've been very sharp with her at our place. The house, I mean. Used to be our place. I still call it that."

Meghan sat in a chair across from him. "She doesn't like being there, she's made that clear. It makes her feel creepy to be there and I'm not," she said. "Her biggest complaint is when she tries to go to sleep at night she has to listen to you and your girlfriend in bed in the next room, giggling and God knows what else. Couldn't you at least make sure she's fallen asleep before you go at it?"

"Yes, well, it's a bit of a moot point, really," said Seth. "Soon enough there'll be plenty more night-time noises to disrupt her, because what I came by to tell you, in person, is, Irena is pregnant."

Seth was a professor of comparative literature at York University, and Irena had been one of his undergraduate students. She'd flirted with him, and he'd encouraged it, but had known better than to act on it while she was still enrolled in one of his classes. On the first day after term ended and the marks were in, she was at his office door. "Now you're free to see more of me," she'd said. Soon enough they were meeting almost daily, at his office, her apartment, even at the house near Lawrence and Yonge he and Meghan had bought with a generous down payment from his parents. Meghan never caught on—it was Irena who forced Seth's hand, making him choose between her and his wife, and by that time he was addicted to her—the affair stirred his blood, and made him feel alive and virile. So Meghan moved out, Irena moved in, and he had a lot of explaining to do, to friends, family, and colleagues. He liked to say Irena was a "mature student," all of twenty-six, so there could be no stigma about it. He was forty-one. And now he was going to be a father again.

Meghan stared at him, but he avoided her eyes.

"Oh Jesus," she said.

"Yep. We're going to have a baby, we're going to get married, the whole bit."

"You sound so enthused," she said sarcastically.

"I want to be. I should be. The timing's not great."

"You stumble from disaster to disaster," she said. "Or maybe you repeat things on a ten year cycle."

There did seem to be a pattern to it, or at least a repetition. A little more than a decade earlier, when Meghan was twenty-one and an undergraduate, she'd taken a course in creative writing at U of T, led by Seth, who was then a PhD student. He came from money, and seemed tremendously sophisticated, well-travelled and worldly to her, a girl from small-town eastern Ontario—Fenolen Falls to be exact. It was an evening class, and a bunch of students went out afterward to a place where undergrads shared pitchers of beer. Seth joined them, and talked almost exclusively to Meghan, and later took her back to his place, where they made sloppy, drunken love. Three nights later they did it again, only sober this time. Prior to this her love life had consisted of a few casual and unsatisfying dorm party hook-ups, so she was feeling like Seth was a major advance, a breakthrough—her first adult romance. They slept together twice a week for three weeks until she figured out he already had a girlfriend, and confronted him. "I've dropped her," he said. "Oh? When?" "Now." After that, they saw each other every night, and within two months Betsy happened—an accident, obviously. Seth expressed true love while lobbying for an abortion, and Meghan had agreed to it, had made the appointment, but at the last minute couldn't bring herself to go through with it. And that's how Betsy came to be.

"Betsy's not a disaster," he protested. "You could say congratulations. She's going to have a sister."

"Half sister."

"I want you and Irena to get along."

"I should be friends with the woman who destroyed my marriage."

"I destroyed our marriage," he said, looking at her finally.

"Is that the new version? The first was, you were too weak, and she came on too strong. She did know you were married, even if you forgot."

"You'll need to forgive her, and me. And in time you will. Give me some credit, I helped set you on your life's path. You were just an aimless girl taking vague courses toward a useless degree, I'm the one who saw talent in your drawing and got you into OCA." There was truth in this—prodded by Seth she had switched to the Ontario College of Art to study design and illustration, juggling classes and motherhood through her early twenties, while most of her peers were partying it up. But she was in no mood to give credit.

"Thank you, Mister Svengali, I'd be nowhere without you."

They locked eyes for a moment. Seth looked away first. Being a man, he hated emotional scenes like this. He'd said what he needed to say, and was actually relieved when Meghan said, "You should go now."

She moved to the front door and opened it for him. On the doorstep he turned and said, "I think Betsy will like spending time with us, once she has a sister. More of a family environment."

"Goodbye." Meghan slammed the door on him. She leaned her forehead against it, and composed herself. After a moment she walked back through the living room, and the phone rang. Without thinking she picked it up. It was work, more specifically her friend and workmate Jan, catching her up on the latest rumours about job cuts and rolling heads. Nothing new or substantial to report, just Jan venting, mostly, until she remembered the real reason she had phoned, that a meeting about a book cover

Meghan was working on had been moved up to tomorrow. She'd need something to present by ten in the morning.

"Can you do it?" Jan asked.

"Yes of course. I'll be up half the night though."

"Don't kill yourself over it."

"I have better reasons to kill myself," said Meghan. "Though I'd rather kill Seth right now."

That started a whole other conversation, and by the time she hung up the phone, and went to the kitchen and looked at the clock, she realised with a shock thirty minutes had passed. Betsy. Through the backdoor window she could see her daughter happily bounding up and down in the air. Up and down, on what? A trampoline. She opened the door and took in the sight of her neighbour Derek watching her daughter from his back yard. His elbows rested on top of the fence and he was drinking beer from a can.

"One, two, three, go for it, Bets!" he shouted encouragingly.

Betsy did a full forward somersault and landed on her feet. Her face was flushed with excitement and pride as she rebounded skyward.

Meghan called out, "Betsy!"

At the top of her trajectory, Betsy met her mother's gaze. Her body froze, and completely forgetting herself she came down hard, catching her feet on the metal edge of the trampoline. It pitched downward and catapulted her—she frantically waved her arms and legs for balance, but in an instant she'd been projected like a missile, head first onto the lawn, crash-landing in a full-on face plant of the kind that wins prizes on Funniest Home Video shows.

Meghan raced over to her in a panic. "Are you alright, are you alright?" she cried out, but Betsy was already pulling herself to her feet. She batted her mom's helping hands away, shouting, "I'm fine. I'm fine! I'm not hurt at all."

"Let me look at you."

Betsy felt her lips. "I've got grass in my mouth," she said. "But it really didn't hurt."

"Grass and dirt," said Meghan. "All over your face."

"Think they used pesticides on it?" Betsy asked.

"I don't know," said Meghan.

Derek piped up. "Nah, the last owners never used anything. They just left it, more or less. They were really old, sweet ancient people. Deaf as posts, both of them—the ideal neighbours for me. Then he died and she had to go into a home."

"Derek gave me the trampoline," said Betsy excitedly. "Do you like it?"

"No," said Meghan, bristling at the idea that the two of them were on a first name basis. "It's old and decaying and I'm sure it wouldn't pass safety standards."

"But it's fun!" Betsy protested.

"It's dangerous. I don't want it."

"Did Daddy leave? You told me I could do anything I wanted once you finished your talk."

"He left, and yes, that's true, I did say that, but—"

"Then I get to keep the trampoline," she trumpeted. She sang it over and over, like a victory song. "I get to keep the trampoline! I get to keep the trampoline!"

"We'll see," Meghan told her. "No promises. Go inside and

get your face cleaned up, and let me talk to our neighbour for a minute."

Betsy ran into the house. Derek took a final swig from his beer and dropped the empty into the dirt behind him.

"I see you two have made fast friends," she said coolly.

"Lovely girl. Full of life," he answered.

"Yes, she is. And the key to that is to let her win some battles sometimes. I wish I didn't have to let her win this one. But I'm afraid I do."

"Excellent plan," said Derek. "Compromise is essential to civilized life. Without it we're just animals."

Meghan let that pass without comment. She was tempted to say, Yes, and speaking of animals, last night I saw you rutting like one. But the way he looked down at her over the fence put her on the defensive, as if he were the judge and she the one on trial, when it should have been the other way round. She stood as tall as she could and said, "You weren't very civilized last night."

"Was I rude?" he asked.

"Yes."

"Then I'm sorry. I don't remember it all that well."

"You were yelling at me in my window."

"I was responding to someone yelling down at me, as I recall."

"But I wasn't rude. You were."

"And I've apologized. I was inebriated, so I wasn't myself. Except that I usually am inebriated, so I guess I was myself. In any case we did kill the noise and put out the party lights, just for you, more or less. I hope you got back to sleep?"

He was smirking—as if he knew she'd watched him and that

girl going at it on the picnic table. Meghan said, "Yes I did, thank you."

Derek looked toward her house. "Betsy loves the trampoline."

"She's got a bike helmet, and knee and elbow pads from a brief interest in skateboarding," said Meghan. "I'm going to make sure she wears them. Are you sure this thing is safe?"

"When it was new, it was top of the line, it's not some cheapy Chinese knock-off. It's not new now, obviously—I salvaged it from the trash but I gave it a good going-over."

"I think I might buy her a new one," she mused.

"You look like the environmentalist type," he said. "Throwing out things that still work should be sin number one."

"But peace of mind trumps all. If you were a parent, you'd understand."

"Don't make it sound like privileged information," he said.

"I didn't mean to sound that way."

"It's common knowledge people worry about their loved ones."

Just then Betsy, her face freshly scrubbed, came bounding onto the deck and down to the lawn.

"Well?" she said expectantly.

"You can keep it," Meghan said. "I might get you a new one instead though."

"Yippee," Betsy shouted. The hug she gave her mother was the most joyful, unselfconscious, and heartfelt embrace she'd given in a long, long time.

10

It was late afternoon when the castle gate opened, and Sylvanne emerged, holding herself erectly and proudly in her finest raiment. Kent, the leader of the besiegers, was napping in the shade of a small tree when a comrade shook him awake. What he saw was a vision walking toward him. Sylvanne's light brown hair fell in waves across her shoulders—there had been no time to find or fashion a widow's cap. Her dress, a type of velvet gown called a bliaut, in a shade of deep forest green that shimmered in the sunshine, she had worn only once before, at the previous year's feast of Christmas. Its bodice was laced at the sides to fit snugly. Hidden under the hem she wore her best sabetynes, for she knew she was likely to be put upon a horse, and her feet would show.

Kent watched as she reached the first knot of soldiers. One of them let out a shout, and now all the others were running toward her. They quickly surrounded her, engulfed her, and lifted her like a trophy upon their shoulders. The mass of men that skittered toward him looked like a giant centipede, and she its unwilling fairy rider. The men delivered her straight to him, dropped her delicately at his feet, then retreated a pace or two, catching their breaths, waiting eagerly to see and hear what would come next. Whatever words were about to be spoken would be repeated around hearths and hunting fires for many years to come, and take on the quality of legend.

Sylvanne had dropped to one knee on being lowered by the men, but quickly regained her feet and her composure, straightening her clothing and hair. To Kent she looked flushed, severe, and altogether lovely.

"You've made this the happiest day of my life, Madame. Are you hungry? Fetch bread and cheese for the Lady!"

"I've come to negotiate terms," she said.

"Eat first."

In short order a soldier handed her bread and cheese on a wooden board. The smell of it almost made her faint, and despite herself, she succumbed to hunger and ripped at the food like an animal.

"Slowly, slowly," Kent warned. "Your stomach will be slow to stretch, I reckon."

"And some for my maid. Mabel! Mabel!"

Mabel pushed her way through the circle of men.

"Yes ma'am."

"Give her food also. And water for us both."

"Of course. Of course. Whatever the Lady requires."

She looked challengingly at the gawking men who surrounded her.

"Privacy while I feed," she said.

A small tent was brought and erected for her. She and Mabel sat on the ground. A cooked chicken in an earthenware bowl was offered through the tent flap, reminding her of the way prisoners are fed in a jail. Sylvanne ate slowly and deliberately, but Mabel attacked it with gusto, wiping fat from her lips with her sleeve, and dropping the bones into the bowl. "My jaw aches from chewing," she grinned. "But my stomach aches most happily."

The tent flap was pulled aside and Kent entered.

"Are we ladies sated?" he asked.

"Oh yes Sir, I never tasted a bird so fine," Mabel chirped eagerly. She dropped her smile when she noticed Sylvanne glaring at her.

"Good then," said Kent. "We'll set out immediately. It's two days steady walk to the castle of my Lord and Master Thomas. Given your condition, and the suffering you've endured, we'll mount you aboard careful, steady horses. M'Lady, you'll have mine, and I'll walk beside."

"But I'm not leaving," Sylvanne said defiantly. "I came out to negotiate, not be carried away like plunder. Why should I go to your Master? He should come to me."

"I'm afraid grave domestic concerns keep him home, m'Lady. And if I may say, negotiation takes place between equals. I have an army of two hundred behind me, and you have a maid with chicken grease on her chin. I have orders to deliver you alive and healthy, and you have no say in the matter."

Sylvanne rose to her feet and attempted to brush past him out of the tent. Kent stepped aside and allowed her to go. Once outside, the sunshine hit her eyes like a blast of fire. She staggered dizzily, disoriented. A sea of peasant faces closed in around her, mostly ugly unshaven men, with a few curious boys among them. An older man called her deary, another asked gruffly, "Where do yer think yer goin?" She heard Kent's voice behind her.

"M'Lady! You're weakened from the siege. You need more rest and nourishment. Please accept your circumstances."

The circle of faces tightened around her, and she felt hands take hold of her arms. She pulled free, then collapsed unconscious onto the trampled grass.

When she came to her senses she was curled up, joggled and jolted, amid sacks full of oats in the back of a rough two-wheeled cart pulled by a dray horse. She was still dressed in her finery, although the green of her gown was now dulled by a coat of dust. Ahead she saw Kent and a dozen mounted horsemen, to her rear came the two hundred soldiers afoot, with Mabel perched unsteadily upon a single horse. The rein was held by a fat oafish fellow walking alongside gingerly, as if there were stones in his shoes. He was sweating severely. Seeing Sylvanne awake he yelled out, "Master Kent, Sir! She arises from her slumber. That calls for a wee stoppage for a morsel, don't you think?"

Kent circled back on his mount, and tipped his cap to Sylvanne. "Are you feeling better, Ma'am?"

Sylvanne made no answer. She'd awoken thinking of her husband, and only after a moment had she remembered he was dead. She looked about her, thinking, I don't even know these men, this country.

"If we keep a brisk pace we reach home before dark tomorrow," Kent was saying to the fat man, who went by the name Gwynn. "Wouldn't you rather we reunite with wife and children under the sun's light, and not arrive to a cold hearth and a dark night?"

"You forget I have no wife, Sir," answered Gwynn.

"No, it's you forget I do."

"The lady looks in need of a cup of comfort, Sir."

"Let her express her own opinion," said Kent. He turned his horse alongside Sylvanne's cart. "Are you in need of anything, m'Lady? A sip of water, perhaps? A stop for relief?"

"How dare you dump me in a cart like a pig carried to market," Sylvanne said indignantly. "I want a horse."

"I told you earlier you could have mine, m'Lady," said Kent.

"If I may say something," interjected fat Gwynn, "I fear my feet are not meant for such gruelling hikes as these. At this pace they'll be bloody stumps by nightfall. Could I take her place in the cart, Sir?"

"Here's a man who feels no shame at being carried like a pig to market," Kent laughed. "It's true the feet of a horseman can grow tender when he's forced afoot, and I worry about mine, in fact. Here's a plan: you will have your cart ride, Gwynn, and maid Mabel will join you there. I'll take the horse she rides, and the Lady can have mine."

And so it was. Sylvanne mounted his fine stallion and slowed it to a walk, falling in behind the cart where Gwynn and Mabel sat, for it was understood that Mabel had a role to play as chaperone; to keep things seemly she was expected to keep her Mistress in her sight at all times. Kent also kept watch, riding discreetly at the Lady's shoulder.

They passed through golden fields where peasants gathering the harvest stopped to gape openly at them. Gwynn kept up a running commentary, remarking how the fields were lush and productive, and the soil of these lands must be very fine. "They belong to the Earl of Apthwaite, and he's been very gracious to let us pass through unhindered," he informed Mabel. "Of course it's not entirely from the kindness of his heart, for young Gerald was deeply indebted to him, and now that he's deceased, the Earl will be quick to gobble up his lands and properties as payment."

Kent told him to shut his mouth, and not speak of such things within earshot of a Lady in mourning. Sylvanne said nothing, but seethed within. After some time they left the fields behind them and skirted dark forests where the ages of trees were measured by centuries. For a stretch the woods enclosed them, and the men and horses were required to walk single file. The cart was wider, and square-shouldered; rogue branches slapped and rapped against it, causing Gwynn to wrap his arms around Mabel protectively. "Hang tight, I'll not let any old tree snatch you from me," he snorted.

"It's what *you* might snatch that worries me," Mabel retorted. "Your hands have already taken liberties for which, if I were upon terra firma, I'd slap your face crimson."

"Shall I let go then?" he asked playfully, leaning close against her. Just then a deep rut jolted the cart and nearly sprang Mabel airborne.

"No!" she cried. "Hang on to me."

"With pleasure."

Mabel pushed against him as if he were a lumpy armchair. "This is the furthest I've ever been from home, and the furthest from comfort, too," she said. "And what's that poking me?"

"In my breeches there's a bone, Madame, though it's made of flesh."

"Keep your flesh well clothed, so that I might keep my chastity intact," Mabel scolded him.

"Chastity? Have you no husband?"

"Never."

"Then you're overripe. The fates must have made this meeting, for I have lost a wife."

Kent and Sylvanne, riding close behind, couldn't help but listen to this banter. Kent turned to her and asked, "And you m'Lady? Ever further from your home?

Sylvanne stared straight ahead. "I have no home," she said.

"I sympathize with your circumstances. I'm certain your mood will improve when you come to know my Lord and Master, Thomas of Gastoncoe. A more honourable man you are never likely to meet."

"Honourable?" Mabel shouted indignantly from the cart. "What's his purpose, stealing a wife away from her husband?"

"I know on the surface of things it's easy to assume the worst in his actions," answered Kent. "But there's more to it than meets the eye. Lord Thomas has a daughter, barely twelve years in age, who now lies gravely ill with the same enigmatic and untreatable affliction that robbed him of his wife, whom he loved ever so dearly. It's said that, of late, this Lady whom you chaperone, the lovely Lady Sylvanne, has come to dominate his thoughts so thoroughly that he believes she alone holds the key to the salvation of his daughter. It was for this reason he wished to consult the Lady."

"Does he not have physicians?" asked Mabel.

"He has consulted as many as could be sent for. All have failed him. Wife dead, daughter waning and wasting away, one day he gave a most unexpected order: Bring Lady Sylvanne to me, says he, but to attain her, refrain from violence as much as you are able. Deliver her in good health and good spirits, using the powers of your persuasion."

"Powers of persuasion?" Mabel repeated incredulously. "Since when is starvation persuasion?"

"It's the fault of her own husband in his obstinacy," Kent retorted. "From the beginning our two hundred could have easily stormed and overpowered that ramshackle excuse for a castle, with its no more than twenty able-bodied defenders—"

"Twenty-six, plus some boys who were willing, but deemed too young," Mabel corrected him.

"Our master's orders were to avoid bloodshed at all cost. He felt that his prize, if gained by bloodshed, would thereby be disposed to hate him, and would be no prize at all. You may or may not know it, but he sent emissaries several times to the Lady's husband, begging simply for a meeting and a chance to speak privately with her. But all petitions were rejected, out of jealousy and mistrust."

"That's a husband's right," Mabel asserted. "It's his duty, in fact, to shield his wife, to keep her close, housebound. He can't be lending her out like an ox at ploughing time."

"She's not to be compared to an ox, that one," Gwynn interjected. "More like a doe, with her big eyes and quiet demeanour. Our Lord will be well pleased to possess her, whether or not she knows anything of wondrous spells or miracle cures for the daughter."

"Tomorrow will bring us answers," said Kent. "What say you m'Lady? Any special aptitude for healing the sick or curing the lame?"

Sylvanne, silent all this time, turned and glared at him with such a fiery rage in her green eyes that he feared she might be a witch, or a demon. As if spooked by her seething emotions, her stallion reared up and shook his mane furiously. Kent leant over to take the reins, calling out calming words to soothe his favourite mount, but the horse was in a lather and wouldn't be pacified. "This is quite out of character," he said. "Perhaps he needs a feed. Next stream we cross we'll stop for water and grazing."

"Thank the Lord for that," said Gwynn, shifting uncomfortably in the cart. "I fear the sores of my feet have been replanted on my poor arse."

11

Meghan was at her desk in her little cubicle on the eleventh floor, scrolling through the font choices of a new design software, when Jan stepped in and asked, "How are you doing?"

"Not great."

"Poor thing. How's Betsy?"

"I haven't told her about Seth and baby on the way, if that's what you mean. One thing at a time. I think she's got a crush on our neighbour."

"Your neighbour. The drunk?"

"The same."

"I saw him once, the day you moved in. He waved over the fence. I thought he was kind of cute. Shaggy and cute."

"In the daylight he can be charming, it's at night he's trouble." She told Jan all about the picnic table incident, and couldn't help but laugh, describing how she'd watched two drunken lovers zipped in their sleeping bag tumble off the table into the dirt. "They were rolling around on the ground like cats in a sack, going *ouch ouch ouch*, but in a silly, giggly way, and then they wriggled out, and I swear to God, *steam was coming off their bodies.*"

"They were naked?"

"Of course they were naked. And then they just ran in the house, laughing their heads off like fools."

"Wow." Just picturing it put a big grin on Jan's face.

"I know. Happy, carefree, drunken fools. I actually felt a bit jealous. She looked so beautiful by moonlight. Like out of a fairy tale. A nymph from a fairy tale."

"Speaking of which, how's your Lady under siege doing?"

Jan was her closest confidante, the only friend with whom Meghan had shared the whole story of her dreams of Sylvanne and the siege. Jan's reaction had been more amusement than concern—she treated it like a soap opera, eager for each new plot twist. "Come on, out with it. Something's happened," Jan cajoled her.

"She's left the castle. Gerald is dead," Meghan blurted out. And suddenly a surge of grief welled within her, Sylvanne's genuine grief at the loss of her husband, and she began to cry uncontrollably, sitting there at her desk. Through her tears she managed to say, "This is crazy."

To her relief Jan was supportive. "It's getting serious," she said. She dabbed Meghan's eyes with a tissue and then stood behind her chair, rubbing her shoulders until the sobs subsided. "Maybe you need some help. I do know a therapist— someone who'd be perfect, and I can help get you in," Jan suggested.

"I'd like that, I think," Meghan said. "I'd like some answers. Or even just to talk.

"Good. Her name is Anne Billings. She's my brother's ex-wife but I've always liked her, a lot more than my brother actually, and she and I stayed friends after they split. You'll like her too, she's super smart but very down to earth. She has a private practice but she's also a professor at the university, and these dreams of yours sound right up her alley—her PhD was all about Wicca, or witchcraft—apparently in academic circles she's made a name for herself that way, using psychology to study mysticism and the paranormal. She's at least sympathetic to stuff like that—if any psychologist is going to take a real interest, it'll be her. I'll call her for you, see what I can do."

12

Betsy kissed her mother goodbye and locked the door behind her, then headed up to the computer. She had only two friends she was allowed to chat with, Sam and Brittany, and neither of them was online. Saturday afternoon. Brittany might have gone out of town for the weekend, and Sam was probably at ballet. Now what? She was instantly bored. This was the second time she'd been truly alone in her life, the second time in less than a week. The first time she'd felt only excitement, this time she felt abandoned. She wandered back downstairs and turned the television to a music channel her mother didn't like her watching. The video showed a singer who looked to be about fifty under his pancake makeup and there were devils in it with blood coming out of their mouths. She watched until it ended and then turned it off. Now what? What she really wanted to do was go outside and jump on the trampoline, but her mother had laid down the law: no jumping without a grown-up watching you. What about Derek, she had asked. Her mother had made a pained face and said, Derek is on the wrong side of the fence, and Derek is to stay there. No jumping on the trampoline until I get home.

So. No jumping, but she hadn't said anything about just *lying* on the trampoline.

The taut black surface of it was hot from the afternoon sun. She lay on her back watching the sky, then played with the orange sunlight through her eyelids, making it lighter and darker by scrunching her eyes shut. Presently she heard sounds from the back yard next door. Derek was working on something again. She heard knocks and clatterings and opened her eyes to see a fifteen foot square of mesh netting, framed on thin pipes, being leaned up against their shared fence. The pipes were junky, salvaged plumbing pipes, and the mesh looked tattered in places, but several layers thick.

A minute later there was a whipping sound, a sharp *whap*, and a golf ball flew into the net, where it was snared like a bird on the wing. The force of it stretched the netting, and the ball slid down to become entrapped in a little bulge of netting that hung over the fence onto Betsy's side. *Whoosh, whap.* Another ball flew into the net, fell and joined the first, resting like eggs in a farm wife's apron.

"What are you doing?" Betsy called out. She stood up on the trampoline to see over top of the fence, and bounced a bit to get a better look.

"Ah. Good morning, didn't know you were there," Derek greeted her. He'd dragged his picnic table to the back of the yard to make some space for himself. At the top of her bouncing arc she could see a half dozen golf balls at his feet. Betsy watched him tap one away from the others, and take his place over it. "Pay attention," he said. "You're about to witness impeccable form." He took several practice swings and finally addressed the ball, staring at it for what to Betsy seemed an agonizingly long time. Then he swung. *Whoosh, whap—whap!*" The ball struck the fence below the netting and ricocheted back at him like a bullet. He tried to twist his head out of the way but it smacked him on the skull just behind his ear.

"Jesus Fucking Christ!" he shouted. Betsy stopped bouncing and stared at him. She covered her mouth to hide her grin. "Don't you fucking laugh!" he shouted at her. But then he smiled himself.

"Do you want your balls back?" she asked, hopping down from the trampoline and going to the fence.

"Of course I want my balls back, what do you think?"

"You should ask nicely," she scolded him.

"Screw you to that. Not everyone is as polite and civil as you, little girl."

"I'm not, really. What's to keep me from keeping these?"

"I'll come over there and wring your scrawny little neck, that's what."

"No you wouldn't."

"Don't try me."

Betsy went to the knothole in the fence. On tiptoes she could see him through it. "I can watch you practice golf from here," she said.

"No you can't."

"Why not?"

"I'll show you." He picked a ball from the ground, came over and stuck it through the hole. "A well-struck shot would knock your eyeball out the back of your skull," he said. Betsy stepped back and watched as the ball fell though the hole and landed at her feet. She scooped it up and rubbed her fingers over the funny dimpled surface.

"Now I have three," she said.

"Where's your mother?" he asked.

"She's inside," she lied. "How come you like golf?"

"Well it's like this, my dear. As Willie Nelson said to Bob Dylan, once you start playing golf, you can't hardly think about nothing else. Direct quote."

"Who're they?"

"Old geezers. Nobody important. Would you like to try?"

He tossed his golf club over the fence, and it came down so close to her that she jumped aside in fright.

"Watch it! You almost hit me!"

"Just making sure you're awake. It's a six iron, perfect place to start."

She dropped her golf ball and picked up the club, holding the grip experimentally, waving it like a baseball bat through the air. "Seems silly, trying to whack a ball with this," she said.

On his side of the fence Derek retrieved another club from a bag lying on the ground. "You're right, it is very silly," he said. "Something for men of leisure to fill the empty days. That's my excuse, anyway."

She took a tentative swing at the ball in the grass at her feet and whiffed completely. She tried again, and missed again. On the third try she connected, and the ball popped up and tapped lightly against the fence.

"I hit it!" she exclaimed proudly.

"Good for you. Now you're hooked. Are you holding the club properly?"

"Why is it called a club? It looks like a stick."

"Just a minute." From a tangle of junk in the back corner of his yard he extricated an old kitchen chair, the kind with a vinyl seat and chrome legs. He carried it to the fence and stood on it so he could look over the top and watch her. She had retrieved the ball and was preparing to whack it again, aiming at the fence, directly at him.

"Wait wait wait. I'm in the line of fire here," he told her. "Turn so I can see you from the side. That's the best way to advise you on your form. Aim toward your house."

"I might hit a window."

"Ha! I don't think you have the biceps to do damage. Keep your hands close together. Choke up a little on the grip."

"What's that mean?"

"Never mind, just swing away."

She gave it her best. Putting aside apprehension and doubt, and drawing on all the strength her girlish arms could muster, she spanked the little white sphere as hard as she could. To her surprise she connected cleanly, solidly—the ball rocketed out of the grass toward the house, and with a delicate *crack* it struck and splintered one of the dozen small panes of glass in the back door. Shards tinkled onto the deck floor.

"Holy shit! Lookit! I broke it," she screamed. "Thanks to

you I broke it!" She rushed up onto the deck to check the damage.

"Not thanks to me," Derek said. "I didn't break it, the ball broke it. Who knew you had such power? You're a natural. Don't worry about the glass. I'll fix it, I promise. I'll get right on it."

Betsy looked anxiously at the jagged splinters that radiated from where the ball had struck the glass. One splinter hung like a loose tooth. She gingerly took hold and tugged on it. It came loose in her hand. She dropped it carefully to the floor.

"Don't be messing around," Derek warned. "You'll slice your finger off—those things are razor sharp."

"I'm being careful," she replied. She pulled another shark's tooth shard loose, then another, driven by an impulse to hide the damage from her mother by tidying up the mess. If all the splinters are removed then the broken pane won't look broken, it'll look clear, like all the others, she thought. She extracted two more splinters, then tugged on a smaller one that refused to budge. Her grip slipped and she felt a sharp pain. She held her hand up and saw blood dripping down into the V between her fingers. She turned to Derek and showed it to him, like a helpless, frightened toddler.

To Derek at the fence it looked like a bloody peace symbol, a crimson V for victory. A thin rivulet of blood trickled down to her elbow and dripped onto the deck. He muttered, "Jesus Christ," then said firmly, "Go get your mother."

"She's not home."

"You told me she was home."

Betsy shook her head.

"Go run that thing under cold water in the kitchen sink. I'm coming over."

She stood frozen by panic, too shocked by the sight of blood to move.

"Do it now!" he shouted. That reached her. He watched her disappear into the house, then placed his hands on the cross beam of the fence, and vaulted up to balance one foot atop it. He swung his other foot up and over, but miscalculated and felt the momentum of his body pitching him forward, then downward, head first. Like a rider thrown from a horse he felt the fence give out under him, an eight-foot panel of slats ripping from its poles and collapsing in a clatter of planks onto Betsy's garden. He came down on top of it, and rolled onto the lawn, unhurt, picked himself up and headed toward the open back door. He found her at the kitchen sink, shaking. He called out, "Betsy! Do you have bandages?" and realized he was yelling.

13

"So what I'm hearing you say is, you don't believe you're dreaming. Instead, in your sleep, you're observing this young woman, this Sylvanne, as she goes about her real, actual life in some other time and place."

"That's it, exactly."

Jan had proved as good as her word—she had phoned Anne Billings and begged her to investigate the curious case of the Lady under siege, who came each night to Meghan in an unbidden, relentless, haunting dream. The psychologist had been intrigued enough to suggest a meeting, and by chance had a cancellation for the next day, a Saturday afternoon. Meghan had jumped at the offer, even though it meant leaving Betsy alone at home again. Now the two women sat in comfortable high-backed armchairs in a book-lined office.

"All right," Anne continued. "Now, while you're sleeping, and watching all this, do you experience any of the sorts of surreal tangents we commonly associate with dreams?"

"None," Meghan answered. "Everything that happens happens at the pace of real life, and there are no weird or bizarre dream-like moments at all, ever. Everything is consistent, and precise, and detailed, and just, *real*. It's like I'm in her head, experiencing everything she goes through, feeling all that she feels."

"So you become her?"

"No, not exactly. I'm still aware of myself too, like I'm inside her, but not her." Meghan paused. "I do know she looks like me, because when she looks in a mirror it's my face looking back at me, but she is definitely not me. She's Sylvanne, a different person entirely, and I'm just in there, watching. I can't influence her, or communicate to her at all. She never acknowledges me. I'm sure she doesn't even know I'm there."

Anne took notes. Meghan watched her for a moment, then said, "Is it common? Is it a condition with a name?"

"Not to my knowledge."

"Can I ask you something?"

"Of course."

"Can you dream something you've never even heard of, then later discover it actually turns out to exist? The story of Judith I told you about, I researched it online—Judith and Holofernes. It's accepted in the Catholic Bible, but most Protestant ones keep it separate, in the Apocrypha. Considered apocryphal, I suppose, not to be trusted."

"Maybe you have heard Judith's story before," Anne suggested.

"You may have forgotten, at least your conscious mind might have. And it's popping up in your dreams."

"I don't think so. I've never much troubled with the Bible." She paused. "God—I'm starting to sound like her. That's exactly what she told her husband."

"It isn't necessary to have read the Bible," Anne suggested. "Perhaps it reached you from another source. You said you were a designer—ever study art history?"

"I did, actually. And I still do from time to time, just looking for inspiration, when I'm designing book covers or promo materials."

"You're very lucky. I'd love to do something like that," Anne said. "I love art, but I have no talent in that direction. So I remain a fan, not a practitioner. I do know that a great many artists have painted Judith and Holofernes. Caravaggio, for one. I saw the actual painting in Rome—I remember thinking the model looked a little too ambivalent in the act to be convincing. If you're going to chop a man's head off, then you need to commit to it totally at a certain point, don't you think?"

"I've never really thought about it," said Meghan.

"There's a better version by Artemisia Gentileschi, another Italian from about the same era, a woman painter, which was rare," Anne continued. "She tackled it several times, I think to a certain extent as therapy—she was raped by her art teacher. Her Judith is all business, getting down to the job as though she worked in a butcher shop."

"I have a ton of art history books at home," Meghan said. "I'll look for it." She thought for a moment. "It's funny, you saying you'd love to be doing something else. I'd have thought your job would be fascinating, but I suppose it's hard, listening to all the weird crap that comes out of people's minds."

"Not as hard as it must be to have the weird crap in your mind."

"Right," said Meghan. "We're here to talk about me, not you."

Anne said nothing, and wrote in her notepad.

"I was hoping you'd say more," Meghan said.

"Unlock the mystery for you? I'm afraid it doesn't work like that."

"What about first impressions? Give me a little."

Anne considered for a moment. "This Sylvanne. Since you began to dream of her, and let's call it a dream for lack of a better term, it would seem she has never been in control of her destiny. She's been the victim of a siege, laid for unclear reasons by a power unseen, namely this Thomas of Gastoncoe. On that front, progress is being made. You are being taken to meet him, and for better or worse, good or bad, there's a goal in mind when you get there."

"*She's* being taken. And the goal is in her mind, not mine."

"In any case, you're on your way to a resolution. Maybe when she meets Thomas, it will become clear."

"I hope so," said Meghan. "I wish she'd hurry up and get there. Why couldn't I be in the head of someone modern, they'd just drive over in their car."

"Yes, it would be nice if they could just straighten it out with a phone call," Anne agreed. They shared a smile. "I think that's enough for today."

"Good," said Meghan. "Sorry if I jump up and run, but I'm really antsy to get home. I've left my daughter alone for the second time in three days, and last time was the first time ever, so I'm feeling super guilty about it. My life is chaos."

"Maybe next time we'll have to talk a little bit more about you," Anne said. "There might be two ladies under siege in this equation."

"I've thought of that," Meghan said. "Could be projection."

"I think there's more than that going on," Anne suggested. "I'm actually quite fascinated by your case, and I do want to see you regularly while we try to get to the bottom of it. I might like to write a paper for a journal of psychology about it, which could make you the star example of an unheard-of condition. Would you be alright with that?"

"Sure," said Meghan. "Do you think I might be channelling a past life?"

"First I'd have to believe in past lives, then in channelling them. Unfortunately I don't."

"Sorry. I know it's unrealistic, but I guess I was just really hoping I'd come here and there would be a breakthrough, in terms of answers."

"Well. Our Lady Sylvanne is on the move. The answers you're so eager for might be coming soon enough, in your sleep."

14

Meghan came in the front door and called out, "Hi sweetie! I'm home." She heard Betsy call from upstairs that she was getting changed, so she headed up to check on her, and also to check the art history books in her studio. She poked her head in Betsy's bedroom and said, "Sorry I got late. Parking was a nightmare, there was some kind of street fair going on. I did phone. Why didn't you pick up? You scared me half to death. You were supposed to look at the call display and pick up."

"I was in the bathroom."

"Well why didn't you call back when you got out?"

Betsy didn't answer.

"Why are you getting changed?"

"I just felt like it." Meghan heard irritation in her daughter's voice, a leave-me-alone tone. She put it down to resentment at being left alone again.

"I'll make some dinner," she said. "Lemon honey chicken, your favourite. With white rice, not brown. But first I need to check on something."

She went to her studio office, the middle room of the three upstairs, and scanned the bookshelves for a particular title. *Italian Renaissance Painting*. She plopped the massive volume on her drafting table and flipped through it randomly. There it was: *Caravaggio—Judith and Holofernes*.

Her eyes roamed the image for a moment. From the first glance she agreed with Anne: Caravaggio's Judith looked too diffident, too decidedly *detached* for someone in the midst of decapitating a general in his own bed, in his own tent, in the midst of his mighty army. Curious to see the other painting Anne had mentioned, she moved to the computer and googled Artemisia Gentileschi. As easy as that, she found the female painter's version of the same event, and again, like Anne, found it more satisfying, more believable. This Judith looked to have righteousness on her side, giving her the strength and certitude to do what needed done. But to Meghan's mind the most striking difference between the two paintings was in their portrayals of Judith's accomplice, her maid Abra. In Caravaggio's version Abra was an old crone waiting patiently like a granny in a buffet line up. Gentileschi's Abra, on the other hand, is part of the team—she plants her full weight on the brute's chest, pinning his arms down while he struggles against the blade Judith slices across his neck.

Before getting up from the computer she gave in to an urge to google Thomas of Gastoncoe, not for the first time. In fact she had done this every time she had used the computer lately, typing his name and Lady Sylvanne's into every search engine she could think of, but she had never turned up anything meaningful. Browsing absently through the results, she heard Betsy heading downstairs. Time to get dinner started.

In the kitchen she rubbed some skinless chicken thighs with olive oil, slid them into a Pyrex dish, sprayed them with concentrated juice from a plastic lemon, slathered on some honey, and popped it in the oven. Betsy came in and stood watching her sheepishly, but Meghan didn't pick up on it. "Can you get me some spinach out of the fridge, hon?" she asked.

It was only when Betsy brought the packet to her at the sink that Meghan noticed the clumsily fashioned mass of bandages that encased the girl's index finger. In alarm she cried, "What did you do to your hand?"

"It got cut," Betsy said timidly.

"How?"

"I was practicing golf with Derek."

"Derek."

"From next door."

"I know who Derek is, thank you very much. And where exactly were you golfing?"

"In the back," said Betsy, wincing in anticipation of what was surely to follow.

"In our back? Derek came over to our back lawn?"

Betsy nodded. "Kind of by accident."

Meghan looked out the kitchen window and with a shock saw that her garden had been violated. A dozen or so heavy slats from the collapsed fence lay scattered in a random pile, crushing her flowerbed. The gaping hole in the fence felt like a breech in her defences. She rushed to the kitchen door, reached for the handle, and stopped dead in her tracks when she saw that a pane of glass had been reduced to a few shards clinging to the frame. She gingerly put a finger through the opening, to confirm what her eyes were telling her.

"I tried to get all the pieces out of it, and got a cut," Betsy said defensively. "He said I don't need stitches or anything."

"You might, by the time I get through with you," Meghan said. Glancing out onto the floor of the deck she saw splattered drops of dried blood. She looked down at her feet and saw that someone had done a very poor job of wiping up similar dots on the kitchen floor. There were faint smear marks from the door to the sink. She couldn't believe she hadn't noticed them before.

"First thing is we're going to take that bandage off and *I'll* decide whether you need stitches or not. Hopefully not, but at least we'll make sure it's clean, and dress it properly. That mess looks ridiculous. Did you put any antiseptic on it?"

Betsy shook her head.

"No, he didn't think of that, did he? Too busy wrecking my fence." Her anger, slow to build, now made her shake with rage. "*First* thing is to give that man a piece of my mind," she seethed. "Or I might just chop his frigging head off!"

She marched out of the kitchen, out of the house, and under a full head of righteousness marched straight toward Derek's door. Betsy followed her as far as their own front step, then called after her, "He went to get a piece of glass! He measured it and everything!"

Meghan took no heed. She rang the doorbell and pounded on his door obsessively, and when it became abundantly clear he wasn't home, it only increased the fury she felt toward him.

15

Meghan examined Betsy's cut and decided it didn't warrant stitches. She cleaned it and rebandaged it, and they sat down to dinner in strained silence. She poured herself a glass of wine, which she never did unless she had guests, but Betsy was too unnerved to make a comment about it. They were both hyperaware of noises from outside, both straining for any sound that might indicate that Derek had returned next door. It began to get dark outside. When they heard an exploratory shout of "Hello?" from Derek's back yard they both almost jumped out of their skins. The missing pane in the window amplified his voice, as if permitting it to trespass into their home. Betsy pushed her chair back and stood up, but Meghan grabbed her forearm firmly and said, "Sit down. We'll finish dinner first. Any repairs he makes will be done on my schedule, not his." From outside they could hear Derek call out a few more times,

quizzically, as if he knew they were in there and couldn't understand why they wouldn't come out. This was confirmed when
he said, "All right, then. I'll be at home when you're ready. See
you." It sounded as if he were talking to an imaginary friend,
or a ghost.

"Good," Meghan said to Betsy. "You've got to put them in
their place." She allowed herself a smile. Seeing it, Betsy felt a
weight lift from her. It was the first flicker of hope that she might
be forgiven. She'd been picking at her chicken, but now she tore
into it with relish. "Is your finger hurting?" Meghan asked her.
She held it up, now properly disinfected under a neat bandage.
"Maybe a little," she said. "Not too bad."

"If somehow it had been my fault, you'd be telling me it's
excruciating," Meghan teased her. "You'd be writhing around on
the floor right now."

"Maybe it hasn't hit me yet," Betsy answered, then worried it
might actually be true.

"Oh, it's hit you," said Meghan. "Unless it gets infected. But
let's not go there."

They were silent again for a minute.

"Mum?"

"Uh huh."

"Before you were married, did you desire Daddy?"

"Where did that come from?"

"Just asking."

"Uh huh."

After a pause, Betsy said, "Derek's been married twice."

Meghan's hackles went up. "Oh?"

"He says sometimes people fall in love because they desire someone. But once you have the person, the desire can go away," Betsy explained. "He told me the difference between desire and love: you can only desire something you don't have, but love is when you love what you have. I think that's what he said." Betsy, feeling very grown-up discussing such a topic, didn't notice that her mother was fuming. "He says what happened to his first marriage, it was all desire, no love. But his second marriage, that was love—but then his wife just disappeared. She just vanished. Why would a wife do that?"

Meghan threw her fork to her plate and rose from the table. "Wait right here," she demanded. This has crossed a line, she told herself. It needs to be stopped, now.

She strode out of her house and was quickly back at Derek's front door, ringing the bell. She could hear music inside, the thump thump thump of hard rock, not a genre she took much interest in, so she didn't recognize the song, even though she could hear Derek singing along, off-key but with serious passion. She caught fragments of it—something about suffering through life without love—and then, through the heavy front door, she heard him howl like a wolf at the moon. She rang the bell again, then rapped her fist on the door until her knuckles hurt. She was livid. She thought, The bastard is going to make me wait until his idiotic song ends. When the song ended she rang the bell again, and soon the door opened, and there was Derek, looking at her sympathetically through a cloud of tobacco and marijuana smoke. She could hear other voices from within, then laughter, then a new song came on, drowning out all else.

"Just a minute," said Derek, and he disappeared, leaving her to stare down a long narrow hallway with a bare hardwood floor scarred by deep random gouges she couldn't begin to imagine the origins of. She heard the blare of music lowered just enough to allow conversation on the doorstep. Coming back down the hall toward her he said, "I yelled for you in back earlier, don't know if you heard me—wanted to tell you I couldn't get a piece of glass cut to size on such short notice, the store was closing by the time I got my shit together. It'll have to be tomorrow. Your back door won't exactly be secure, but what the hell, it's only one night, and nobody knows about it except you and me."

"I want you to stay away from my daughter," Meghan said.

"Yeah, sorry about the little accident. Bit of a disaster, I did tell her not to touch that glass—"

"I'm not talking about the glass, or the accident, which wasn't an accident so much as an inevitability, given the hazardous things you keep encouraging her to do. I'm talking about discussing who you desire and how you desire them with a ten-year-old girl who's home alone."

Her words sobered him—in fact he looked as though he'd been slapped. "But she *asked* me," he protested. "She asked if I'd ever been married, and I said, Yes, twice, and she asked Why didn't any of them last, and I said, You're too young to understand."

"Right," said Meghan caustically. "Then you went ahead and explained anyway."

"No, I tried to put her off," he replied, "But she told me she was plenty old enough to understand, that her dad says she's wise beyond her years and knows lots of things she shouldn't. And I said, Like what? And she said, My homeroom teacher's bisexual, which means he can fall in love with a man or a woman." He raised an eyebrow and asked, "Did you know her homeroom teacher is a bisexual?"

"No, I didn't, in fact," she said through clenched teeth. "Anything else I should know about her?"

"She loves you. She's very worried about you. She hates her dad for wrecking a good thing. She hates being forced to visit him. She's a nice kid. Very smart. Feisty."

His words had the momentary effect of draining all the fight out of her. Her shoulders drooped. Suddenly she felt more tired than anything. "That, I knew," she said.

"Right then, I'll see you tomorrow," Derek said brightly. "I'll aim for an early start, up with the songbirds, decked out in amateur carpenter's gear. I'm looking forward to it. I haven't worked with putty in years."

Meghan felt a need to reframe and reiterate the message she'd come storming over to deliver. "I may not like you, but she does," she told him. "I'd tell you to stay the hell away from her, but we're neighbours, she's bound to see you, and ordering her not to talk to you would make her want to talk to you all the more. Just keep your distance, especially if you're drinking or smoking pot, or messing with any other substances like that. If you do see her, be nice. She's a fragile kid."

Derek shook his head. "Fragile? You're projecting. That kid is tough as nails. She was such a trouper—that was a nasty cut, you know—there was blood everywhere. Grown men faint at less, some anyway—I felt lightheaded myself."

Meghan sized him up anew. "I can see why Betsy likes you, you're a child. If she were a few years older, she'd see right through you."

"I wasn't counting on her as a friend for life anyway. She'll make her own choices, she already does. She likes me—big deal. I may not be terribly presentable or successful on your terms, but I am in no way responsible for an ugly divorce that's messing up her ten-year-old head."

His words tore at her, adding another blow to a heart already battered and aching with a mother's guilt. She wanted to cry, but ordered herself not to. "You're mean," she muttered, but the thought trailed off, unfinished. All she could think of was Betsy, and the impossible sum of things known and unknown that would be required of her to make her daughter's life right again.

Back in her kitchen Meghan found Betsy doing dishes at the sink, and scolded her. She had told her not to get the bandage wet.

"It doesn't hurt," Betsy said.

"It doesn't matter," she said sternly. "Go get into your pj's and I'll change it for a dry one."

"How'd it go with Derek?" Betsy asked.

"Oh, we had a lovely chat," Meghan said acidly. "There's no glass until tomorrow."

Betsy looked at the empty window pane in the door. It was close enough to the handle that anyone could reach through and unlock it.

"What are we going to do about the door?" she asked.

"I'll figure something out."

"Like what?"

"Go and get ready for bed," Meghan told her. "Just give me five minutes to sit and think of something."

"How come it's always five minutes?" Betsy wondered.

"Go!"

She did as told. Meghan slumped into a chair at the table. She could actually feel a draft of cool night air coming through the empty pane. One small little puncture in her home had altered everything. She really wished she was handier with tools. Was there a way to nail the whole door shut without wrecking it? Then she realised she didn't have any tools in this house, the tools she was thinking of were all Seth's tools and they were all with Seth. She hated herself in this moment for having to rely on men to fix things, for never having learned self-reliance of the practical sort. Maybe it's time to change that, she thought, maybe tomorrow I'll tell Derek to forget it, and I'll go to Home Depot or whatever and get a pane of glass myself, and some putty or whatever they use, and do it myself. How hard can it be? I'll be like the women on those home reno shows that get all empowered by doing it for themselves. But then she thought, who am I kidding—I never watch those shows because I never want to be those women, I'd rather hire a plumber than get all excited about figuring out how to hook up a faucet. I just wish there were female plumbers, I'd hire one in a second. After she'd crawled around under the sink I'd make coffee and we'd dissect our disastrous love lives.

In the end she rigged up a sort of early warning defence system at the door. She rummaged around for a bit of rope, tied it around the door handle and then up to an unused hook some previous occupant of the house had mounted on the wall nearby. She pulled the rope as snug as she could and knotted it, and found that when she tried to open the door the rope allowed no more than a four inch gap. Of course an intruder could always cut the rope, but they wouldn't be expecting it, and dealing with it would take time. For a second line of defence she stood a roll of paper towel on the floor next to the closed door, and set a wine glass on top. The glass would topple and shatter if anyone opened the door, at least in theory. She didn't feel like testing it with an experiment. For the third line of defence she would sleep on the couch in the living room downstairs, with both her cordless phone and her cell phone by her pillow. Betsy would be upstairs in her bed as usual.

When she was certain Betsy had settled safely to sleep, Meghan lay down on the living room couch, checked the phones one more time, pulled her duvet to her neck, and thought, I've gone to a whole lot of trouble to make myself feel secure enough to fall asleep, and I've completely, abysmally failed. But no wonder, when there's a hole in my door big enough for a raccoon to come through. Are there raccoons in this neighbourhood? Of course there are, they're all over the city. One could jump in and not even knock over the wine glass.

She told herself she was being absurd, adding wild animals to her list of worries, which served to remind her of all the other worries on her list. The fridge in the kitchen grumbled and groaned like a hungry man's stomach, and every change in tone made her eyes pop open. This is ridiculous, she thought. I will never get to sleep like this. And yet she was so tired that sleep came quickly.

16

On the afternoon of the second day of their journey they ascended a low, wooded ridge. At the summit the land was cleared for grazing, and afforded a view down the other side. A pleasant river snaked through neatly tended fields, and in the distance a village appeared to nestle against the walls of a stout castle much larger and more grand than the one Sylvanne had known. The men called out happily at the sight of their homes.

As they descended through the fields women and children toiling at the harvest dropped their rakes and scythes and rushed to greet them. There was much merriment, and if some embraces were overly tearful, at least they were tears of joy. Sylvanne rode aloofly among the peasants, aware of eyes upon her, but looking neither left nor right. In front of her the oaf Gwynn had lifted Mabel from the back of the cart to walk with him, and was introducing her to one and all as his betrothed.

Mabel blushed like a girl paid her first compliment, and protested only mildly.

One farm wife broke from happy reunion with her husband to stare at Sylvanne unabashedly. "So this be the great Lady herself," she proclaimed. "I can see why our Lord obsesses. Quite the fair flower, ain't she?"

"Beauty's not enough," her husband added. "She'll need to perform."

"If she's half as eager as I am, m'Lord will be delighted with her," she grinned, jumping up into his arms and wrapping her legs around him with such force that he tumbled to the ground with her on top, to the laughter and teasing of the many merry onlookers.

More and more peasants and villagers joined the happy throng. They paraded into the village and crushed together in the narrow lanes leading to the castle, which soon loomed over them. Then suddenly they stopped, having reached the point where a lowered drawbridge spread across a narrow moat. Kent dismounted and took the reins of Sylvanne's horse in his hand. He yelled for the disorderly mob to make a passage for them, and they squeezed through the crush onto the stout timbers of the bridge. Sylvanne looked over the side at the blue waters of the moat and saw half a dozen pure white swans approach, gliding closer as if to have a look at her. "Even the birds are curious, Madame," Kent laughed. Then they passed from the sunlit bridge into the shadowed passageway of the barbican, then through it and back outside into sunlight. The castle had two walls of defences, with the space between—the bailey—occupied by stables and liveries,

servants' quarters and storage sheds. Here the cobblestoned path
to the inner sanctum was lined with maids, menservants and
vassals, a flood of faces all freely gawking up at the Lady upon
her horse. On their master's orders, no one spoke, and after the
carnival-like chatter of the peasants outside, the sudden silence
gave Sylvanne a chill.

They passed through another gate to the inner courtyard,
where yet another gaggle of onlookers waited at the bottom of a
long stone staircase. Their finer attire showed them to be courtiers and noblepersons, but they gaped at her just as openly as any
peasant had. Kent held out a hand and helped her dismount from
her horse, and when she wobbled for a moment, unsteady on legs
made stiff from the long journey, a murmur of concern went
up from the crowd, as if this first impression marked an inaus-
picious portent. A single voice called out, "Welcome, m'Lady,"
but was shushed by the others. Sylvanne composed herself, and
allowed Kent to lead her up the staircase. Behind her she could
hear a buzzing of low voices, of whispered, pent-up remarks that
exploded into chatter as she passed through the doorway and
entered the castle.

The hall was murky and dim. She blinked her eyes to speed
their adjustment, as Kent guided her further within. They made a
left turn, then a right. Light fell upon them from a high window.
They reached a dead end in the hallway, and stood before a heavy
wooden door. Kent rapped upon it, and a voice bade them enter.

Kent stepped aside to allow Sylvanne to pass, then followed
behind. She stepped into the room, and saw that it was dominat-
ed by a large canopy bed, its four heavy oak posts ornately carved

with coiling, climbing snakes. Upon the bed, under rumpled white linen, slept a young girl, no more than twelve. Standing over her, with his back to the door, was a man. He brushed a wisp of hair from the girl's forehead, and felt her cheek with the back of his hand.

Kent cleared his throat. "She is here, m'Lord," he said.

Thomas of Gastoncoe turned around. "There you are," he said. He searched Sylvanne's eyes for a glimmer of recognition, and found nothing but seething anger there.

"Do you not know me?"

"I expect you to be Lord Thomas," she replied.

"Yes, yes, you can guess who I am, but do you recognize me? Have you not seen me before?"

"Never," she said coldly.

"But you have. I was at your wedding. That's how I know you."

"I swam in a multitude of new faces then," Sylvanne said. "Preoccupied with my own passage from girl to wife, I remember few."

"It was a magnificent feast, given by your husband. Nothing spared."

Sylvanne gave him a withering look. "Indeed, it was the happiest time of my life," she said. "And now I find each new day to be my unhappiest."

Thomas dismissed Kent with a glance. With a bow, he left them.

"I'm sorry to hear about your husband," Thomas told her. "A fine man, but stubborn. We passed good times together at the jousts. I was something of a mentor to him in those days, trying to curb his impetuous nature. We used to talk about going off crusading together. I was surprised when he didn't go with his father. What was the nature of his illness?"

"You know full well," Sylvanne spat.

"I apologize if you believe this unfortunate siege contributed in any way to his death."

"An apology changes nothing. He's dead, and we live."

"Yes," he responded. "And how is it that he died, while every other person in your retinue, everyone from maid to valet, from soldier to charwoman, survived? I know of some who clambered down over the walls and deserted you, but even of those who stayed within, how was it that he was the first and only one to die?"

Sylvanne returned his gaze defiantly. "He refused to eat while others went hungry," she said.

"And you were not so noble? Or so impractical? You ate while he starved? If so, m'Lady, you are as much responsible for his death as I. Or did he eat somewhat? Or did he eat nearly as much as others, and only now, in death, do you seek to raise him to a false sainthood of self-denial?"

Sylvanne began to cry. She turned her back to him, hating herself for showing him this weakness. Thomas spoke with sympathy. "I don't mean to make you suffer more for it. You've lost a spouse, I know what emotions that arouses, what torments bruise your heart. All I mean to suggest is that, considering that every other person placed in his circumstances survived, then some other malady must have caused his death. And I apologize if my actions in any way hastened it."

He came to her, and placed a hand gently on her shoulder. She jumped at his touch, twisted away from it, and turned to face him, enraged, electrified.

"Don't you dare touch me," she growled. "Don't you ever lay a hand on me." She stepped back, eyes darting madly about the room. She spotted a short sword in a scabbard hanging over the back of a chair, ran to it, unsheathed it, and held it with two hands, aiming it toward him so that the tip was chest high. Thomas was alert, and wary, but not frightened, for his martial training had included techniques for fighting unarmed against a swordsman. Not that she was any swordsman—he could tell that from the awkward, insubstantial way she waved the blade at him. The fury that burned like passion in her eyes failed to translate into menace with a weapon. He smiled at her, and the hint of condescension in his eyes drove her mad. In a frenzy she charged at him, wildly slashing with the blade. He ducked nimbly behind one of the posts at the foot of the canopy bed, and when Sylvanne lunged fiercely at his head her sword came to an abrupt halt, embedded in the bedpost, perfectly bisecting one of the ornate snakes carved there. Sylvanne tugged on the hilt, struggling with all her strength to free the blade, but she couldn't make it budge.

Thomas watched her in amusement for a moment, then stepped around the bedpost and grabbed her by her wrists. In a calm, unruffled voice he called for Kent, who entered immediately. "Help me pacify the Lady," Thomas commanded. "I want her hands tied securely, but as comfortably as possible. And afterward free this damn blade, but carefully, without causing further damage to the poor furniture."

In short order Sylvanne sat sullenly in a chair by the bedside, her hands roped together behind her back. In the fading afternoon light Thomas lit a candle and turned his attention again to his daughter Daphne, still asleep under white linen sheets, oblivious to the high drama that had just transpired.

"There there, my darling," Thomas whispered to her. "Daddy's here. I'll keep a candle burning day and night. Promise me you'll keep a candle burning too. We'll keep a flame alive, won't we?"

Daphne lay mute and still. He studied her thin, sallow face for a moment, watched the feeble rise and fall of her breast as she breathed. "She was once so full of life," he whispered. "You should have seen her."

Sylvanne was unmoved.

"I know I shouldn't expect your sympathy," he said to her. "But will you hear me out, let me explain myself?"

Sylvanne closed her eyes. "If I could close my ears against your voice the way I shut my eyes against the light, I would."

"This is not what I envisioned at all," he told her, his voice tinged with disappointment. "I sought you as an ally, and now you've made yourself a captive. I wanted, and still want, needed, and still need, your help."

He waited for her to open her eyes, but she kept them shut. He fetched a chair and placed it beside hers, sat in it and leaned close to her face.

"I'm grateful that you cannot close your ears, for what I'm about to tell you requires they be wide open, and your heart and mind also."

Sylvanne made no response. She continued to keep her eyes closed.

"So be it," he said. "Listen to me carefully. Do you imagine that the future will be very much different than our present age?" He paused, then, realising it was futile to attend an answer, continued, his voice filled with an agitated enthusiasm. "Can you imagine that mankind might move forward, with fantastic inventions? Machines that can fly like giant birds, transporting people in their bellies, or astonishing glowing objects that make all of human knowledge available to anyone? Can you imagine such things might be possible?"

She opened her eyes at last and looked at him neutrally. Taking this as encouragement he spoke even more excitedly. "I don't just imagine these things. I see them, in my dreams. Since the death of my dear wife some months ago I dream them every night without fail. But what I experience is more than a dream—I inhabit the body of a man. He's a man of the future— a freeman, neither owned nor owing to anyone. An everyday man, not a great king, nor a renowned poet, nor respected physician, though I wish he were. There's nothing remarkable about him at all. But every night when I lie down to dream I become entrapped in his thoughts and actions. I watch his world, this staggering complex world of the future, so much of which I can't comprehend, through his eyes, from a place I occupy in his mind. Derek is his name. Does that name mean anything to you at all?"

He looked at her expectantly, and from the hard glare he received in return it was clear she thought he was insane.

"At first, on waking every morning," he continued, with less confidence than before, "I obsessed and tormented myself as to what these night visions of mine could mean. Then, suddenly, two months ago now, a new person entered Derek's world—my world. This person, a woman, looks exactly like you. Not like a sister, or cousin, in appearance she is you exactly. Her name is Meghan. Do you know that name? She has a daughter, Betsy, two years younger than my own. Meghan? Betsy? Derek?"

Sylvanne looked at him without comprehension. His voice became more desperate.

"Do you know what a television is? Television—wondrous machines. Have you ever, in your dreams, watched a television?"

"You're mad," she growled.

"You think so?"

"You've destroyed my life, for nothing."

He sagged back in his chair, distressed by the thought she might be right. At that moment his daughter Daphne began to cough, softly at first, then more violently. He rose from his chair to look upon her. Just as suddenly as she had started coughing, she stopped. He watched her settle back into sleep.

"Whatever I've done was for her," he said. "In the future, you see, they possess amazing medicines, and such clever interventions as to make us poor primitives look like mere beasts, poking and prodding in ignorance at our wounded flesh. I inhabit Master Derek's head, but have no influence upon him, for if I did, I'd make him busy himself with seeking out and consulting the best medical authorities of his time and place. But I can't—I can't convey to him my daughter's symptoms, or make him take any interest in the science of healing the human body. I'm merely dragged along impotently with him through the life he leads, which I can't help but judge to be a dissolute, pointless existence. Through his eyes, from time to time I catch tantalizing glimpses of medical knowledge that might save my poor daughter's life, but they remain mere glimpses, nothing near to specific diagnosis or remedy. The knowledge is there, tantalizingly close, yet inaccessible to me. And then, just when I began to despair at the cruelty of it, the hopelessness, I saw a woman, a beauty like yourself. Not merely *like* you. You. Exactly like you, she looks, in all features of face and body, and even to the graceful way you carry yourself. She, or you, came to occupy the dwelling next to his. Do you understand me? I thought if I could talk to you, you might know of this other world, of this Meghan, and have her talk to Derek—do you understand?"

"You wish me to speak to people you've dreamt? You are mad."

"Am I? If so, I'm sorry."

He turned away to keep her from seeing a tear streak his cheek. He wiped it with his sleeve and turned to her again. "I've already lost a wife," he said. "I can't stand to lose our child. I can't stand it."

Sylvanne was unmoved. "If it's pity you seek, don't ask it of someone so ill-treated by you," she said. "For what you have done, God will spare you no mercy."

"From what I've seen of the future, there is no God," Thomas answered. "It's every man for himself, and every woman too."

There was a gentle knock at the door, and Kent entered, followed by Mabel, who was excitedly chattering to him. "And such gorgeous draperies! Must have come clear from Persia, I should—" She cut herself short as she realised into whose presence she had entered. She glanced from Lord Thomas to the sickly girl upon the bed, then to Sylvanne, seated in a chair in an odd posture, wondering at first why her Mistress kept her arms behind her back.

"Her rooms are ready, Sire," Kent announced.

"Madame, wait till you see them—you've never dreamt of such luxury!" Mabel gushed.

"My dreams come up short, do they?" Sylvanne replied, not taking her eyes from Thomas.

He ignored her remark, and informed her, "I've had several fine steers slaughtered for my returning soldiers to feast upon, and made certain the choicest cuts were set aside for you. If beef is not to your liking, feel free to ask the kitchen for any fish or fowl you please, cooked to any taste your palate fancies. You'll be served meals in your rooms, for now. You're staying in my wife's quarters. I've tried to make it as comfortable as possible."

"Have you changed the sheets since she died?"

He met her icy glare with a gentle, supplicating look. "Please don't hate me," he pleaded. "Go and eat what I've offered, then have your maid bathe you, aided by my wife's former maidservants, whom you will find to be sweet-natured, trustworthy girls. Then sleep. Perhaps in restful sleep you'll feel your pain subside, and your heart begin to soften."

"He talks of softening my heart while he keeps my hands shackled," Sylvanne said.

"Of course, of course," said Thomas. "How thoughtless of me. But you must promise to be good."

"You don't know the meaning of that word," Sylvanne snapped.

"Yes, well. Eat. Bathe. Sleep. Tomorrow is a new day." He gestured to Kent to take her away.

17

"Hello, anybody up? Good morning! Hello!"

Meghan woke with a start on the living room couch. The room was bright with sunlight. She threw off the duvet, and staggered to her feet, bumping the coffee table she'd pulled close the night before to keep her two phones within arm's reach. In her groggy, half-wakened state she thought at first one of them must have rung, but which? No, a voice had called, that's what it was—she turned and could see across the kitchen counter to the back door, where Derek knelt outside, bringing his grinning, expectant face close to the broken window pane.

"Slept on the couch, did you?"

Meghan came to the kitchen in her pyjamas. "I didn't feel comfortable sleeping upstairs, knowing the door wasn't lock-able," she explained. "Don't!"

It was too late—Derek had already stuck his hand through,

unlocked and turned the handle, and given the door enough of a push that the wine glass, perched precariously atop the paper towel roll, teetered and crashed to the floor tiles. Derek flinched at the sound, and closed the door sheepishly. "Sorry about that," he said. "Didn't know you'd booby-trapped the place."

"Jesus Christ," Meghan answered irritably. "Don't try to come in until I sweep up." She rummaged in the cupboard under the sink for a dustpan and a hand broom, and set to work brushing up splinters of glass on her hands and knees. Derek watched her through the closed door. She felt his eyes on her and realised self-consciously that on all fours like this her thin pyjamas were stretched tautly across her behind. She stood and then lowered herself to a squat instead, not that it made much difference. She was still a woman in pyjamas being watched by a man through a window.

"I've already been to the hardware and got the glass, it opens at seven a.m. for tradesmen, you know, even on Saturdays," Derek nattered from the sunshine of the deck. Through the missing pane she could hear him well enough. "They're all there, too, the poor bastards, working weekends. You have such a nice little deck here. Very cozy. Great view of my place, all the prized possessions piled in my back yard. It looks a mess, but believe it or not I know where everything is. And don't ask me if I want coffee."

"I wasn't about to," Meghan grumbled. A couple of the slivers of glass were so microscopic the broom was passing over them, leaving tiny glinting irritants that stoked her annoyance.

"And don't make any for yourself, either," he said cheerfully. "I brought you one, and some croissants. I asked myself, does she seem like the croissant type or the Danish type? Went with the croissant—you can add jam to a croissant, but scraping the jam from a Danish, it's just not done."

"That's very good thinking!" chirped Betsy, prancing into the kitchen all smiles.

"Stop right there," Meghan ordered. "Don't come any closer in bare feet."

"You I got tea," Derek said to her.

"Black tea?" Meghan frowned. "She's too young for caffeinated drinks."

"I bet she likes Coke," Derek responded. "That's got a hell of a lot more caffeine than an innocent cup of tea."

"She doesn't drink sodas either," Meghan answered sharply.

"You're always getting me in trouble with your mother," Derek teased Betsy.

"I drink ginger ale, sometimes," she announced.

"That's not caffeinated," said Meghan. She stood up, surveyed the floor, and decided it passed muster. She went to empty the dustpan with its shards of wineglass under the sink.

"How'd you break that?" Betsy asked.

"I didn't. He did," said Meghan curtly. At the door she unknotted and removed the rope she'd strung the night before, her last line of defence. She opened the door and let him in. He crossed the threshold carrying a bag of croissants in one hand, and in the other he balanced the coffee and tea, one atop the other in their plastic-lidded paper cups. "Better be careful!" Betsy giggled delightedly, and Derek played to his audience of two, like a court jester or a clown at a birthday party, pretending to almost stumble and bobble the drinks. His cavalier style, which Meghan saw as deliberately courting disaster and further spillage, infuriated her. And yet when he set the cups upon the kitchen table, and turned around to look at her with his big open face, a strange emotion seized her.

The events of the previous night came flooding back to her, and her mind filled suddenly with images of the same sharp blue eyes, broad forehead and large mouth, seen precisely as Lady Sylvanne had seen them, in the bedroom of a sickly twelve-year-old girl. She was looking into the face of Thomas of Gastoncoe.

"Something wrong? Derek asked.

His words made her aware that she'd been blatantly staring at him, as if he were a painting, or a photograph.

"Mom, you look like you've seen a ghost," said Betsy.

"Not a ghost," she said, flustered. "I'm fine, really. Derek has come to fix our door, so why don't—"

"And our fence," the girl interrupted.

"That's right, and our fence, so why don't we let him get on with it?"

"But we haven't had our breakfast."

"He has, I think." He nodded in confirmation. "Let's go get properly dressed, come back and eat up quickly, and get out of his way."

"You won't be in my way," said Derek. "And this won't take ten minutes. The fence is another matter, it'll take a bit longer. I bought a couple of two-by-fours to reinforce it."

"That'll be fine," Meghan said. She fought a continuous urge to stare at him. Thomas of Gastoncoe. A dead ringer.

"I'm going to have a sip of tea," Betsy announced, putting on a British accent. To her great surprise, her mother didn't say anything in response. She picked up the paper cup and brought it to her lips, and still Meghan paid her no heed. She sensed that her mother was suddenly preoccupied with Derek, and the feeling brought a pang of jealousy.

"I'm drinking it!" she declared.

"Fine, go ahead," Meghan answered absently. "I'm going upstairs to get dressed." She hadn't figured out how to broach the matter of her dreams with Derek, but she knew one thing: it should not be done in pyjamas.

Upstairs she was about to pull on a pair of jeans and a tank top—her usual Saturday uniform—when she decided a shower would clear her head and help sort her thoughts. Under the warm spray she gave her mind up to Sylvanne and Thomas. They had finally come together, they had clashed, and she had lived it—she had felt the ferocity of Sylvanne's hatred of him, and it made her shudder. Then she recalled how Thomas has spoken the name Meghan, how he had described her. He called me a great beauty, she remembered, and the flattery pleased her. It's too long since I've heard anything like that from a man, she thought, smiling to herself. Drunken Derek yelling "You're cute when you're angry!" doesn't count. She remembered how Thomas had spoken of Derek's life with incomprehension—what were the words he'd used? Dissolute and pointless. Dead on. With a sudden shock she realised she had left her daughter alone downstairs with that very man, a man she barely knew, a man she habitually described to friends as the obnoxious drunk next door.

She dressed quickly and hurried back down to the kitchen. There was no one there and the pane had already been replaced in the back door. Through the window she could see Derek pulling nails from the fence planks with a hammer, while Betsy, still in her pyjamas, was bouncing on the trampoline, landing on her feet one time, her bum the next. They were happily chattering to each other like old pals. Meghan opened the door and stepped out onto the deck.

"What the hell do unicorns need a horn for anyway?" Derek was asking. "Narwhals are the only other mammal with a big pointy pole sticking straight out their foreheads, and they *use* theirs, to dig up food from the sea bottom, but a unicorn eats grass like a horse, does he not? A horn's only going be a nuisance in that case, getting in the way all the time."

"They need the horns to defend themselves," Betsy replied.

"From who?"

"Lions and tigers and things."

"Your unicorns have wings—they're not going to stand around poking their head at a bunch of hungry lions, they'd fly away."

"They do have wings, you're right." Betsy slowed her trampoline act so she could examine her pyjamas, which were covered with supercute My-Little-Pony-style cartoon unicorns, with manes like the hairdos of homecoming queens. "A Pegasus is a horse with wings."

"Those are Pegacorns," Derek proclaimed. "Those are some

clever marketer's idea of what six year old girls want to cuddle up with."

"I'm not six, I'm ten," Betsy protested.

"Doesn't matter. You were hooked at six. Or three. Now they've got you for life. At ninety-three you'll be dusting your little glass menagerie of crystal unicorns and porcelain Pegasuses, or would that be Pegasi? My own dear mother treasures a shelf of little glass birdies in her nursing home, I swear on a stack of Bibles. They're her best friends, I'd say."

Betsy finally noticed her own mother, standing on the deck. "Mom," she called. "Derek says unicorns are a crock."

"Don't lie," Derek scolded her. "It's most unbecoming in a child. I said no such thing."

"You did!"

"I never used the word crock. They're mythical beasts, myths are never a crock. They're beyond that, like Santa Claus or the tooth fairy."

Meghan came down into the garden. "Time you got out of those unicorns anyway," she said. "Go get dressed. And then, my dear, I think it's practice time on the piano."

"Really? You haven't made me practice it in weeks."

"Exactly."

Betsy attempted a cartwheel on the grass. Her form was excellent, a perfect whirling swirl of a circle that brought her to a standing stop in front of her mother. She beamed up at her. "I'm getting good," she squealed happily.

"Practice makes perfect," said Meghan. "Same for the piano."

"You're forgetting one thing," Betsy said, holding up her bandaged finger.

"If you can do cartwheels on that hand, you can play a piano. Anyway, your pjs will get all grass-stained if you're not careful," Meghan said. "Go get changed."

"In a bit."

"Betsy, I need to talk to Derek. Alone."

Derek set his hammer down. "Sounds ominous," he said.

"Is it about me?" Betsy asked.

"No."

"If it's about me, I have a right to listen," she insisted.

"It's not about you."

"Is it about your dreams?"

"Possibly."

"Mommy has strange dreams," Betsy said to Derek.

"So you mentioned," he answered. "She's lucky to remember them. I never do. Or maybe I'm the lucky one, I guess it depends on the dreams."

"Hers are really strange—"

"Betsy," her mother cut her short. "Go inside, get dressed, and I want to hear that piano for a good half hour before I see your face out here again."

"You don't have to yell," said Betsy.

"I wasn't yelling."

"It's most unbecoming in a mother." She smiled at Derek, expecting him to appreciate what she thought was a splendidly clever echo of a phrase he'd just used himself, but he was looking down around his feet for a can of beer he'd set there. He picked it up and drained the last remaining dribble. "Just let me grab another, be right back." That left Betsy alone under her mother's withering glare. She slunk into the house.

"Aren't people supposed to wait until noon for that?" Meghan asked when Derek returned.

"Maybe. But then I'd have to keep track of the time." He took a swig from the can and said, "Working in the sun like this gives a man a thirst."

Meghan said, "I'm not sure how to broach this. You're going to think I'm strange."

"Normal is strange to me," he replied.

"This is not normal. Betsy's right. I do have very odd dreams these days. It's really one dream that continues every night, and related to it, I need to say something to you."

"I'm all ears."

"Have you ever heard of anyone named Thomas of Gastoncoe?"

Derek shook his head no. From inside the house the first notes of the piano could be heard. Betsy was playing a childlike, somehow compelling version of Good King Wenceslas.

"Well, Thomas is someone who looks just like you," Meghan continued. "And I have reason to believe he might be in your head, listening to me now, so I'd like to speak directly to him, if I may."

Derek looked amused. "Fire away."

Meghan clasped her hands together at her waist, like a child composing herself to sing in front of strangers. "Thomas," she began. "In my dreams last night I heard what you said to Sylvanne. I was there, in her mind. If there is anything I can do to help you, to cure your daughter's illness, to bring her back to health, I will do it. I'll start by advising you to give her lots of fruits and vegetables. Oranges, if you can get them. Or lemons or limes. Vitamin C, but you don't know what that is. It can't hurt. Try chicken soup. Go to Sylvanne, and tell her what Daphne's been eating, and what medicines her doctor has been giving her. Tell her, make her listen, and I will hear it."

She studied Derek's face. He looked back at her neutrally.

"And one more thing," she continued. "I know Lady Sylvanne has already tried to attack you with a sword, so your guard is up. Keep it that way, don't ever drop it, because she wants your head. She means to kill you. Her husband planted the seed on his deathbed, he told her to learn the story of Judith and Holofernes, from the Bible—if you don't know how it ends, well, Judith got into his bed and cut off his head."

Meghan took a deep breath and exhaled. It felt very good to get that off her chest, regardless of what Derek might think of her. "There. That's it, I'm done," she said.

Derek looked around for his hammer. "All right then," he declared. "This fence will be finished in just a bit."

Meghan watched him pick a slat up from the ground and pull a nail from it with the hammer's claw. "Thank you for taking this so well," she said.

"How do you know how I'm taking it?" he asked. "All you're seeing is the surface politeness."

"And what's underneath?"

"Loads of things. Bemusement. It's kind of cute. Then bewilderment. What the fuck is she talking about? But mostly it's a pleasant surprise—it's nice, it makes you more interesting. You're more complicated than I thought."

"Now you're smirking."

"Am I? It's hard not to."

From inside the house they could hear Betsy's rendition of Good King Wenceslas collapse into childish random bashing of the keys.

"I better go keep her on course," Meghan said. Derek nodded and turned back to his work.

18

Thomas had for many nights been in the habit of staying up late at Daphne's bedside, propping himself up with pillows on a divan, watching his daughter by candlelight. Some nights he called for the night nurse and returned to his own bedroom to sleep; on others the soft pillows and dim flickering light caused his eyes to droop and shut, and in the morning he would awake to a cold room, sore-necked and fully clothed. This night was something new—when he awoke the candle was still lit, and the night nurse stood over him with a look of concern on her face.

"What is it?" he asked.

"I thought you called me, Sire."

"I did no such thing."

"You were talking quite strenuously," she suggested.

"Was I? Yes, likely I was."

He remembered now, and remembering, he sprang to his feet in excitement, colliding with the hapless nurse in his zeal. He caught her by her arms before she fell, righted her, then hurried to the bed and his sleeping daughter. He leaned in close and whispered eagerly, "She hears me, Daphne. The woman of my dreams hears me."

To the nurse he barked, "Go and see that Lady Sylvanne is roused and brought to me—No, on second thought, I'll pay her a visit. I must speak to her at once."

"Then should I—" the night nurse began, but he had already hurried past her out the door.

The guardsman on duty outside Sylvanne's room had fallen asleep, a young soldier hardly more than a boy propped up against the stone wall, resting his cheek on the pole of his halberd. When Thomas snatched it from him and brought the bayonet-like tip to his chin, the poor lad nearly died of fright. "Forgive me, m'Lord," he pled.

Thomas tested the blade of the oversized axe and proclaimed, "I should behead you here and now."

"As you wish Sire, as you wish," the young man sputtered.

"I wish you would stay awake," Thomas scolded him. "Now find the key and let me in. If you're unlucky I'll remember this later, but for now I'm intent on a greater purpose. Hand me that candle."

The soldier did as told. Thomas entered a small anteroom, where he could make out the maid Mabel lying on a small cot against the wall. Fussing in her sleep, she turned and rolled away from the candle's light. The door to Sylvanne's room was open a crack. Thomas pushed it wide and entered. She lay upon a large bed in the center of the room. He moved quickly to her bedside, and called her name softly.

Sylvanne heard a voice, and felt herself shaken awake. She opened her eyes and saw Thomas standing over her bed, whispering, "M'Lady, m'Lady."

She recoiled from him in fright. As she gained her senses her fear turned to fury.

"You'll not have me," she whispered. Finding her voice, she shouted for Mabel.

"Have you? You misjudge me," Thomas chided her. He announced eagerly, "I bring wonderful news—the woman of the future, the one of whom I spoke, who looks your twin, who lives in my dreams—she also lives in dreams, or so it seems. She told me she is inside you, she has seen me, and it's my hope that she is watching me now, and hears me as I speak."

"How dare you come to me in the night like this," Sylvanne hissed. "Have you not compromised me enough? Get out!"

"Madame, Madame. I know now what you are about. You have no more secrets from me. This Meghan—from her vantage point inside your mind, she sees all, and can tell me what goes on there. Judith and Holofernes! You see! I know all about it. She is the one who told me—how else could I know?"

"Mabel!" Sylvanne screamed. From the other room came the sound of Mabel grunting as she woke. She came running quickly, quite disoriented, and made more so by the sight of Lord Thomas in her Lady's chamber. Sylvanne fixed her with an accusing glare. "What lies have you been telling this man?"

"Nothing, ma'am. I've spent no time with him at all."

"M'Lady, whether you believe me or not has no further relevance," Thomas interjected. "I speak to another, one whose soul has migrated the centuries and lodges now in your mind. She is unfelt by you, that much is apparent. Yet she sees me, and hears me, and when I communicate with her you become a mere vessel of transmission. When the sun rises in a few hours I intend to bring you to Daphne's bedside, where you will listen to my physician describe his remedy. Through you that other entity, the woman Meghan, whom I pray may be my daughter's saviour, will be informed. Even though you don't intend it, you do me a great service, and I am grateful."

He spoke with such enthusiasm that Sylvanne almost believed him for a moment. She put a hand to her chest as if seeking her heart's pulse. "I don't feel her," she said.

Thomas answered without hesitation, "I'm certain she is there. I do not merely believe it, I know it, absolutely."

A few hours later, with the arrival of daylight, the three of them gathered at Daphne's bedside—Thomas, Sylvanne, and the Physician, a portly, ruddy-cheeked man of middle age named Blunt, who had laid out his tools upon the bed beside the girl, spreading them atop the same swath of coarse hemp cloth in which he normally kept them wrapped. He took hold of Daphne's forearm and removed a filthy bandage. On her white flesh, just below her elbow, a pus-filled, swollen wound gaped grotesquely. Thomas and Sylvanne watched as he took up a rust-flecked scalpel that looked more suited to woodworking, and gently scratched it across the wound. Pus gushed out and soaked into a dirty rag he had placed under her arm.

"And so you see, this is how I've been attending to her of a morning, for some weeks now," he pronounced. "Of the four humours, she withholds too much yellow bile—this is how we encourage it to the surface so as to drain it off. As you can see, the blood itself is corrupted." With the scalpel he made a small incision near the wound. Blood began to trickle down her arm into the rag, soaking it crimson red. "It's absolutely vital to allow some blood to escape, in order that poison burble out with it. The poison concentrates around the wound."

Thomas turned to Sylvanne, and said gravely, "Do you see what is being done? Give it full attention." To the Physician he said, "An authority I trust has opined that fresh vegetables and fruits, oranges in particular, might be beneficial."

"Oranges?" the Physician scoffed. "Worst possible thing. Too acidic. And besides, where would you get them?"

"I've already sent someone to the south," Thomas said. "I'm hoping that he might with luck find a trading ship arrived from Spain."

"I've thirty years experience. Never heard of oranges causing anything but cankers in the mouth. Do you wish to give her those?"

"There's plenty you don't know," Thomas replied.

"I'm not a magician, although I wish I were, Sire. I use what cures I've found success in previously. Fresh vegetables? In this case I trust more in what I've prescribed—the bark of an oak sapling, boiled with the guts of a songbird, given morning and night. Oak for strength, and the songbird to restore her to girlish vitality. Grant me some credit, and excuse me for speaking plainly, but she has lived much longer than her mother did after she acquired similar symptoms. You should have engaged me in her mother's case, instead of those quacks you relied upon."

"But I see no progress here," Thomas protested. "She declines more slowly than her mother, that is certain. Yet she still declines." Again he turned to Sylvanne. "Look upon her as closely as you can," he exhorted. "Take in every clue, as much as your senses can absorb."

Sylvanne stood over Daphne and reached out to her face, solemnly stroking her cheek with her fingers. The absence of sympathy or pity in the gesture unnerved Thomas as he looked upon her. Suddenly Daphne's eyes opened. She looked quizzically into Sylvanne's face.

"Do I know you?" she asked.

"This is Lady Sylvanne, darling," Thomas interceded. "She's come to help you."

"You're an innocent in this, and I wish you no ill," Sylvanne said neutrally. "But your father suffers delusions."

"Stop," Thomas demanded.

"He fantasizes that I might cure you, yet he gives me only reasons to wish him suffering and grief. Do you think that wise of him?"

"Close your mouth!"

Daphne, confused and troubled, looked plaintively to her father.

"Daddy?"

"She doesn't mean it, darling."

"I do—" Sylvanne meant to say more, but Thomas slapped his fleshy palm across her mouth. She bit at it, and he swore at her, vulgar words he immediately regretted using in front of his daughter. He yelled for the guard to return her to her quarters. The same young man from the previous night was still on duty. He made to take hold of her, but Sylvanne snarled at him, "You needn't handle me. I know the way."

"Before you go, I'll say one more thing to you," Thomas told her. He came and blocked her exit, looking straight into her eyes. "I speak now to that other. To Meghan. Did you see? Did you see enough? I pray you did. Please let me know it. I live for this exchange."

Sylvanne returned his gaze, staring at him with a fiery rage. "Are you finished? Then get out of my way." He stepped aside and she strode out the door.

Thomas looked at the bite marks she had left across his palm. He held it up to the Physician. "Lucky she didn't break the skin, or I'd have need of you too," he told him.

On the bed Daphne shuddered for a moment, like an underfed puppy. She looked at her father with wide, inquisitive eyes. "Daddy, why did she say you killed her husband?"

"It's a long story, my darling," he sighed. "Not one I'm prepared to tell just yet. Perhaps if all goes well."

19

Mabel sat by the window watching kestrels circle in the cloudless sky. She rubbed a hand over her belly, which ached contentedly—she had eaten several hearty meals now, and could feel a sense of vigour reborn in her body. She had to admit she was taking well to life in this grand castle, and felt no regret at having to quit Squire Gerald's drafty, ill-kept little keep. As soon as the thought came to her, she scolded herself, wondering, 'Have a mere handful of dinners and a soft feather bed converted me so quickly to snobbery? Mustn't forget where my loyalties lie—it were a tragedy what happened to my Master Gerald, and for my Mistress to be widowed so young. Mustn't lose sight of that.' She was pulled from these thoughts by the sound of voices in the hallway. Then the door opened and her Mistress was returned to her.

"What news, Madame?"

"Nothing of import. The girl awoke."

"And how is she?"

Sylvanne looked at her sharply. "What care you how she is?"

"But I, I didn't mean her health, ma'am," Mabel stammered, although that's exactly what she had meant. "I meant how is her personality—is she a pleasant girl, or a brat, is she sweet or is she spoiled?"

"Don't ask such things of me," Sylvanne responded harshly. "I can't allow myself to pity her, even if she were pleasant." She thought a moment. "Your interest in her is too keen for my liking. I'm still asking myself how our captor came to know of Judith and Holofernes."

"Oh ma'am, please do believe me when I promise you my purest loyalty," Mabel cried obsequiously. "I would never plot against you. Never would I share your secrets."

"That man Gwynn you rode in the cart with, on the journey here—you formed an attachment to him, it was obvious. Perhaps you mentioned it to him, forgetting in a moment of agreeable conversation that your words might have consequences."

Mabel blushed at the mention of Gwynn. "I don't think so, ma'am," she replied. "In fact I'm quite certain I never said such a thing to anyone at all. I swear it. On my heart, believe me Madame. I couldn't stand to be mistrusted by you."

"I don't know who, or what, to believe anymore."

Sylvanne sat wearily on the edge of her bed. Mabel watched her shoulders rise and fall with each breath. She came to her Mistress, touched her shoulder tenderly, and began to loosen the buttons on the back of her dress.

"Confide in me, Madame."

"I spoke very cruelly to the girl," Sylvanne said ruefully. "And again to you, just now. It's not in character for me to say such things. I feel such a stranger here, a stranger even to myself." She let her neck slump forward as the dress loosened, and Mabel rubbed her shoulders gently under the fabric. "My dear husband has charged me with a solemn obligation, which I promised to carry out. And I've never broken a promise in my life. I will fulfill my duty, because I must. But it isn't easy—to do it I need maintain a fire, an angry burning flame of righteousness, that leaves no room for weakness, or pity, or doubt. And in that state of mind, cruel words come naturally from my mouth." She rose and let Mabel pull the dress from her arms, stepped out of it, and elected to put on a simple housedress, a deep blue kirtle with pale yellow cuffs. "I'm glad you are here with me, Mabel. You're the only one in this place who remembers me the way I was, the way I truly am. I don't truly wish harm to anyone."

"I do know that Madame," said Mabel. "I've observed you a long time, long before you were elevated to the status of a Lady, remember? Why, I used to buy milk and cheese from you in the marketplace, when you were just a simple girl bringing goods to sell. Everyone in those days remarked on your sweetness and sincerity—there wasn't a more vibrant, openhearted girl in all the world, I don't reckon! It's no wonder Master Gerald plucked you from among the common folk and made you his queen."

"I should have refused him," Sylvanne mused. "I should have married a carpenter, or run away with a travelling minstrel."

"No, no, Madame," Mabel chided her softly. "There's no point dreaming of what wasn't and never can be. None of us can change the past."

"In this place I'm expected to change the future," Sylvanne said unhappily. "Lord Thomas has a heart so set on curing his daughter that he tolerates me, and treats me as a guest, knowing full well I intend to kill him. Isn't that peculiar?"

"I suppose it is," Mabel agreed. "At least on the surface. From what I've seen though, Madame, the man possesses love in abundance. He loves his daughter desperately, that much is apparent. And a desperate man will grasp at any straw, no matter how peculiar it might appear to others."

"Don't defend him to me, Mabel," Sylvanne said abruptly. "I need you as an ally, and an accomplice, just as Judith had her Abra."

"I doubt if I'm as brave as that maid," Mabel responded.

"I don't require bravery from you, but rather stealth, and cleverness at thievery—those are the skills you'll need. You treat our captors with deference, good humour even. I've noticed that whereas my every move is monitored, they like you already, and give you leeway."

"If I do wish to appeal to their good natures, Madame, it is only so that they might treat us both better," Mabel defended herself.

"Yesterday and this morning you've been allowed to fetch meals from the kitchen—do they watch you closely in that duty?"

"Oh yes, ma'am, there's a soldier at my side throughout."

"Does he hurry you? Impede you from talking to others?"

"Not exactly ma'am. The cooks are ladies of my age, and they like a wee gossip. The guard allows it, for it grants him time to chat up the younger maids."

"It sounds as if he barely watches you at all." Sylvanne said. "The kitchen must be busy as a beehive, a place of some clutter, where knives are plentiful."

Mabel felt a sense of dread at these words of her Mistress, but tried to hide it. She hoped her face showed sympathy and support. "I can guess your intent, Ma'am. It wouldn't be easy."

"Not easy, but not impossible. Please obey me in this, Mabel. Stealth has been lost to me, for I'm kept under lock and key. You are more fortunate, you move more freely, and that puts me at your mercy. I can't succeed without you."

"I'll try my best, Ma'am."

"That's not enough. You know how much this means. You must hurry, for I fear delay—I intend to fulfill my duty to Gerald quickly, before I lose my nerve. Bring me a knife, quick as you can. Promise me you'll succeed, and keep to it."

Before Mabel could answer, the door was flung open, and without announcement Thomas entered. "Ladies, I come to inform you that I've started Daphne on a brand new regimen of fresh vegetables," he proclaimed. "That'd be squash, beans, and carrots, all boiled up in a nice chicken broth. She ate it heartily, safe to say she devoured it, which brought joy to my heart. I've had good news from the south: oranges are procurable in the port, they will be two days in arriving."

A jubilant smile stretched across his lips. Mabel met his gaze with a smile of her own, a more careful one, making sure that her Mistress did not see it. Sylvanne had turned away, toward the window, to the rooftops, the treetops beyond, and the kestrels that continued to whirl in the sky.

"Did you hear me?" Thomas asked her. She didn't respond. "I said, did you hear me?"

Sylvanne turned and looked at him dispassionately.

"That suffices," he said. "I'll leave you ladies to your rest."

He bowed, stepped lightly to the door, and closed it behind him. Mabel cautiously offered an opinion. "He seems a decent man," she said.

"Mabel, please!" Sylvanne demanded. "Such remarks are not helpful when I'm doing my best to hate him."

20

Meghan rang the doorbell and waited impatiently, clutching the handle of a large leather art portfolio. She glanced at her watch. Cutting it too close, she thought. She decided she could still make her ten o'clock meeting if she limited her chat with Derek to three minutes. Another minute passed, another ring of the bell and knock upon his door for good measure, and she was preparing to bolt, when the door opened, and there stood Derek, groggy-eyed and rumpled in pyjama bottoms and a tee shirt, bed-head hair hanging limp like seaweed exposed at low tide.

"Good morning, I have a meeting I can't be late for, so I'll keep it short," she began. "I'm speaking to Thomas now. I just wanted you to know I was there at your daughter's bedside, I took it all in, despite Sylvanne's indifference—"

"Come in, come in," Derek muttered sleepily, stepping back and bidding her enter with a half-hearted wave of his arm.

"I don't have time," Meghan told him. "Let me say this: Thomas, I'm glad you're giving her fruits and veggies, that's a great start. Now the next step, get that crazy doctor away from her! He doesn't know what he's doing! He's killing her. That whole system of medicine he practices, of trying to balance the four humours—it's all bullshit, it's been discredited a long time ago. Now we worry about germs and bacteria, which are like tiny little bugs you can't see, but they're having a field day in that nasty wound on her arm that your doctor keeps poking and gouging at daily. Just clean it up and leave it alone! Boil some water, let it cool to lukewarm, and clean out that wound, clean it thoroughly, I want all the pus gone. Then wrap it in clean linen, and keep it wrapped. Change the linen twice a day. Don't let the pus build up, pus is bad, not good! And no more bloodletting, she needs all the blood she's got, poor thing! You hear me?"

"What the hell is this about?" Derek grumbled. "I haven't had my coffee—"

"It doesn't matter, Derek. Thomas will get it, that's what matters."

"Thomas has left the building," Derek mumbled.

"No, let me finish!" Meghan insisted. "I'm not speaking to *you*, I'm speaking to Thomas. This is important. Thomas, I think you need to sit Sylvanne down, and tell her the full story, so I can give a proper diagnosis. What are the symptoms, where does Daphne hurt, how often does she have a bowel movement, spare no detail. Do you hear me? I hope you hear me."

"Remember I told you it was cute, this weird little mania of yours? It's not cute. Not at seven in the morning."

"It's after nine. I'm sorry Derek, I've gotta run."

She scurried down his steps to the street, the sound of her heels clattering on the concrete sidewalk as she hurried to her car. She heard Derek call out, "It's not cute—it's creepy!"

A minor traffic accident involving a bicycle courier had snarled traffic, and by the time the elevator doors opened on the eleventh floor, Meghan glanced at her cell phone and saw she was twelve minutes late. She hurried past reception down a curving carpeted path between cubicles, and poked her head into the conference room, to find that Jan was the only person there. "Debra told me if you were more than ten minutes late to forget it. Now what do we do?" she asked. Debra was their boss.

Meghan picked up the phone on the conference table and punched in Debra's extension. "Debra? So sorry. Traffic was an absolute bitch." When she hung up Jan said, "That was very brave—using the phrase absolute bitch when speaking to one."

Meghan laughed. "The meeting's still on, she'll be here in a sec." She laid out her designs on the table and waited. A sec turned into five minutes. Jan said, "She's doing it deliberately, to let us know she's the alpha male around here."

"I thought you'd say alpha bitch," Meghan whispered.

In an even lower whisper, Jan replied, "I was going to, but she might stick her snout through that door any second." Then she asked brightly, at normal volume, "How are you, anyway? How are the dreams? Still under siege? Did you meet your Thomas yet?"

"I have, in fact."

"What's he like?"

"He looks exactly like Derek, my neighbour."

"What, the hunky drunk next door? The midnight flasher?"

"The very same."

"You've been dreaming of your neighbour this whole time?"

"There's more to it than that. Much more. Incredibly more. It's complicated—"

"I saw him once, when I helped you move in—"

"I know, you told me. You think he's cute."

"Shaggy-cute. A woolly bohemian. And Thomas looks like him?"

Meghan nodded. "Thomas is in better shape. He's more serious. He carries himself better," she said.

"Always the way."

"What do you mean?"

"The dream man is always better than reality."

"Jan. It's not a joke."

"Of course not," Jan replied. "I need to get a second look at your neighbour, see what we're dealing with here."

"You've already seen him."

"I glimpsed him in his back yard, from your deck. He waved. Had a nice smile. Since then I've only heard about him from you. Is he still acting like a complete jerk?"

"Not always. Betsy and he are like best buddies now. He gets along with her better than I do."

"She's missing her dad," Jan said.

"Who's utterly preoccupied with his prize student, and the baby she's so kindly growing for him."

"Men are such idiots."

"Most of them," Meghan agreed.

"And what about Thomas, is he an idiot too?"

"No, actually." For a moment she pictured him in Daphne's room, tending to his sickly daughter by dim candlelight. "In my dreams he's kind of..." she paused, searching for just the right word to describe him. "Admirable."

"I thought you were going to say hot," Jan teased.

"Jan, I beg you, take it seriously," Meghan scolded her. She was surprised to hear Sylvanne in the tone of her own voice, and in the odd phrasing. I beg you.

"I've been very supportive up until now," Jan protested. "But if you're going to tell me that after all this, the man of your dreams looks just like your neighbour, well I'm telling you sister, now is the time to rejoice and give thanks that he's been gift wrapped and delivered almost to your front door."

"More the back door, actually," Meghan replied. She began to tell Jan the story of the shattered pane of glass, and had reached the part where she first noticed the sloppy clump of bandages wrapped around Betsy's finger, when Debra suddenly arrived, sailing into the boardroom without so much as a nod of greeting and setting herself straight to the task of assessing the designs Meghan had laid out on the table top. They were cover designs for a novel called *Enemies with Benefits*, all variations on an image of two teary women commiserating. In one they were in a swank cafe while handsome men circled like predators, in another they sat cross-legged facing each other on a comfy couch, with a box of tissues between them half-buried in a pile of scrunched-up used ones. Debra wasted no time in giving her opinion.

"This work is not to your usual standard, Meghan."

"I think it's true to the book," Meghan defended herself. "The book is all about women processing, and here we see women processing." In truth she had barely flipped through her galley copy, she'd relied on the blurb prepared for the catalogue.

"But there's more to it than that," Debra said sternly. "We talked about this, I'm certain. I'm sure I told you what I've been telling everyone—*Bridget Jones* was about one woman, *Sex and the City* was about four, well, this one splits the difference and is about two. Two best friends comparing sex lives—bright, gorgeous young women in their twenties who expect the men they meet to measure up to their high standards, to be their intellectual and emotional equals, and yet they wind up navigating an urban wasteland of eternal adolescents, Game Boy addicts and porn freaks eager to subject them to every bizarre sex act known to man."

"Like that show *Girls*?" Jan said.

Debra winced. "Yes. But we can't *say* that, we have to differentiate it. We're expecting this book to be *huge*, the film rights have already brought six figures. It's for a new generation of women who think Sarah Jessica Parker is a wrinkled old hag. It's edgier, more explicit—there are passages of severely kinky sex, enough that men might be tempted to read the thing too. But, Meghan, I see nothing in your designs, nothing here at all, to alert people to that."

"Maybe she could be stirring a cup of tea with a riding crop," Meghan suggested, with just a hint of sarcasm.

"You don't get it," Debra rebuked her. "These girls don't drink tea, they chug Red Bull."

"Do you really think men will wade through pages of women's chatter for a few bits of kinky sex?" Meghan asked.

"It's more than a few pages. And we have to let them know. Give them the option."

"We should change the title, to something that really zeros in on the no-strings-attached sex they're having," Jan interjected. "Saying friends with benefits to describe a relationship is something women do. It's a cute pun, to make the point that they keep ending up having sex with men they don't even like, but we need a stronger word than benefits. Something funny yet depraved, so men will sit up and pay attention. They love depravity. Any hint of it and men rent the DVD."

"Then they fast forward through it," Meghan asserted. "Novels don't have fast forward."

"It's like that website that tells you to the second where the naked bits are in every movie ever made," Jan added. "Men search that. They memorize it like sports statistics."

Debra directed their attention back to the design. "Think of it as a movie, because it's going to be one soon enough," she intoned. "You're designing a movie poster to lure men as well as women to the local Cineplex."

"Think kink," Meghan said.

"Exactly. A Helmut Newton kind of thing, only more contemporary, realistic but influenced by computer animation. And I need it by Thursday."

She turned on her heels and left the room, taking all the

tension with her. Jan and Meghan exchanged looks of relief. Then Meghan sighed deeply. "She told me I'm slipping," she worried. "First time for that."

"She's stressed. Everyone is. She has no more clue than we do what they're plotting upstairs. The whole imprint could be shut down tomorrow, and she'd be on the street with the rest of us. We're still young and adaptable enough to land on our feet, but she's fifty-six, divorced, and higher up in the food chain, where chances of a lateral move are slim to none right now."

Meghan gathered up her papers into her portfolio and suddenly felt a wave of self-pity wash over her. "At least her kids are grown," she sighed. "I've got a child to worry about, I'm getting divorced, too. I'm thirty-one, but I *feel* fifty-six."

Jan gave her a gentle hug. "There there," she said soothingly. She looked into Meghan's face. "Your eyes do look awfully tired. I'd say try to get some sleep, good old-fashioned restful sleep, if that's possible. Can't you take a break from those dreams of yours?"

Meghan shook her head. "I wouldn't even want to. It's hard to explain, but now that I've met Thomas, I feel I have a purpose. I promised I'd help him cure his daughter. I used to dread going to sleep, now all of a sudden I can't wait. I can't stand the suspense."

"What do you mean, you promised him?"

"I did promise. I told him I'd help him, through Derek. Don't look at me as if I'm nuts, please—you'd understand totally if you could see how desperately, pitiably ill Daphne looks, lying on her bed. Her skin is grey in colour, and translucent, I swear. My biggest worry is that I've reached her too late, that I'll sleep tonight

and discover she's passed away." The thought of it made her eyes
moisten. "I couldn't bear it," she said, fighting back tears.

"Girl, get a grip," Jan said. "Whatever happens in that world,
this is the one you live in. Concentrate on making this one work."

"You do think I'm nuts."

"Let's just say I'm worried about you. How was your session
with Anne? Was it any help? Did she have any insight?"

"No, not really. I'm seeing her again in a few days. She wants
me to be her guinea pig." She forced herself to smile. "I'll be fine.
I know what needs doing. I'll go home and do it."

21

In her upstairs studio Meghan arranged a scattering of new drawings, all of them variations on the same image: a woman in black lingerie pumps gas into a Mercedes, while her lover sits watching her from the driver's seat, one black glove visible on the steering wheel. It was a scene straight out of the book, which she had forced herself to read, but had ended up skimming, mostly. Young urban women taking risks with strangers, that was pretty much the theme of it, and this scene, Meghan felt, captured both ends of the spectrum of possibilities—a girl could make herself vulnerable like that and be incredibly turned on, or just as easily the anticipated erotic jolt could fizzle into self-consciousness and public humiliation. Meghan looked at her sketch and knew she would need to fix it—the model would have to be leggier, more gamine-like, to bring out the vulnerability. She knew Debra would be expecting a minimum of three ideas, and this was only the first, but instead of setting herself to the task, she put the sketches aside, sat down at the computer, and Googled *medieval medicine.* While she scrolled down the choices, Betsy stuck her head in the door and said, "Are you finished?"

Meghan shook her head. "Uh-uh."

"Then why are you on the computer?"

"I need to check something."

"When can I use it?"

"When I'm finished."

"Can I come in now?"

"Not yet."

Meghan had banned Betsy from the studio for the afternoon—she didn't think it appropriate for a ten-year-old to watch her sketch images of kinky women in erotically-charged situations. "I'm just taking a break for a minute, and then I'll be back to work."

"Why's that woman putting gas in her car in her underwear?"

"This is exactly why I don't want you in here—too much explaining." Meghan got up to shut the door.

"What am I supposed to do?" Betsy whined.

"Watch TV. Read a book. Draw something."

"I need my own computer."

"I gave you an iPad , you lost it, remember?"

"I didn't lose it, it was stolen."

"You took it to school, you came home without it, that is all I know."

"I left it in the cafeteria for like, not even five minutes."

"Betsy. I'm closing this door."

"I need another one. I'll help pay for it, out of my allowance."
Meghan shut the door.

Betsy wandered downstairs to the kitchen, swung open the fridge
door, and randomly scanned its contents, in hopes of finding
something good, like chocolate pudding or cake. But there was
nothing like that. In fact it scared her a little how empty the
fridge was, another sign that her mother was losing it. From next
door she heard a sound that she guessed must be Derek whacking
a golf ball again, and went out to investigate.

The elaborate frame of plumbing pipes and netting he had so
recently constructed was gone. From the deck she could see that
he'd come up with a simpler strategy: his ball was now tethered
to a six-foot-long elastic band attached to a spike in the ground.
He set the ball between his feet and reared back for a swing, when
Betsy called out in a singsong voice, "I can see yooouuu..."

The disruption made him carve a huge divot out of his scrag-
gly lawn. He spotted Betsy on the deck and said, "There you are.
How's the finger coming along?"

"Better. Is that a real ball?"

"No, it's hollow, and plastic. But for some reason, even though
I've set it up so it can't hit me, and I know it won't hurt even if it
does hit me, my body doesn't believe my mind—every frigging
time it comes flying back at me, I bail. It's turning my smooth
swing all spastic. What happened to your trampoline?"

"My mom locked it in the shed. It's part of my punishment
for the broken window. Plus she said it's too dangerous."

"Ridiculous," Derek spat. "You're overprotected. You'll never learn to deal with dangerous things unless you're given dangerous things to deal with."

"What happened to your netting?" she asked.

"I took it down. When I wasn't using it, it loomed too high above me, like a prison fence. Gave me the creeps, especially at night. This is better. Simpler is usually better."

"What other games do you have?" Betsy asked.

"None. Golf is infuriating enough."

"I have badminton, do you like it?"

"Like it? I love it," he exclaimed. "In my day I was fourteen-and-under regional champion, or I would have been if I'd bothered to enter. Wicked drop shot, I had. But that was mostly indoors, and I love it even more outdoors—it's the only game besides golf where you really have to watch what the wind is up to—a capricious little gust can ruin what you expected was a perfectly placed shot."

"Shall we play?" Betsy asked excitedly.

"Oh let's," he answered, gently mocking her. "But we'll have to play blind badminton."

"What's that?"

"We'll make the fence the net, which means you can't see the birdie until it comes fluttering back at you."

"Brilliant!" Betsy cried. She was thrilled. She ran inside to retrieve her racquets and shuttlecock, and before long a spirited game of blind badminton was underway.

❖

Up in her studio Meghan was lost in the world of medieval medicine, educating herself as to the properties of the four humours. The familiar musical peals of Betsy's distinctive laugh reached her faintly from the back yard. She got up and went to the back bedroom window to have a look. Below her Derek and Betsy, in high spirits, were whacking the birdie back and forth over the fence.

"You know if you win, you get to declare yourself blind badminton champion of the universe, because we're the only two players known to exist," Derek was shouting, his voice ragged from exertion.

"Even if I lose, I'll still be second in the universe," Betsy yelled back. "I'll get the silver medal!"

"No, you'll be the worst, worst in the world. Shit!" His return shot hit the fence and fell back in his yard. "Pardon my French. Okay. I'm serving. Ready?"

"It's ten eight," Betsy called out.

"For me," said Derek.

"No, for me!"

"It was nine eight for me."

"No it wasn't!"

"Don't mess with me, girl," Derek scolded.

"You're the one messing."

"Whatever. Finish this game, then I need a cigarette."

"But ten eight for me, right?"

"Fine. Still plenty of time to whip your ass. I mean butt."

"Ass is a donkey," Betsy laughed.

"True. And people do whip donkeys, right on their ass."

"Asses have asses!" Betsy giggled. "Damn it!" She muffed a shot. "Ten nine."

"Watch your language," Derek teased her.

"Which one, asses or damn it?"

"Both."

"You say them all the time!"

"I'm allowed. When you stop living with your mother, you're allowed."

"She didn't hear me."

"I think she did. Check the window."

Betsy looked up to see Meghan looking down at them.

"Mom! Come out and play."

She shook her head.

"Come and play! It's called blind badminton, because of the fence!"

Meghan opened the window wide enough to speak through. "Sorry honey, I've got so much work to do."

"You always say that."

"I'll be down in a bit."

"Your bits take hours."

"Smoke break," Derek announced.

"It won't be hours," Meghan said.

"Come now or forget it," Betsy warned her.

"I'm closing the window," Meghan answered. She did, and disappeared inside.

Derek sat on top of his picnic table and lit a cigarette. On her side of the fence Betsy entertained herself by batting the birdie straight up into the air, again and again, counting each successful swat out loud, to see how long she could keep it aloft. At eleven she stopped—"I think a bat flew by!" she shrieked excitedly.

"Too early for that," Derek said. "Unless he's messed up. How's your mother doing, by the way?"

"She's getting better, I'd say."

"I don't know about that," Derek replied. "Had quite a lot to say to me at seven thirty this morning, and none of it made the slightest bit of sense. Which is fine, I suppose." He sang a few lines from a pop song: "*Wish I knew what she was thinking, Wish I knew if she was sane, Wish I knew if it was only a game.* Do you know it?"

"Never heard of it," Betsy said.

"What do they teach you kids in school? Are the seminal bands of the 1980s so easily forgotten? The Jones of Ark?" He sang another tune: "*A human being, is only really being, when he is being, loved.*"

"But why does everyone need to be loved?" Betsy asked. "It's very unfair if it's not their fault no one loves them. Why do the people in songs always go all crazy when they can't have love?"

"Generally speaking, if pop songs are to be believed, love and the lack of it are the primary cause of madness, suicide, and crying all night," Derek replied.

"Someone's at your door," Betsy said.

"What?"

"Your doorbell rang. The front one."

"You heard it from here? I'm getting old." Derek got up and headed inside through his open back door. "Should have kept my head out of the speakers at those long-ago rock shows."

"Shouldn't smoke," Betsy yelled after him.

"I don't smoke with my ears."

A few minutes later Betsy was playing with a stray golf ball she'd found, rolling it around on her badminton racquet, when Derek reappeared with a friend in tow, exclaiming, "Come meet my new friend Betsy! You'll like her, she's ten."

Betsy climbed up to her deck to get a look at them. Derek spotted her there. "Betsy, look who's here. A sight for sore taste buds, my old buddy Ken." Ken nodded to her. He had his long hair tied back in a ponytail, wore a black tee shirt that said Stay Heavy, and was doing arm curls like a weight lifter with a twelve-pack of beer in each hand. "Gimme one of those, I'll lighten the load," Derek demanded. "Two dozen beers here—if I'm quick enough, I'll get eighteen to your six."

"I have no interest in alcoholic beverages," Betsy said haughtily. "To me they taste awful."

"Youth is wasted on the young, so the old get wasted," Derek said.

"Why do you like it?" Betsy asked.

"You're too young to understand, unless that homeroom teacher of yours is a drunkard too."

"No, only a bisexual. But he told us once he had a love-hate relationship with cocaine."

"Me too, still do," said Ken. "Love it when I have it, hate it when I run out."

"You do know too much," Derek said to Betsy. "Don't be in a hurry to put away childish things."

"What's that supposed to mean?"

"Stick to lollipops and dollies as long as you can."

"I'm already past those things," she said curtly. "I like online chat."

"Give her a beer, then," Ken said, ripping open the flimsy cardboard case and handing Derek a cold can.

Derek's eyebrows lifted mischievously above a rogue's grin. He held the can out toward Betsy. "Would you like one?"

Just at that moment Meghan came out onto the deck. "She most certainly would not," she said sharply.

"We're just joking around," Derek smiled. In a teasing voice he added, "The young lady has already informed us she has no interest in alcoholic beverages."

"Hilarious," Meghan scoffed. "Betsy, time for dinner."

It was a warm summer evening. As she ate her meal in the kitchen, Betsy strained her ears to eavesdrop through the open door on the conversation of the men outside, catching only fragments of phrases from the increasingly drunken rhythms of their speech. She ate quickly and got up to head back out, but Meghan stopped her. "I don't want you going out there."

"But you always tell me I need more fresh air."

"It's not so fresh. They're smoking like chimneys, the two of them."

"Outside smoking doesn't count."

"You can go use the computer if you want. Chat with your friends for a while, then it's bath time, then bed."

"What are you going to do?"

"I need to talk to Derek for a minute." She felt a need to talk to Thomas, to tell him of Sylvanne's plot to get a kitchen knife, and reinforce her insistence that Daphne's bloodletting stop. She'd been researching the antiseptic and antibiotic uses of medieval herbs, and wanted to tell him to apply vinegar and lavender oil to the wound on her arm, and add garlic and onion to the vegetable soups prepared for her. She also wanted to raise the possibility of tuberculosis as the cause of Daphne's sickly cough.

Betsy trundled upstairs to the studio, and Meghan cleaned up the dishes. Occasionally she heard laughter from the men, and a loudly hooted expletive here and there. Better get out there before they're incoherent, she thought. She wiped the counters and dried her hands, then went out the back door. There was only Ken in the back lawn, lazily swinging a golf club. He lifted his head and saw her, and stared at her quite brazenly, her long legs in particular, making her wish she was wearing something more concealing than short shorts and a tank top.

"Where's Derek?" she asked.

"Gone out to get cigarettes and papers," he replied.

"Papers?"

"Rolling papers. Come on over—I sold a bike today, one of my motorbikes. I got some serious cash for it, and now it's like, Let's Party!"

"I'll pass," Meghan said. "Got things to do."

"Should I tell Derek you're looking for him?"

"Sure. Tell him it can wait until tomorrow."

"Will do."

She went inside, irritated that she had something important to say to Thomas, but couldn't. There was an hour to fill before Betsy's bath and bedtime, and what she really wanted to do was get back online and continue her research into tuberculosis, autoimmune illnesses, and medieval medicine, but with Betsy at the computer she decided instead to pick up her galley copy of Enemies with Benefits again, hoping a scene she'd somehow missed in her cursory skim-through would now jump out at her and beg to be illustrated. She spread herself out on the living room couch, but after a few minutes she realised she was sweating. The room was stuffy in the heat. She decided the best place would be out on the deck, but that meant putting herself on display to the drunks next door. It would have to be the lawn—the fence would grant privacy.

There was no one in Derek's back yard when she went out. She brought a picnic blanket to spread on the lawn, and flopped down on it with a couple of cushions from the patio chairs. In a few minutes she could hear, but not see, Derek and Ken emerge from the house and settle back into an evening of drinking beer around a picnic table ashtray. She perked up when she heard Ken say, "Your neighbour wanted to talk to you."

"What about?"

"Didn't say."

"Apparently she's having dreams about me." Derek said.

"Sounds promising."

"Yeah. Some dude that looks just like me, some ancient prince in a castle."

"Doesn't matter. Nice ass trumps craziness any day," Ken remarked.

"She truly believes there's someone listening in my head, and she needs to talk to him. Thomas, his name is, and she'll be like, 'I'm talking to Thomas, not *you*.' I've told her there's no one else in there, it's all private property, but she doesn't care, says it doesn't matter whether I'm aware or not, he's there, all right. He's in there."

"Don't let her see the real you," Ken advised.

"Too late for that! Don't you remember me yelling at her the other night? Up at her window right there? In spite of that I've landed in her good books. Christopher Hitchens to the contrary, there is a God. I'd do her in a minute. She's gorgeous, don't you think?"

"Like I said, nice ass trumps craziness."

"Everything's nice about her."

Meghan, now fully focussed on her eavesdropping, waited for more, but instead there came a prolonged silence. She pictured the two of them lost in thought, hiding in a cloud of cigarette smoke. Then Ken said, "Someone like her might be good for you."

"What do you mean?" she heard Derek say.

"Well. It's just. Well you know. She'd have been about the same age, now."

"Don't even go there," Derek said quietly. "Although I know you care. And I'm glad you care." Then there was another prolonged silence. Then Derek broke the sombre mood with a sudden loud, elongated yowl—Meghan pictured him rising from the picnic table and stretching like a noisy cat. "You're my best friend, old Ken," he sighed affectionately. "It's been a long strange journey and back through all of that, and here we are, still the best of buds."

"Smoking the best of buds," added Ken.

"Gimme a hug," said Derek.

"Fuck that."

"No, come on, do it. No one's hugging me these days. Every human needs a hug."

"All right then, for charity's sake. Lonely old Derek."

Meghan heard the beavertail claps of the manly backslaps that are inevitable when drunken men hug each other. She'd begun to worry about how she was going to sneak into her house without them realizing she'd been listening to them, and seized this moment to scurry up onto the deck unnoticed. She lingered by the door for a moment, taking in the sight of two middle-aged fools clenched together in that dishevelled yard.

"I can't believe I'm doing this," Ken said.

"It feels great. *A human being, is only really being, when he is being, loooooved,*" Derek brayed.

"That song sucked. You can let go now."

"No fucking way. I'm loving it."

"Small doses, man. Everything in small doses."

"But not love. Never say that about love."

22

Sylvanne sat on her bed while Thomas paced her room. He'd been speaking for some time about his wife, most especially the history of her illness. "She suffered no convulsions, or twitching or spasms to serve as signposts of what was to come. No, it was just a gradual malaise, a sickly cough such as anyone might have in the winter season, only this one lingering into spring, and growing more bold with the lengthening days. Her pulse weakened till she could scarcely rise from her bed in the morning, and lay there much of the day. Some days, by sheer strength of will, she would pull herself to her feet, unsteady as a newborn foal, and make her way to the chapel for prayers."

Sylvanne tried to distract herself from his words, for she feared that such a sad story might arouse sympathy within her, and weaken her resolve. She encouraged her own mind to wander back to her former life, well before the siege, when she and

Gerald had been newlyweds, when he had loved her keenly. He had written poetry for her, not only before they were married, but afterward as well, in fact the later poems became even more ardent and explicit in describing her charms, because by then he'd gained intimate and detailed knowledge of them. How she wished she had committed some of his poems to memory, for she knew not what had become of them in the siege. She hated herself for being able to recall only a handful of random lines in full, for it made it all seem so wasted, as if Gerald, the poems, her former life, none of it had ever really existed. She was lost in such thoughts when Thomas, in his pacing, stopped and stood directly before her, mouthing words she barely heard.

"The soup and the vegetables are working wonders," he said. "And now that we have ceased to open her arm for bloodletting, the infection grows less livid. The oranges I expect to arrive before dark tonight. If not, then tomorrow."

Sylvanne turned away from him and looked out the window. "Look at me when I speak to you," Thomas ordered her. "I need to be sure this is heard. There's been such vast improvement already, I wish there was some way I could thank you. I am of course addressing Meghan with these words. There's an unreality to it, for although I address myself to someone who has already proven herself helpful, sweet, and kind, yet I speak these heartfelt words of thanks to the sullen face of one who can't bear to look upon me."

Sylvanne met his eyes. "Why should I look upon you, when you speak not to me, but some imaginary creature?"

"You have a point," Thomas said. In softer tone he continued,

"It's my mistake—I should know by now not to expect much from you in the way of sympathy. I wish you would be helpful. Come along now Sylvanne, I wish to show my daughter again to the woman Meghan, who dwells inside you. Come, we'll go see Daphne now."

Sylvanne made no effort to get up.

"Come."

"No."

"Dear Meghan," said Thomas, exasperation in his voice, "Forgive me if I resort to driving this uncooperative lady like a beast of the field. Know that my intentions are pure. Grant me one moment."

He left the room only briefly, then came striding back through the door straight to Sylvanne on the bed. He carried a fresh-cut switch in his hand, a whip suitable for herding cattle or goats, and without hesitation he slapped it down hard on the table next to the bed, so that a pewter goblet tumbled and fell to the floor. Sylvanne involuntarily jumped to her feet.

"You're a bastard," she spat.

"I'll do whatever it takes to save my daughter," he told her. "If you stand in the way of that, you will suffer. Do you understand? Now. Do I need shackle you, and drag you there, or will you walk beside me?"

Sylvanne stood and walked toward the door. "This must be what hell is like," she said wearily. "A place where all action is coerced by threat."

Daphne was feeling much better—she was sitting up on her bed, knitting with raw wool, attended to by a servant girl named Beth. As Thomas and Sylvanne entered she called out brightly, "Daddy, I'm knitting you a winter scarf."

"Wonderful," said Thomas. "How has she been?"

"Fine, Sir," answered Beth. "Her fingers are much more nimble than my own, and she never drops a stitch."

"What colour shall we dye it?" Daphne asked excitedly. "Shall we use beetroot to make it red?"

"I prefer a nice green," said the servant girl. "It's a colour not seen enough in winter."

Thomas leaned forward to give Daphne a kiss. "Red suits me fine," he said. "Red as the blush in your rosy cheeks, my love." But the smile on his face quickly disappeared, for Daphne began to cough violently. Sitting on the bed, he took her in his arms to comfort her, holding her until the cough subsided. "There there, my darling, you've overdone it for one day," he said softly. "We can't expect you to be fiddle-fit on a few days' good soup. Full health will take some time." He told Beth to fetch a drink of water, which he brought carefully to his daughter's lips. Then he turned to address Sylvanne.

"You can clearly see she's looking so much better, and it's all down to you, Meghan. I don't know how to repay you. Words of gratitude are inadequate to the soaring feeling that has filled my heart these past days. I wish I could embrace you, but the woman who stands before me will have none of that, I'm certain."

"For once you know my feelings," Sylvanne said.

"I'll make do with embracing my darling daughter, who

needs love along with her vegetables." He tenderly took Daphne in his arms.

"Thank you Daddy," she sighed. "It feels so nice."

"Poor dear," he worried. "You're so light and thin. As if made of feathers, not flesh and bone and skin." He held her at arm's length and looked searchingly into her eyes. "Promise us you'll get better."

"I want to," she said, her voice a whisper.

"I'm glad. Keep wanting."

Daphne glanced over her father's shoulder and met Sylvanne's eyes. She took a sudden fright, chilled by the hostile glare that was returned to her.

"Why does she stare at me so coldly?" she whispered in her father's ear.

"Don't be frightened, my dear. There is someone who cares about you very much, inside her. Very much. She's hidden from sight, but she is there."

"I wish I could see her."

"She sees you, and that is what matters. Trust me, darling. She is there."

23

Betsy woke in the middle of the night to the angry wail of a car alarm. She parted the blinds to peek down at the street below and recognized Derek's beat up old two-seat sports car, screeching back and forth to squeeze into a tight spot between two SUVs. The one in front had been bumped—aglow with blinking orange parking lights, it blared an angry cycle of blips, whoops and wails to wake the dead.

Derek's car lurched one last time and settled in place. Betsy saw him stumble from the driver's seat, slam the door behind him and stagger toward the still-screaming SUV. With his palms squished protectively against his ears, he kicked ineffectually at the back bumper a few times. Meanwhile from Derek's car a woman emerged and sauntered over to him, a little unsteady on high heels. Betsy couldn't make it out, but whatever they said to each other made them laugh. Then the woman stepped up and laid her hands on the SUV's sun roof, and in that very instant it stopped screaming, and for a moment the dark deserted street returned to an almost spooky calm.

"You've got the magic touch," Derek whooped gleefully. As she stepped to the curb, he held out a hand, and when she took it he pulled her to him, kissing her so roughly the two of them nearly tumbled.

"Careful," she playfully scolded him. "Not out here, let's get inside where it's private."

"I can't wait to get inside," Derek murmured, and the woman said something back Betsy couldn't catch. She watched as Derek led her to his door, and heard it slam shut behind them. She stared at the shadows of tree branches swaying on the street for a moment before she lay back down to sleep.

At noon Derek was sitting at his picnic table in a threadbare housecoat, the Saturday Globe and Mail spread before him, smoking a cigarette and drinking coffee from a chipped mug. Betsy's head appeared over the top of the fence, looking down on him like a mischievous angel.

"Is that your breakfast—coffee and a cigarette?" she asked.

"No. Coffee and a cigarette is what's popularly known as a whore's breakfast," he answered irritably. "Throwing in a newspaper elevates it to an intellectual's breakfast."

In a singsong Betsy asked, "How was your Friday night?"

"If you want to be my friend, you need to learn something: Don't bug me when I'm reading the morning paper."

"I saw you with someone last night," Betsy said teasingly. "Is that your girlfriend?"

"Did you hear what I just said?" Derek scowled.

"Is she still inside?"

"No. She turned out to be a head case and I kicked her out. Didn't you hear the yelling?"

"You kicked her out? In the night time?"

"Screw off, little girl," Derek muttered. "You hear me? Get lost. I'm sick of looking at you."

Betsy's mouth fell open, and the tiny gasp that came from it was the sound of her heart shattering. She dropped from sight behind the fence; seconds later Derek saw her scuttle up the steps to her deck and dash tearfully inside the house. He felt a pang of remorse, and almost called out to her, but in his hung-over mind the urge to apologize was trumped by a fierce desire for peace and quiet, caffeine and nicotine.

An hour later he was still in his housecoat, stalemated against a brutal hangover, stretched out atop the picnic table using his rolled up newspaper as a pillow, snoozing in the sun.

"Hello Derek. Are you awake?"

He opened his eyes and saw Meghan looking at him, from the exact spot Betsy had occupied earlier.

"First the daughter, now mommy dearest," he muttered darkly, shielding his eyes with the crook of his elbow.

"She doesn't need to be verbally abused on a Saturday morning."

"Is that what I did?"

"From what she told me, yes you did. I have enough to worry about without you adding to it."

Squinting in the sunlight, Derek dragged himself to a sitting position, tugging at his housecoat to keep his privates covered. Meghan caught a glimpse of his thigh and glanced away quickly to avoid having to acknowledge that something might have briefly been on display. Glancing down, Derek satisfied himself that he was decent, then fumbled for a cigarette.

"Here's my theory of worry, yours to take away at no charge," he told her. "Physically, we humans are hardly more evolved than our mammalian brethren, but mentally, through some fluke of evolution, we've developed a massive consciousness, which compels us to build elaborate empires of worry in our minds. Upon death, like our physical bodies, these worries dissolve into maggot food. Why worry about maggot food?"

"I'm not. I'm worried about my daughter."

"Are you?"

"Yes."

He took a deep drag on his cigarette. "Don't you think your lady under siege is an appropriate metaphor for your own life?"

"I already have a therapist, thank you. She made the same observation, but I'd already thought of it myself. She at least believes me when I tell her what I've experienced."

"She's paid to dole out sympathy. Or pretend to."

"Maybe I should pay you then," Meghan said sharply. "I suppose I should be grateful you're willing to listen to me, that you haven't told me to get lost. But it would be so much easier if I thought you believed me."

"What difference would it make if I did?"

"It would help me a lot. I could pass information to Thomas without you getting all strange about it, and letting me know by smirks and grimaces that you think I'm a freak."

"This Thomas, what is he like? He looks just like me, correct?"

"His face is the same, but he's better groomed. He holds himself well. He's very fit—he spends much of his time in training, for jousts and warfare. So he gets lots and lots of hard exercise. And there's no junk food in his diet, it's pretty much coarse bread and meat, from what I've seen. So yes, he's like you, but in better shape, and better turned out. Super-fit people are never slobby, it seems."

Derek sucked in his paunch and sat up straighter on the picnic table. "I'm actually in pretty good shape for a man of thirty-eight," he said.

"If you say so," Meghan answered. "Now if you don't mind, I need to say a few things to Thomas."

"As if I could stop you. Round two."

"All right then. First off, Thomas, I've been doing research into natural antibiotics. Those are plants that might help heal Daphne's arm where that surgeon's been hacking at it. To help kill any infection there, vinegar and lavender oil are strongly antiseptic. They should be used when cleaning it, although I'm sure they'll sting. Thyme and tarragon are good in her soup, and onion and garlic too. I was going to suggest myrrh, the same stuff the Wise Men brought to baby Jesus—it's a tree sap with wonderful antibacterial properties, but it would have to come from the Middle East and I doubt you'd be able to get it. Now secondly, I have a theory, based largely on the sound of that cough of hers, that Daphne might have a lung disease called tuberculosis. The most obvious symptom of it is night sweats. So I'm asking you: does she perspire a lot in her sleep? If she wakes soaked in sweat I feel we're halfway to a diagnosis."

"I'll make sure he gets the message," Derek assured her. "Maybe I'll sing a little song for him about tuberculosis—rhyme it with psychosis."

"Please don't say things like that. It's not helpful."

"It's my nature," he said. "I'm just messing with you. I do have some sympathy—I may not believe what you tell me, but I believe *you* believe it. I don't doubt your sincerity."

"Right. It's my sanity you wonder about."

"Since you put it that way, yes."

"I have an idea," she said. "I'm going to ask Thomas something. Thomas, I need to convince Derek here that I'm not mentally ill, and I think there's a way you can help me. Can you please think of some really private, obscure thing you know about him? Something you've observed from being in Derek's head, something no one else could possibly know? Please, share it with Sylvanne, and I'll hear it, and then come back to Derek with the evidence, with rock-solid proof, and then he'll finally have to believe me that there is, in fact, a Thomas in his mind."

Derek thought a moment. "Thomas, listen up. Porn habits are off limits, bud."

"Please. That's the last thing I want to hear about," Meghan sighed. "I'm fully aware of all the deviant crap that clogs the internet, and if you're looking at it you're just one in a billion, apparently. That's not what I want Thomas to tell us. I'm hoping for something more personal, something absolutely unique to you."

"If he's in there, and truly the gentleman you describe, he'll respect any real secrets I have, and not go blabbing them."

"His goal is to cure his daughter," Meghan said. "He'll do whatever it takes. This could be the swift kick we need to get you motivated to help us save a child. So Thomas, please do it. Give me something good from the private world of Derek."

24

A girl in the kitchen offered Mabel some meat from the leg of a boar, yesterday's supper reboiled. She said no, knowing wild boar was a dish Sylvanne did not care for, but she did manage to take a few pieces and stuff them in her mouth. "Just a wee sample," she joked. Then she returned with breakfast for herself and her Mistress: boiled eggs still in their shells, some rye bread roughly sliced, a bowl of warmed butter to dip it in, milk in a pitcher, and warmed cider in a jug. The guard helped her carry it from the kitchen to her Lady's chambers, then excused himself with a nod and a bow. As the door shut, Sylvanne looked upon her maidservant expectantly.

"Well?" she asked. "Did you manage it this time?"

Mabel shook her head regretfully. "No Ma'am."

"I'm growing impatient with you," Sylvanne spat. "How hard can it be? From a kitchen full of them I ask only that you slip a small blade unnoticed into your apron, and hurry it to me."

"It's not so easy, Ma'am," Mabel said apologetically. "I'm watched, always. But I promise the day will come when the proper opportunity presents itself, and I will act."

"Make haste, Mabel," Sylvanne exhorted her. "The more healthy that child grows, the harder it becomes to contemplate ruining her happiness. Every day I'm taken from this room to sit with father and daughter, where despite myself I'm affected by them. I can't help it, when I'm exposed for hours on end to the loving attachment I see them share. Then I'm brought back here to be locked up and left to daydreams and queer thoughts. Do you know what I was thinking, just now? That perhaps I should kill the daughter along with her father, for her own good, to spare her a life of wretchedness. She's already lost a mother—would she really want to go on living, sickly as she is, and fully orphaned? Mightn't she be happier drowned like an unwanted kitten?"

"Oh, no, Ma'am, you mustn't think such things," Mabel cried. "To punish the guilty won't bar you from heaven, but to harm the innocent surely will. And that child is sweet-natured and innocent."

"I know that, and thus I contemplate putting her out of her misery. Is it strange to imagine that killing someone could be a favour to them?" Before Mabel could answer she continued, "I'll kill her father as a favour to my late husband, because it's my duty to do so, but why stop there? Why not kill the daughter, or kill myself even? I've never killed before—I may discover I like it, and go on a spree."

"Madame," Mabel pleaded. "I worry for your sanity. You obsess on your singular duty, and that can only be unhealthy."

"How can I not obsess?" Sylvanne muttered angrily. "Do I have anything else here to occupy my mind?"

In a careful, tentative voice, Mabel asked, "Might I give you some advice, ma'am?"

"Yours is the only voice that speaks to me," said Sylvanne. "So speak freely."

"Well then. You're not making your task any easier by so clearly showing everyone here your true intent. They see it, one and all, in your face, your actions, and even your words. When you are in the presence of Lord Thomas you're sullen, unhelpful, and your words are ice cold. You claim a desire to imitate the life of Judith, but as I recall the story of that heroine, she didn't approach that villain Holofernes with fury on her face and foul curses on her lips. Just the opposite—she tempted that great brute. She led him down the garden path to his own destruction using soft sighs and feminine giggles, gestures meant to enchant a man, and make him forget himself."

There was good sense in these words, Sylvanne knew. Clearly, seduction would serve her better than the brooding anger she displayed to Lord Thomas. In a voice laden with self-reproach, she said, "I haven't found a way to disguise my unhappiness. It's too fresh, too strongly felt."

"Our Biblical model accepted her need to play seductress, ma'am," Mabel continued. "She behaved uncharacteristically for a greater purpose. And so should you, if I may say. So should you. Be sweet to the daughter, become her friend and companion, so that the father will look upon you tenderly. Match his tender regard with your own. Make him fall in love with you."

Before Sylvanne could give expression to her thoughts the door opened, and a guard informed her of his orders: she was to be brought at once to Daphne's bedroom. Pointing to the untouched breakfast upon the table, Sylvanne said, "Give us a few moments, there's a dear," in a voice she intended to sound honeyed and demure. To her own ears it felt fake, it fairly reeked of insincerity, but it produced the desired effect on the guard. He looked at her uncertainly, then nodded, and left the two women alone. As the door closed Mabel saw her Mistress smile for the first time in a very long time, possibly since the siege had been laid. "You might be on to something, sweet Mabel," Sylvanne mused. "Come with me to the girl's bedside, and let's see whose heart I can win."

25

Daphne sat up in her bed, watching with delight as her father juggled three small oranges. A dozen more nestled in a wooden bowl on her sheets. "They came all the way from Spain, where it's sunny and warm," her father crowed. "I expect they'll soon make you sunny and warm as well. They are sweet, yet almost sour, and that's very curious. I'm told they only grow in lands that never see snow."

In a chair by the bedside, the servant girl Beth had been assigned the task of peeling and segmenting one of these exotic, mysterious fruits onto a silver plate to present to the young lady. Thomas glanced at her, and saw that she had grown bewildered and frustrated, for the skin of her orange was tough and dry, and when she ripped at it, chunks of the watery interior came away with it. Her hands were dripping juice onto the plate, yet she dared not wipe or lick them. Seeing the mess she was making of it, Thomas grew ill-tempered. "Useless girl, give me the damn fruit," he barked, and taking it from her platter, recomposed himself to a more gentle manner, bowed to his daughter, and handed her a new plate with the pulpy fragments upon it. "For you, my dear," he said grandly. "Now don't eat the skin, that dry rind, but suck from it the moist innards."

Daphne picked up one of the least mangled fragments and tasted the pulpy flesh. "It's good!" she cried, and both Thomas and Beth applauded happily. She tore into it, then another piece, then another.

"For the price of one of these, I can feed a soldier of my guard for a month," Thomas told her.

Daphne sucked the juice from every segment, licked the plate, and demanded eagerly, "Give me another."

"That's two soldiers," Thomas hooted delightedly.

"Let me unwrap it myself this time," she said. "I want to lick my hands, and not waste so much as a single drop. Beth, you look so funny, with your hands wet with juice, yet afraid to wipe them. Lick them, go ahead." The servant girl looked doubtful, but Thomas scolded her to do as told, and she timidly touched her sticky fingers to her tongue, immediately curling her lips and making a bitter face. Daphne laughed. "Perhaps you got the sour part, for I've tasted nothing but sweetness."

Thomas handed his daughter her second orange. "It might be easier if I slice it for you," he suggested, pulling his table knife from its sheath.

"No, no," Daphne protested. "You'll spill the juice, and a knife shouldn't be licked. There must be a way to do this, so as to keep the segments intact, and the juice trapped within." She applied herself to the job, while Thomas watched closely. Meanwhile a guard ushered in Lady Sylvanne, followed by Mabel.

Thomas greeted Sylvanne excitedly. "Ah, there you are at last. I called for you because the oranges have just arrived. Have you ever tasted one before?"

"Never," Sylvanne replied. She met his gaze, and he was surprised to find that her eyes were placid, not the churning seas of rage he had come to expect.

"No, I shouldn't have thought so. Well here is your chance— you may have one if you like."

"No thank you," she said softly. "If I partake, there'll be one less for your daughter." Inwardly, she almost gagged on the words. But she could see that Thomas was quite taken aback by them.

"If these do the trick, I'll get more," he told her. "For some reason I'm feeling generous, and want to share them. What about your maidservant? Mabel, would you care to try one?"

"I—I don't know, Sire," said Mabel cheerfully, unable to hide her pleasure that such a nobleman would remember her name.

"Have one," he commanded.

"But I've never tried one, Sire."

"Go ahead," he urged, holding out an orange to her.

Mabel looked to her Mistress for guidance, and Sylvanne, forcing herself to smile, nodded her permission. So she took the orange from his hand, brought it to her mouth, and bit it, unpeeled.

"No no no, my good woman, you have to peel it first," Thomas laughed. "It's not an apple. Here, watch my daughter—she already seems to be getting the hang of it. The goal is to separate peel from fruit without spilling any goodness from it, but to be honest we know as little as you about how to properly accomplish such a thing. So, while you and she conduct your experiments, I'll take the opportunity for a private word with your Lady."

To his surprise Sylvanne seemed amenable to the idea. He led her to a smaller dressing room off the main room, leaving the door open so that there would be no hint of impropriety.

"You're very cooperative today," he told her.

"I'm the same woman," she replied. But she looked and sounded different to him—in every previous meeting she had snarled at him through clenched teeth, her body tense with hostility. Now it seemed as if she were, if not exactly comfortable, at least making an effort to be a good and gracious guest. He wondered at the change but did not press her for an explanation as to its origins. Instead he simply allowed himself to be pleased by it.

"By now you're familiar with the way in which I need to address you," he said. "I'll speak to the other, to Meghan, if I may."

She nodded her head slightly, granting permission.

"Meghan, when you asked me to supply an intimate detail, gleaned from my observations of Derek in his private life, I admit I was quite worried at first. So much of his life is a puzzle to me, and I feared some things that strike me as singular and wondrous would strike you as everyday occurrences, hardly worth noting. I make no claim to comprehending those machines of the future you call computers, which he manipulates so easily, with no more thought than I would bring to using knife and spoon. He presses a button and manoeuvres through a labyrinth of pictures, sounds and movements of a miniature reality, flattened like a painting. Then there is the television machine, from which he sits at a distance, and gives his full attention for hours on end, as one would indulge the ramblings of an aged uncle who talks but never listens, and never knows when to shut his mouth. Television has taught me so much about his world—I remember the first time he applied paste to his teeth, and scrubbed his mouth before the mirror—I found it astonishing. Over time, however, as he watched his television machine, I saw other people also brushing theirs, all of them crediting this paste for their lustrous white smiles, and not a tooth missing in any of their mouths."

Sylvanne listened to him with a faintly encouraging smile. Beneath it, she was thinking how strange it was to feign interest in words that seemed to her the ramblings of a lunatic. But she nodded politely and bid him continue.

"I apologize, Meghan, for I can't help but digress in my telling of it, to give Sylvanne some insight into your world, and of my own wonderment at what I witness there," Thomas intoned. "I will try to adhere to the subject, to speak of Derek, and to fulfill your request for some telling detail of his private life. Just this very day there occurred a powerful incident I'm eager to report to you, one that begins with a sister, leads to a mother, and ends with a wife and daughter.

"Have you met his sister? I think not, for I myself have never laid eyes upon her. She communicates with him via the telephone, another wondrous device that poor Sylvanne has no understanding of, do you my dear? Can you imagine holding someone's voice against your ear, even when they themselves are miles and miles away?"

Sylvanne shook her head. "Tell me how it's possible," she gently urged him.

"Would that I knew! Miracles are not given a second thought in that great age to come. But again I need remind myself that I speak now to inform Meghan. The story I tell concerns Derek's mother, and in a bizarre way, it concerns me as well, as you shall soon see. Derek has a sister, younger than him by a few years, named Claire, who telephones him frequently to converse of matters that oft times strike Derek as trivial. Usually he indulges her, but occasionally he cuts her short. Just yesterday Claire telephoned in a state of high emotion, made plain by the tremulations of her voice. She had only just returned from a visit to their mother, who is an ancient woman by the standards of our time, but not by yours, Meghan—I believe she has attained the age of seven and seventy years.

"This woman's faculties are not what they once were. The health of her mind declines. Claire called to report that this day had marked a dreadful turn for the worse. Mother had failed to recognize daughter, and what's worse, insisted that she had never laid eyes on her before. She could not be persuaded otherwise, despite Claire's best attempts through story and anecdote to jiggle a key into her mother's locked mind, and thereby cajole a remembrance. 'Oh Derek, it was awful,' Claire lamented. 'I tried everything I could think of, I showed her pictures of us together, talked to her of me and you and Dad, but there wasn't a glimmer of recognition from her at all—she just stared at me blankly, and told me to leave her alone.'

"Now Derek, for his part, did his best to soothe his sister, who was sobbing through the telephone, and promised to visit his mother straightaway, to take her measure himself. And to his credit he did so—he immediately changed his clothes and set forth across the city in a horseless carriage of shining metal. Oh Sylvanne, the wonder of it! Thank you for listening so earnestly, I'm certain this sounds nonsense to you."

"Not at all," she lied.

"After some time he reached his mother's place, called a nursing home, a huge edifice chock-full of elderly folk and the servants who care for them. On a high floor he knocked on a door, behind which his mother kept a single small room of her own, and heard her bid him enter. When he did she greeted him warmly. 'You've come, have you?' she asked.

"'Yes, mom,' he said. 'How are you keeping?'

"'Oh fine. How are you, Thomas?' That's right, Thomas—she called him Thomas. Derek was naturally taken aback by this, and so was I, for as she said my name I felt she was looking into Derek's eyes, and through them looking exactly into my own soul. Indeed, this lady, and especially the look in her eyes, did stir in me remembrances of my own dear mother, God rest her soul. The resemblance was startling, and for a moment I felt as if I were in my mother's presence once again. Derek naturally had a different reaction. He became agitated, and corrected her. 'I'm Derek,' he said.

"'But you look so much like Thomas,' she replied, very matter-of-factly.

"'Who is Thomas, mother?'

"'He lived a very long time ago, I'll tell you that.' She paused as if remembering something. 'He was a good boy,' she said. Meghan, I can't tell you what an odd tingle I felt as she said that. I swear I heard my own mother's voice.

"Derek, unnerved, saw fit to change the subject at this point. 'Claire came to see you this morning,' he reminded her.

"'She did?'

"'You don't remember?'

"'No. I'm forgetting some things, and remembering others.'

"'You seem lucid enough to me.'

"'I'm fine.'

"'What have you been up to?'

"'Don't ask stupid questions. What is there to get up to in this prison for the aged and infirm?'

"'That's more like it,' Derek replied. 'That's the cranky old crone I call mother.'

"'You watch your tongue. You'd be cranky too, living like this. It's no life. I'm ready to move on.'

"'Mother, really, poor thing,' Derek answered. 'You've been saying that off and on since Dad died. Twelve years ago.'

"'Has it been? Feels like I just—he was in the tub, you know. Always loved a bath. I went to check on him when he didn't come downstairs. I knew instantly.'

"'Yes. You've told me before, Mom.' Then Derek went to her and gave her a very tender sort of hug, a genuinely sweet and sentimental gesture. She felt hollow-boned, like a bird. 'I'm going to give Claire a call, tell her you're back to normal,' he told her.

"'Pah,' she spat. 'I haven't felt normal for twelve years.' And it was just at that moment, as he held her in his arms, that he looked past her onto a shelf, and his eye alighted on a small picture, which those in the future call a photograph—they are like miniature paintings, perfect in their likenesses of those they portray—and there he saw his own self, Derek, holding with obvious affection a woman and a girl.

"'Where did you get that?' he asked his mother.

"'What?'

"'That photo.'

"His mother looked upon the photograph, and said, 'You must have given it to me. You married a beautiful girl, my boy, and little Ginny looks so lovely there. How are they keeping, anyway?'

"And Derek said, 'They're dead, mother. You know that.'

"His mother for a moment seemed genuinely shocked, staggered by the news. 'They died in a car crash, seven years ago,' Derek told her.

"'I'm sorry,' she said to him softly, in the very frailest of voices. 'I'm forgetting things, Thomas. Remembering others. So much death, and so unfair.'"

Sylvanne had done her best to feign an interest, but had some time earlier stopped listening to him, and had allowed her mind to wander. She came back to herself now, and found Thomas staring at her expectantly. "Is that the end?" she enquired, in a voice she meant to sound meek and tender.

"Don't you see, Sylvanne? Once again, his mother called him Thomas! And once again, I had the sense she was looking through him, directly at me."

"Yes, I do see," replied Sylvanne, straining to sound concerned, and helpful.

"I hope so," Thomas answered. "In any case, Derek stayed on for quite a long time, until the daylight faded, and the view of the city from their high window turned into a speckled pattern of lights. In that time they talked of many things, large and small. He bade her sit on a soft chair, while he sat on a stool and massaged her feet. She was very pleased by that. But from time to time he glanced at the photo on her shelf, and memories filled his mind, of happy times with a wife and daughter, and of the grief he suffered at their loss."

"Poor man," she said.

"Yes. In his own home there are no pictures of them at all. But again, Sylvanne, if I may address Meghan directly once more: I've produced here the secret you asked for, gleaned from his now-so-dissolute life: the man once knew the happiness a wife and child can bring. Not so different from me, after all."

From the other room Sylvanne could hear Daphne and Mabel happily experimenting with oranges. "That's all I have to say," Thomas said finally. "Likely to you just a jumble of disjointed words, all of them meant for Meghan—if you found them overly strange or in any way frightening, I apologize, for it was not my intent."

"Don't trouble yourself," Sylvanne replied. "I'm not the sort of flower that wilts under a summer's sun."

Thomas studied her. "No, I suppose not. You've been through so much lately, and yet you stand as proudly in your posture as any woman I've ever met."

"I'll take that as a compliment," she answered.

"It is. I've noticed the same trait in your twin, the woman Meghan. She carries herself erectly, and her gait is as lovely as that of a young doe. The women of her age do not dress with our sense of modesty, in kirtles that skim the floor, no indeed, they bedeck their bodies in minuscule scraps of fabric, and call it fully clothed. At first it's shocking, but—"

"Daddy! I'm walking."

Through the door they could see Daphne in a long white nightdress, taking tentative steps across the room, her face glowing with achievement. Thomas eagerly hurried to her, and took her hand.

"This is wonderful, my darling, wonderful," he cried. From the doorway between the two rooms Sylvanne watched as he led his daughter around the room, as if escorting her toward some imaginary, celebratory dance floor.

Mabel sidled over to her Mistress, and in a low voice, enquired, "What did he wish to speak of, Madame?"

"It doesn't matter. Gibberish of some sort," Sylvanne muttered. "I took your advice to heart, and behaved most genially toward him. I pretended a great interest, which encouraged him to jabber about his dreams of the future until I nearly lost all track of meaning in his words."

"See there?" Mabel said brightly. "It didn't kill you to make nice."

"No, I suppose not," Sylvanne said. But she felt troubled. In pretending to like him, she had felt her feelings move to a precarious place, a place at odds with her purpose. She watched Thomas chatting playfully with his daughter a moment. "Look at him, so contented. He possesses an abundance of love, or so it appears—it would be child's play, I now see, to make him fall in love with me. But I sense a risk in this newfound strategy—if I'm to show him kindness, and more, then kind acts might lead to kind feelings within me, the same way charity warms the heart of one who gives."

"Charity can't be bad, m'Lady."

"But it can, I fear. No soldier can afford it, once war's declared and the battlefield bloodied. War was made against my husband, and though I be a woman, I feel myself the last man standing of his ragged little army. Except for you, dear Mabel, I'm all alone. Alone and unarmed, but I haven't yet given up the fight. I need a knife, Mabel. Bring me the knife."

26

Derek opened the front door to find Meghan on his step, carrying a heavy leather satchel. "Can I come in for a minute?" she asked.

"On one condition—you say nothing about the squalor."

"I'll hold my tongue."

"And possibly your nose."

She followed him down the hallway toward his living room. "I can only stay a minute, so I'll say this quickly and without a lot of—" she stopped in her tracks, struck speechless seeing his living space for the first time. It looked like an indoor version of his back yard. A pigsty.

"Now remember what you promised," Derek said. "As you can see, I'm a packrat, I can't stand to throw out perfectly good trash."

"It's not that," she replied. "No matter how it looks, it's a bit disconcerting, to come into a place with a floor plan just like mine next door, and see how someone else uses it."

"Which is a polite way of saying you couldn't live like this. I know what you mean about identical layouts, though. A dozen near-identical houses run cheek by jowl up this side of the street, and in every one of them the walk from the bedroom to the toilet is three steps north, seven steps east, two south, drop your drawers. I bet at rush hour, seven in the morning or eleven at night, all sixteen toilets flush simultaneously. We might as well all be rats in a Skinner box. Now, what exactly can I do for you?"

"A couple of things." She sat herself down on Derek's old couch, opened up her satchel, and spread several medical books on his coffee table. "These are for you to read," she said. "I've saved you some trouble and marked with Post-It Notes the pages that look promising—there are a bunch of conditions I think might apply to Daphne. They're all cross-referenced. I hope you can read my handwriting on the notes, sometimes it gets pretty tiny. I've been insanely busy with work so I haven't had time to sit down and go through them properly. You, on the other hand, seem to have all the time in the world, so I'm hoping you'll have a look at least. Ideally you should read them out loud—I think if Thomas hears them spoken, he'll be more likely to understand. Thomas, if you hear me, it's no slight on your intelligence, me saying this to Derek. It's just there's a ton of medical terminology, some of which I don't understand myself."

"I thought his daughter was getting better," Derek said.

"She is. She actually got up and walked, which is like a miracle.

But I still want to cover every angle. She still hasn't been properly diagnosed."

"Speaking of daughters, yours has stopped coming out to the back yard."

"I know. She's been shunning you because of how you treated her the other morning, and now she's giving me the silent treatment too, brooding in her room. Her father told her he's going to have a new baby. She's not taking it well."

"I didn't know that part. I thought you two are still married, that you'd just recently split up."

"That's right."

"Guy moves fast."

"Guy moves sloppily, is more like it."

"And the mom to be? It's not your former best friend or something sordid like that, is it?"

"Not exactly. A student of his."

"Does Betsy know her?"

"Why do you care?"

"I don't know. I do, a little. I like Betsy. I am sorry I growled at her."

"I think she feels she's been replaced, and her dad's going to abandon her. And I'm dealing with deadlines and don't have time to deal with it. Right now I have to run to a meeting, which if it goes well will give me a chance to catch my breath and pay some attention to her. God knows she needs it."

Derek nodded, but said nothing in reply.

"It's nice of you to worry about her," she added. "Especially since you told me the other day worry is maggot food."

"I didn't say I practice what I preach," he smiled. "I'm a human being. We're all liars and hypocrites."

"Not always," she protested. "Sometimes we're good. Thank you for asking about her. I'll tell her you did."

"Whatever. Is that it?"

"No. There's something else. Thomas has spoken to me. He spoke to Sylvanne, exactly as I asked him to." She hesitated, searching for the right tone. "It was very cute. He was amazed you brush your teeth."

"Jesus Christ. He's going to have to do better than that."

"Oh he did, he did. He's smart enough to figure out tooth brushing isn't all that rare and exotic in this day and age, so he moved on to something else he saw you do yesterday. You went to visit your mother, because your sister asked you to. She was worried because your mom didn't recognize her anymore."

Derek raised an eyebrow.

"Your mom's only seventy-seven, but she must have some kind of early-onset dementia. Her memory is going. She lives in some kind of home. A big building with lots of floors, lots of elderly folks."

"Uh huh."

"And when you got to her room, she was thrilled to see you, and you were quite relieved that she recognized you—and then she called you Thomas."

Derek's open face turned thoughtful. "Know what?" he said. "This is getting weird."

"That's what Thomas said too—he looked at your mom and was shocked at how much she looked like *his* mom. But he felt a connection when she looked at you—at him—and then when she said his name he knew she felt the connection too. He just knew it."

Derek studied her face carefully, looking for some hint that this might still be an elaborate practical joke. If not, what was it? She met his gaze, and they locked eyes.

"What is your game?" he asked.

"It's not a game."

"Whatever it is, it's pretty good," he said. "Except for one thing. There's an orderly on her floor named Thomas. As we walked to the elevator she said hi to him. Did your Thomas tell you that?"

"No, he didn't. Don't tell me you're still holding out on me, Derek! That orderly is irrelevant, he wasn't in the room when you spoke to your mother. No one was, except you and her. Now how could I possibly know all the intimate details of a conversation that only you and your mother shared? How could I know what your sister said to you on the phone?"

"I don't know. You're not the type to hack a phone line, you wouldn't have the skill set. But you could have hired someone—tapping into a cordless is easy as tuning into a radio. Or you could listen in by putting your ear to our common wall here—I'm loud when I'm on the phone, and I pretty much repeated the conversation to my sister when I got home. Or maybe you've drilled a hole through the wall, or hidden a mini-cam. Maybe you've hired a private detective to stake me out, tail me across town. I've seen the movies, I know what lengths an obsessive female will go to, to ferret out a man's secrets."

"What reason could I have to obsess about you?" Meghan cried in exasperation. "Have you looked in the mirror lately? Have you looked at how you live? Have you looked at *where* you live? You know what this room screams to me? Three things—cockroaches, bedbugs, and head lice. All harmoniously coexisting in perfect, squalid harmony. I'm sorry, Derek, squalor is not attractive, to me or to any other woman on the planet."

"I have no trouble finding women, thank you very much."

"Right. You bring them in at two a.m. and they're out by three. But this is all beside the point. The point is, I came over here with what I thought was clear and obvious proof, thinking you'd finally have to accept the truth—why can't you face up to it?"

"Put it this way," he said. "I'd prefer if you turned out to be just plain old-fashioned nuts. It's not even pejorative. More like welcome to the club."

"I'm not nuts," she answered. She took a deep breath. "Look, I'm sorry I got my back up. I'm the guest here, the one intruding into your space, your life, and it's not my place..." She hesitated, like a high jumper staring at the bar, visualizing what it would take to make the leap. After all the cutting things she'd said to him just now he stood before her without malice. He still looked upon her with an open, unguarded face, willing to hear her out. She felt her nerve almost fail her, and then she spoke. "In your mother's room there's a photo. Of your wife and child. They're dead."

"I see." Derek's eyes showed a flicker of bewilderment. "Why didn't you just tell me about that, right off the bat, instead of all the minor details first? Why pussyfoot around?"

"I felt like I don't know you well enough." She wondered if she saw a tear at the corner of his eye. He brought a finger up to touch it. She herself felt like crying.

She looked at his smooth, honest face. He said, "It's true. I found a great woman and I married her. And we had a lovely little girl. It's not a secret I keep hidden, but I'm surprised you know about it." His words, and the casual, matter-of-fact way he delivered them, left Meghan a little at a loss.

"I'm sorry," she said.

"Don't be sorry." He stared at her evenly, with just a hint of defiance. "The wound has healed, Meghan. What you're seeing are the scars."

She had an instinct to comfort him, to touch his arm, but something in his eyes kept her at a distance.

"I'm going to go. I didn't mean to invade your privacy and bring up things I probably have no right to know."

"We're neighbours," he said. "If we ever became *good* neighbours you'd have heard about it eventually."

"We can be good neighbours," she said.

"Deal."

She glanced at the medical books on the table, "You will look at these, won't you? It would mean the world to me."

"Sure. I will," he said. "I'm still not sold, but I'm running out of plausible explanations for the things you tell me. So I'll have a look, just to be on the safe side. If there's a Thomas, he might learn something. I might too."

27

Sylvanne was combing Daphne's hair. She picked up the young girl's long tresses and piled them atop her head. "I prefer my hair down, not up," Daphne told her. "I have a neck like a stork, so I like to keep it cloaked."

"But this is the neck of a swan," Sylvanne disagreed. "How gracefully it curves from your bodice to your chin. Any handsome knight would fall off his horse at the sight of you."

"You really think so?" asked the girl, blushing.

"Have you seen yourself in a looking glass lately? The little stork is growing into a lovely swan, for certain," Sylvanne insisted.

"You're thinking of that fable about a duckling who's ugly."

"I'm thinking of a pretty girl named Daphne."

Sylvanne planted a sweet peck of a kiss on Daphne's neck. Just at that moment Thomas entered, and saw it, and saw his daughter, dressed in day clothes, rise from her chair and come to him, radiant and beaming.

"Daddy, do you like my hair this way?" she asked, doing a little pirouette to show it off from all angles.

"I can honestly say I do," he replied. "You're looking quite the lady."

"I wish I had some fancy soirees to attend," she mused. "I wish I lived in the capital. I wish a prince would see me like this."

"That's three wishes," Thomas said tenderly. "Don't spend them so freely. Save one for getting well."

"I am well," Daphne insisted. "Sylvanne says I'm well enough to go riding, and I think we should all three go out on horseback together, this very day. This very minute! She's been telling me all about the horses she kept when she was my age. Her father's farm had two sturdy draught horses she brushed and fed, and rode them bareback in the summers. She had two, and I've never yet had one."

Thomas glanced at Sylvanne. She smiled back at him discreetly. Her hair had been fashioned into one long braid, and pinned up, displaying her lovely neck to fine effect.

"If wishes were horses..." Thomas said dreamily. "Well, I suppose a horse is a reasonable wish for a girl. We'll find you one."

"Today?" Daphne cried.

"No, not today, but tomorrow I'll put out word. There may even be something appropriate in my own stable, although off-hand I can't think of one. They've all been bred for warfare, I'm afraid. Very spirited bunch. You'll need something gentler, a sweet old mare with a motherly streak."

"But I want a spirited one," Daphne demanded. "And it should be chestnut in colour, and bigger than a pony. Sylvanne says ponies are for girls, and I'm a young lady now."

"Suddenly it's Sylvanne, Sylvanne, Sylvanne," Thomas said good-humouredly. "Has she convinced you to regard the perfectly apt word girl as pejorative?"

"She recognizes what's there for all to see," Daphne replied. "You said yourself that I'm looking quite the lady."

"And does Sylvanne herself have anything to add on this subject?"

Sylvanne smiled slyly. "Nothing needs adding," she told him. "The young lady is so articulate and polished in her language, I fear that by comparison my own voice sounds as waves slapping an empty boat."

"Hardly," Thomas replied. "Your voice is the wind that fills the sails."

Sylvanne made a little show of whispering to Daphne like a girlish conspirator, "I think your father just called me a windbag."

Daphne giggled, and gleefully scolded him, "Daddy, did you call Sylvanne a windbag?"

"My my, how women like to twist men's words," Thomas replied. "No wonder we have such trouble speaking from the heart."

"Say something from the heart," Sylvanne urged him. "And I promise this time, we won't make fun."

Thomas hesitated. "Yes. Well." A distant look came to his eyes. Sylvanne and Daphne waited. He put his hand to his chest, and said, "I'll beg off, if I may, for I'm afraid my heart's a little tender, just at the moment." His voice trembled slightly. "My dear Daphne. With your hair up like that, you look so much like your mother."

"Daddy. I'm sorry," Daphne said softly.

"Don't be. I'll leave you two now to your fun."

Sylvanne stood quickly and took hold of his wrist to stop him from going. "No, no. It's really time for her to take a rest. I'll leave you two."

Thomas looked down at where her hand touched his skin, and felt a tingle surge through him. Her eyes were two pools of sparkling, radiant light. "Your demeanour is so altered these past days that I can scarce believe you're the same person, Lady Sylvanne," he said. "You've captivated my impressionable young daughter, and caused this room to ring with girlish laughter for the first time in many a moon. I thank you."

"She's good company," Sylvanne said modestly, letting her hand fall from his wrist. "She brightens my days, as well."

"I do wonder at this sudden change in your deportment, however," Thomas continued. "It seems to signal a change of heart, and the abandonment of your husband's wishes. Or could it be playacting, a ruse, an emotional Trojan horse by which you hope to penetrate my defences?"

Sylvanne didn't flinch. She met his eyes squarely. "The only person in the world I trust at the moment, my maid Mabel, has advised me to look for trust in others, by granting trust to others. So I'm giving myself up to you—in hope that your actions in bringing me here were for an honourable end, and that I might in some way help you achieve them."

Thomas studied her. "Nothing would please me more than to return that trust," he said. "Customarily, in listening to the words of others, I can only guess at their true feelings. But in this case, I expect I'll discover the truth or falseness of what you say, in my dreams. For I have an ally, a spy in your mind, fair Meghan, your twin."

"Then I pray this Meghan is not a liar," Sylvanne said.

"No. She has nothing to gain by that," said Thomas. "She's a truth-teller, and a mind-reader, inside you even as we speak." He looked directly into her eyes again. "Just now I think I see her in there with you. It's as if your eyes are the windows to not one soul, but two. Can that be true? Or is it because when I dream, her eyes are as beautiful as yours?"

"You frighten me."

"Don't be frightened. There's nothing you can do to change the truth."

"Pray, let her read my mind, and make her report. Call for the guard, for I've grown suddenly weary, and wish to retire to my room."

Thomas walked her to the door and watched as the guard led her away. He was still tingling from the radiance of her eyes, so powerful he'd put it down to the presence of two souls. He asked himself again, Could it really be that I saw Meghan in those eyes?

"Daddy, will we go riding tomorrow?" His daughter's voice returned him to the moment.

"First we need a horse, before we make plans about riding one."

Daphne picked up a comb and ran it through her long hair. "Do you like Lady Sylvanne?" she asked.

"I do like her," Thomas replied. "I'm not sure I trust her."

"I wish you would," the girl said.

"And why is that?"

"Because you're in need of a wife."

"A few days ago you were terrified of her," Thomas reminded her.

"She's different now. And you're in need of a wife."

"You're in need of rest. And you're awfully young to be a matchmaker."

"Mother told me something, before she died. She said she hoped you would marry another, to give me sisters, or a brother."

"Did she? That sounds like something she would wish for. Thinking of others, even at the end."

"Can we go riding tomorrow?"

"You've asked me that. Don't mount the saddle until there's a horse underneath."

28

"How did Derek react, when you told him you knew that his wife and child had died?" Anne asked. Meghan had come for her second session.

"He told me the wounds have healed, but he has scars."

"What do you think he meant? Keeping in mind that there are many levels of meaning."

"He meant end of topic. Change subject now. He didn't want to talk about it. He said he was open to talking about it, but he didn't want to talk about it."

"Do you think the wounds have healed?"

"Maybe they don't. His little girl must have been about four when she died. I think of Betsy, when she was four, to lose her like that..." Meghan shivered at the thought.

"Humans are often surprisingly resilient when tragedies happen. We're animals like all the others—priority one is to keep living. And if you're going to live, you may as well try to find happiness. Or re-find it."

"That's true."

"Other people do move on, and rebuild their lives."

"That's true too."

"How does he react to you when you try to talk to Thomas through him?"

"Well, he'd been resistant, but at the same time kind of humouring me, partly because he finds me attractive. But when I told him about his wife and child, he started to wonder. He agreed to read the medical texts I gave him, so that's progress."

"He finds you attractive. How do you know that?"

"I eavesdropped on him the other night. I didn't do it deliberately, I was trapped in my back yard, not wanting him to see me."

"Why was that?"

"Because he was drinking, as usual. He had a friend over, and I thought if he saw me he would say something idiotic, something to ridicule or mock me just to entertain his friend, so I sat on my little patch of lawn, out of sight below the fence, waiting for him to be distracted so I could slip back inside the house. I couldn't help but listen. He called me gorgeous." She smiled, a little embarrassed.

"And how did that make you feel?"

Meghan broke into a wide grin. "That's the all-time classic therapist's line, isn't it?"

"These things are classics because they're tried and true," Anne smiled. "So. How did that make you feel?"

Meghan thought a moment. "It's funny, you know. Coming from someone I'd been thinking of as kind of a loser, like Derek,

I was flattered, but not totally flattered. He is good looking, I guess—I mean if I thought he was ugly I wouldn't have cared less what he thought of me. But," Meghan hesitated a moment. "I don't know. If Thomas were to say it, I would feel totally flattered."

"Why?"

She thought a moment, then said suddenly, "Am I in love with Thomas?"

"Only you would know. Are you?"

"Oh my God. I admire him, and feel such sympathy for him—his daughter has been so sick, and he's so desperate to make her better, working so hard to help her get well. I want to comfort him, give him hugs. And then, just looking at him, apart from all that—the way he carries himself—it affects me, somehow. He's very proud, I would say. Strong. And honest. And serious. I just wish I could *be* with him."

"And what does Thomas think of you? Does he ever say?"

"He has. Several times. He's called me a beauty, and also said he likes the way I carry myself. He thinks I walk elegantly, like a young doe." She paused, enjoying the warmth of a pleasant reverie. She could see Thomas clearly in her mind, standing by the fireplace in Daphne's chamber. "Now that Sylvanne's making nice to him, he's able to look at her more naturally, more comfortably. Last night they locked eyes, and it was eerie, but I felt he was looking through her, and seeing *me*. It was the first time I felt that." She felt her pulse quicken, remembering and reliving that moment. "It's just so totally unfair. Why do we have to be centuries apart? If he were here, I'd give him my love in a second."

29

A small brook meandered across a field of golden wheat shimmering in the autumn breeze. Daphne rode in front, on her horse, her very own horse, a sweet old chestnut mare named Mathilde. Despite her protestation that she was a young lady, and should ride as ladies do, Thomas had insisted she wear a boy's breeches and ride like a boy, straddling the saddle, that being the safer technique for a novice. Behind her he rode next to Sylvanne, who sat side-saddle on her big black horse, as a lady is expected to. Daphne reached the brook, and Thomas called out for her to wait there. When they caught up he allowed his horse to dip its head to the water and drink. He dismounted to take a drink himself in cupped hands.

"My mount is forever thirsty," he said. "Look how he sucks it up by the gallon, like an elephant's trunk."

"Mine wants only to run and run," Sylvanne replied.

"Let her run toward home then. It's time we turned back."

"One more jaunt!" Daphne pleaded excitedly.

"This is far enough," he told her. "Beyond here the path narrows, the woods grow dense and wild."

"Oh *please*, Daddy?" she begged.

"All right," Thomas relented. "But this may be your last time riding in that fashion. Next time we'll have you adopt the proper posture of a lady on horseback. Now take your mount no further than that first copse of alders. Then you turn around smartly and come straight back."

He and Sylvanne watched her horse step cautiously across the rocky, knee-deep stream. On the far side she kicked her heels into its belly, and it began a disciplined canter away over the open field toward the trees. "This outing has brought colour to her cheeks," Thomas observed. "My physician tells me that's a bad thing. I wonder what our friend Meghan would say?"

"Perhaps you'll dream the answer," Sylvanne smiled, mirroring the look of ease and contentment she saw upon his face.

"I do fall asleep these nights hoping for answers," he replied. "Last night I was eager to see Meghan, that she might help me to solve the puzzle of your change of heart."

"And what was her verdict?"

"None. I passed the whole night with Master Derek, for she paid him no visit. To give him credit, he diligently and devotedly perused the medical books Meghan gave him, offering commentary of his own as an adjunct to the texts, addressing me as if I were an old friend. He read deeply on the subject of something called tuberculosis, but neither Daphne nor my wife could be said to perspire much in the night, which is a primary symptom of that malady. Crohn's disease, and Multiple Sclerosis, if I pronounce it correctly—he seemed to think auto-immune conditions of that sort might be responsible for my poor daughter's state, but I can only wonder at the meaning of auto-immune. Much of it was lost on me, I'm afraid. Quite frustrating. And on top of it, as I said, I wanted to see Meghan, so she might tell me what you're up to."

"Poor thing," said Sylvanne teasingly. "Left to your own devices to determine my sincerity."

"I do know what I wish the answer to be," he said, and for the first time she caught a hint of flirtatiousness in his voice. But just at that moment the mood was shattered—they heard the startled scream of a horse, and in the distance saw Daphne's mount rearing on its hind legs, terrified by the sight of a wild boar darting out of a nearby thicket. The horse bolted, galloping in full flight toward the woods. They saw Daphne's feet slip from the stirrups, her body slide dangerously from the saddle, her hands desperately clinging to its mane.

In a blur of movement Thomas pulled his horse from the water and climbed aboard, urgently sending it to a full gallop. But Sylvanne, already aboard her mount, had a head start, and as she turned her horse to the chase she expertly hauled up her dress and swung a leg over the beast to ride full saddle. It was she who reached Daphne's horse first and, grabbing hold of the reins in one hand, expertly turned the horse's head, forcing it to take on the pace of her own mount. The horses slowed from gallop to trot, and soon enough to a tranquil standstill. "There, there," she cooed softly. "Are you all right, dear girl?"

"She wouldn't listen," Daphne whimpered, tears streaming down her face. "I don't like this horse at all."

"Do forgive her," Sylvanne said soothingly. "That boar was as large as I've seen, and mean looking, and gave poor Mathilde a nasty shock. It frightened her as much as she frightened you."

Thomas arrived, his old warhorse panting heavily.

"Are you all right, my darling?" he asked.

"No," she replied. "I've been treated to a nasty shock, thanks to Mathilde." She slapped her horse's neck childishly. "Sylvanne says I should forgive her, but I don't feel like it."

"I'll wager she's sorry to have scared you, and a little embarrassed," Thomas suggested. "I didn't expect a stolid old mare like that to spook so readily. Next time try to keep your head, and rein her in when she wants to run wild."

"I'll try, Daddy."

Thomas glanced at Sylvanne astride her saddle. "So much for a lady's proper posture," he said to her. "My finest horseman couldn't have ridden better."

"Some positions are more expedient," Sylvanne replied coyly. She stood in the stirrups and lifted one leg over the horse's back to return to side-saddle, affording Thomas a brief glimpse at her bare calves under her dress. He looked into her face, and saw that she had caught him looking, and despite himself he blushed. In her eyes he saw an unspoken challenge, a mix of confidence, flirtatiousness and bemusement. In his eyes she saw that he was smitten.

❖

By the time they arrived back at the castle Daphne was barely able to stay upright in the saddle, so great was her exhaustion. She showed no interest in food nor drink, so they put her straight to bed, where she fell instantly asleep. Thomas and Sylvanne stood at her bedside awhile, watching her frail chest rise and fall in the soft candlelight.

"Do you think it was too much for her?" Thomas asked with concern. "Her breathing is so hurried."

"She's reliving her adventure, that's all," Sylvanne reassured him. "Stimulation of that sort can only be good for her. Her blood will be renewed by it."

"I hope so," he said. "Certainly her arm is looking much better. It's healing well, and that's thanks to advice from the future—clean dressing and vinegar have very nearly banished the infection there. Earlier today I had even considered her fully recovered." He watched as his daughter's breathing calmed, and felt some relief at the sight. Then he turned and studied Sylvanne's face. "I don't know how to thank you for your quick action on horseback," he said earnestly. "Once, when I wanted to thank Meghan with a kiss, I was rebuffed by you. Will you accept a kiss for her now, and one for yourself?"

"Perhaps. On the cheek only. Not the mouth."

"Of course," he replied. He took her face in his hands, and planted three soft kisses, one on each cheek, and one on her forehead. "One for Meghan, one for Sylvanne, and one for the future," he pronounced softly.

Sylvanne smiled up at him like a lady in love.

"Sleep well," he said. "The guard will take you to your chambers."

She looked into his eyes imploringly. "Is a lady to be thanked, and kissed, and yet still treated as a prisoner here?"

"I'm afraid so," he replied, his voice tinged with regret. "Everything is strange, I know. But life is change, and if things continue along their course, I'll soon have you dine at table with me in the Great Hall, as a proper guest should. A guest of honour."

"I'd like that very much," she told him. She reached for his hand, and held it in her two hands, playfully examining his sturdy fingers one by one. He let her do it, marvelling at the intimacy of this simple act, until stronger feelings of attraction and desire took hold of him, and fighting them, he pulled his hand away. Without another word, she turned to leave, fixing him with a dazzling, triumphant smile, a smile that kept him awake half the night, for the more he dwelled upon his memory of it, the more he recalled a hint of malice in her shining eyes.

30

Mabel lived for her thrice-daily trips to the castle's kitch-en to collect meals. The kitchen was in an outbuilding in the bailey, so it was quite the jaunt just getting there. First she was brought down from her Lady's chambers in the castle keep, through the Great Hall, which often as not was crowded with courtiers and visitors, sycophants and supplicants, a lively cross section of folk, from ratcatchers to ropemakers, tinkers to needlers to ploughmen to garlic sellers, all hoping for a word with the Lord on some issue of import to them. Then she skirt-ed the chapel, and exited the castle through a stout gate into the open air of the bailey, past the quarters for the knights in training, where handsome young boys and men engaged in all kinds of simulations of acts of war, past the workshops where the clothiers and embroiderers toiled to keep all the servants and courtiers dressed so well, past the brewery where the ale wife produced as creamy and potent a beverage as Mabel had ever tasted, to the great kitchen with its massive, ever-smoky oven, where a dozen maids busied themselves producing the wheat, rye and oat breads that were the staple of everyone's diet, and an equal number of butchers and cooks prepared meat and game of all sorts, all of them chattering in that smoky cacophony with a teasing, good natured camaraderie that was to Mabel a blessed and cherished antidote to the dismal hours she spent locked away with her brooding Mistress.

Meal times were extremely regular. Breakfast at seven, dinner—the main meal of the day—at eleven, and supper at four o'clock. Mabel could feel herself grow impatient as those times approached, and any delay in the arrival of her guard was agony to her. Today the guard had been at least half an hour late, and she had felt herself on the verge of leaping from a window. Even Lady Sylvanne, so typically bound up in her own thoughts, noticed Mabel's agitation, and remarked, "Am I really such painful company as all that? I've taken your advice, and tried to be more likable to our captor. Please don't expect a similar performance here in private. Here I am myself, and I am sorry if you suffer for it."

"No, no, Ma'am," Mabel protested. "I wish only for my Mistress to be herself. To be at peace. To be contented."

"Really? I've only asked one thing of you, and you've failed me thus far," Sylvanne said sharply. "I don't ask for peace and contentment. I ask for a knife. Bring me a knife. No more excuses, Mabel. I want it today. Do you hear me?"

Mabel nodded. Before she could speak they heard the long delayed knock upon the door. It swung open, and a handsome lad, so young as to be unable to grow a beard, beckoned her to follow him.

"You're a new one—what happened to the other, the one who usually accompanies me?" Mabel asked him as they descended toward the out-of-doors.

"I just follow my orders, m'Lady."

"Oh, I'm not a Lady, I'm a servant, just as you are. You can treat me as you would an auntie. A boy so young and fair as you, I feel as if you *should* call me auntie."

"I'm neither boy, nor servant; I'm a squire, a knight in training," the young man said huffily.

"Well pardon my ignorance," Mabel said teasingly. "Perhaps I should call you Your Majesty."

The boy said nothing further, and soon enough they neared the kitchen. Just outside the open double door Mabel was surprised to spot Gwynn, pulling a chicken from a wicker basket for the cook's inspection. There were nine birds squeezed in there, and he sought the fattest, but they were so jumbled up together—tumbling, pecking at each other, and squawking indignantly at their loss of freedom—that he mistakenly grabbed hold of one of his skinniest birds, a sorry specimen that had lost the feathers on its chest to an unknown ailment.

"They're not nearly so plump as last week's," scoffed the cook, a brawny old crone by the name of Hellen.

"Plumper, ma'am, plumper," Gwynn proclaimed. "Now that I'm home from my military adventures, I've got 'em back on a proper diet. Feel that thigh there, lots and lots of fat and tender meat."

The cook examined the bird's naked belly. "What, have you been plucking her while she's still alive?" she demanded.

"No, no, it's common in that breed," he lied. "They moult at this time. I'm telling you, this bird, nicely basted, would suit the table of the Lord himself."

"Don't tell me my business," she barked at him. "I must have meat, so I'll accept your poultry, however piss-poor. Boiled, it'll serve to fill the bellies of the men at arms, they're not particular."

"Let me show you a more typical foul, this one," he exclaimed, retrieving another squawking, thrashing bird from the basket. "Aha! Now here's a real beauty!"

Just then the young soldier interrupted to announce, "I've brought the Lady's servant for to take her dinner."

Gwynn looked round excitedly. "Why Mabel," he crowed. "Here we be talking of tender meat, and speak of the devil, here *you* be! I've been wondering about you, and how I was to catch a moment for a chat. Are they treating you well?" He looked her over thoroughly from head to toe, without shame. "You look plumper too—it suits you, truly it does."

"Sir, you make me blush," replied Mabel.

Gwynn called into the kitchen to the girls and women working there. "Ladies, come out, come out for a moment, I wish you to make the acquaintance of my new wife." He called toward the nearby ale house, where a handful of vagrants and drunkards could as usual be seen loitering in a strip of shade down its side wall. "Come one, come all, I've an announcement to make! Here's my future bride—feast your eyes upon my prize! I'd marry her today if I could and be a widower no more. This one is robust and cheerful, all I look for in a spousal companion."

Mabel, flattered by his attentions, responded with mock severity. "Don't get ahead of yourself. I'm still prisoner here."

"The spoils of war, you are, but I won't let you rot. My boys need a mother, too!" He pointed to three snot-nosed feral brats, wrestling in the dust of the yard.

"Concentrate on your business," the cook scolded him. He ignored her, holding a chicken by its neck for Mabel's inspection, encircling its flapping wings and tucking it almost tenderly under his arm.

"You'll be feasting on one of my birds by suppertime, my dear," he proclaimed. "They tell me the master demands only the best for you and your lady. Cookie here will select the finest of the fine, and I'll decapitate, gut and clean them, all for a modest sum of course."

"Chickens were one of my duties back home," Mabel told him. "May I have a look?"

"No time for that," stated her young guard. "We're here for one purpose."

Gwynn raised himself up and towered over the lad. "I'll take charge of her," he informed him. "Go over to the barn and chat up the milkmaids awhile, there's a good boy. And don't forget, the hay in the loft is comfortable and soft."

"I don't mind a-meeting them girls," the young man replied.

"Wash your face and hands on the way," Gwynn advised him. "Girls like a gentleman. Cleanliness is next to God-given good looks, ha!"

The guard wandered off. "I admire your array of knives," Mabel said, looking over his collection of tools.

"Most belong to the kitchen," he replied. "These three are mine. Tools of the trade. You won't find a sharper blade anywhere hereabouts."

Mabel picked up the largest of the three. "May I borrow it?" she asked.

"What for?"

"I lack a tool to trim the cuticles of my lady's fingers and toes."

"Ha! That's too massive for such a delicate job. Take this one."

He handed her the smallest knife. The blade was hardly longer than her middle finger, and about as wide. She raised it experimentally, holding the handle so that the blade protruded from the bottom of her fist, and made a jabbing motion in the air.

"Sits well balanced in the hand, does it not?" Gwynn said proudly. "I carved the handle my own self, according to my own principles."

"It's beautiful," Mabel said.

"Consider it a present. The first of many, I hope."

"You truly are aggressive," she remarked.

"A man needs to be, to gain what he desires."

The old cook interrupted. "I desire you to slay me some poultry, and leave your romancing for another day," she snarled. Glancing across the yard, she announced, "Ah! Young guardsman makes a hasty return. What happened, lad? Did you meet your milkmaids?"

The guard felt the back of his head, and checked his hand for blood. "Their father was lurking about, and drove me off with a stick," he told them.

"Don't despair, my boy," Gwynn said cheerily. "The girls will love you the more that you suffered for them."

The cook picked up a wooden mallet meant for softening meat, and threatened Gwynn with it. "Shall I crack you a good one then, so your lady love here grows more fond of you?" Then she did just that, whacking him across the back of his head.

"Owww!" Gwynn cried. "Leave off, crazy old crone!"

"Love hurts, hahahahaha," she cackled happily.

"Are you all right?" Mabel asked, coming near and inspecting his head tenderly. He knelt down and leaned against her like a dog wanting to be petted.

"You see? It works!" the cook shouted happily.

31

In her chamber Sylvanne weighed the knife in her hand. "I was hoping for a tool with greater substance," she muttered.

"This is better," Mabel asserted. She didn't tell her Mistress it was a gift from Gwynn. Instead she said, "If I'd stolen a larger blade, ill intent would be suspected, should it ever be discovered. One of this size is more readily explained. We can say we need it to trim wicks and toe nails and the like."

"I suppose you're right," Sylvanne said. "It will draw less attention to itself, and therefore be more easily manoeuvred behind his back." Hesitantly, and lacking confidence, she practiced a stabbing motion, bringing the blade toward herself, as if stabbing him in the back as he embraced her. She thought, Could I really do that, when the time comes? Could I harness the fury it would need?

"You'll need to lure him close, ma'am," Mabel counselled. "You'll need to use all your charms to draw him to your bed. Honeyed words and gestures spin the loveliest of webs."

"I'll spread a deep colour over my lips. I'll wear my golden belt low upon my hips," Sylvanne murmured.

"Now you're talking, ma'am," Mabel praised her. "Make him as potter's clay in your hands."

After dinner Thomas paid his usual evening visit to Daphne's chamber, and found Sylvanne dressed in the exotic costume of a gypsy woman, holding his daughter's hand and guiding her through some intricate dance steps, while the servant girl Beth clapped time on a tambourine. Daphne was likewise dressed up for make-believe, in the shimmering clothes of a Moorish harem girl.

"Daddy, Sylvanne is teaching me how to dance," she giggled excitedly. "Shall I show you?"

"I am all eyes," Thomas replied. "Where on earth did you get these outfits?"

"Sylvanne's been telling me tales from the Arabian nights," Daphne replied. "I said I wished to go there, but she said why not bring Arabia to my bedroom? She gave specifications to the sewers and embroiderers, and they made all these just to please me. Aren't they splendid?"

"They are. Almost too splendid. Too revealing, for a girl your age."

"Oh don't be a prude, and watch me dance," she admonished him. Slipping tiny silver cymbals onto her fingers, she tapped out a faint beat for herself as she slid across the stone floor in beaded silk slippers like a wisp of cloud in a blue sky. Her movements, while graceful, showed her to be in that gawky phase of life when a girl is all boney limbs and large feet. Thomas, the doting father, was nonetheless entranced at the sight. But soon enough her concentration lapsed, her feet stuttered, and she lost her place in the dance. She stamped her feet in frustration, hung her head and pouted like a child.

"I never do it right," she cried. "You show him, Sylvanne. You do it beautifully."

"Me? No no," Sylvanne demurred. "This dance is meant for a young girl to attract a husband, not for an old widow to perform in public."

"It's not public, it's only Daddy and me," Daphne insisted. "Besides, you're almost family, you spend more time attending to me than anyone else, and you're the best company. Daddy, tell her to perform. Don't tell her, demand it!"

"I would like to see it," Thomas said.

"Goody-good," Daphne shouted. "Then you must. You must!"

The girl slid the cymbals from her fingers and handed them to Sylvanne, then retreated to give her space to move. Sylvanne took a deep breath, and began to tap a beat with the cymbals, softly at first, then building in strength as she gained confidence in the purity of her rhythm. She began to dance. With her hair loose and flowing, and her wrists describing small circles in the air like songbirds chasing their tails, she had never looked lovelier, Thomas thought. He glanced at Daphne, who looked thrilled and absolutely mesmerized. His eyes were drawn back to

Sylvanne as the dance progressed and matured into a creation of extreme sensual enticement. Her hips swayed to the perfect beat of her fingers, and presented her body as an offering to him. He looked searchingly into her eyes, and was certain he saw desire reflected back at him.

32

Derek opened his door in the afternoon to find Meghan there, standing uneasily on the front step. He hadn't seen her for two days. "I just have a minute," she said. "I want to thank you for looking over those medical texts I lent you. Thomas says you did."

He shrugged. "You said yourself I have a lot of time on my hands. Did he get anything out of it?"

"Some. The medical terminology mostly left him muddled. He said he found it a jumble."

"So did I."

"But at least you read it. Thanks. It did some good. He said she doesn't suffer night sweats, so I've discounted tuberculosis. And Daphne actually seems to be getting better by the day, so maybe it was just down to the infection in her arm. I'm hopeful. Cleaning that up has made a big difference already." She paused. "Now do you mind if I say something to him?"

"Never suppress a generous impulse. The motto of someone I used to know."

She knew he was talking about the wife he had lost. There was kindness in his eyes, and she sensed a movement within him, something stirring in his heart, as if goodness were a hibernating bear awakening there.

"That's a good way to live," she said. "Is it your motto too?"

"I try."

"So I can say something?"

He nodded.

"To Thomas?"

Again he nodded.

"Okay." She took a deep breath. "It's always hard to start," she said. "I'll just plunge in then. Thomas—I can plainly see you're falling for her, and I can understand why. You're vulnerable, and lonely, and she's offering you a shoulder to cry on. She's become kind and sweet, all the things you sincerely wish she would be. On top of it she's grown more and more flirtatious, she's playing the total temptress. But don't forget I'm in her head, and I can feel everything she's up to. All this playacting as if she likes you, and teasing you, this dancing for you, presenting her body and subtly offering it to you, well, in a way it's fake, and in a way she was right to worry—it's affecting her, she's starting to waver, she's starting to like you and be attracted to you, which might be a good thing except at the same time it's making her crazy with guilt because it's a total betrayal of her duty to her poor dead husband." Meghan was aware she was starting to sound frantic, but she couldn't slow the torrent of words. "I'm totally blown away by the strength of her loyalty and duty and honour that's all bound up in a promise to her husband to kill you, and now she doesn't really want to do it anymore but she feels like she must, and it's driving her out of her mind! The sooner she does it the better—that's what she's thinking now, she absolutely must do it quickly before she loses her nerve! So Thomas—she still intends to kill you, I know you don't see it, you see only a pair of lovely eyes gazing at you so seductively these past days and nights. She's trying to get you to lower your guard. She's planning to plant a knife in your back. So be careful!"

Meghan caught her breath. She'd been addressing Thomas, but of course it was the friendly, slightly mocking face of Derek looking back at her. "Thank you for putting up with this," she said.

"You should really come in and sit down," he said. "I'll get you a glass of water. You look dehydrated."

"No, no, I'm fine," she protested. She bent down to rummage in a satchel at her feet. "There's one more thing I need to show you. To show Thomas."

"Come in, come in then. Here I thought you were done, now there's visuals to go along with the audio."

She followed him into his living room, and from her satchel she pulled a colour photocopy of Artemisia Gentileschi's painting of Judith and Holofernes, showing the gritty, indomitable heroine hacking away at her hapless victim's neck. Blood flowed in rivulets down the white linen sheets. She handed the image to Derek. "Look at this. This is what she wants for you. For Thomas, I mean."

"That's nasty," Derek said.

"Please be careful, Thomas," Meghan continued imploringly. "I can tell you this much—she has a small knife now, one her maid brought from the kitchen. She intends to lure you to her bed, and give herself up to you, and then when you're defenceless, and blind to everything but desire, she'll stab you with the knife. The provocative dancing, the demure looks, all the seductive behaviour that's put you under her spell, it's an act. When she moons at you lovingly, it's a falsehood. That's the way you need to think of it."

"Sounds to me like the web's been spun, and she's already caught him."

"He is smitten," Meghan agreed.

"Men are helpless in the face of a good-looking woman who knows her power. She looks like you, right?"

"Yes."

"Then he's a dead man."

Meghan ignored the compliment. "I don't want him to die. That's why I'm warning him."

"If I were him I'd go for it," Derek said. "Getting a woman to do all the work for once is like manna from heaven—there's not a man alive who would pass that up."

"Don't, Derek," Meghan said curtly.

"Don't what?"

"Don't mess around with this."

"I'm not, I'm not," he insisted. "Listen, if he really is in my head, he might like to hear some advice, man to man, bro to bro."

Meghan looked doubtful.

"Hey Thomas, go ahead, go for it," he continued. "Let her

lead you to the boudoir, bud. Let it get naked, and hot and heavy, so hot she won't want to stop—"

"Enough," said Meghan sharply.

He ignored her. "All you have to do is find the knife where she's hidden it, toss it away before she can use it. She'll break down and cry, and *give up*, that's the best case scenario, and you'll be right where you want to be to comfort her. Things'll warm right back up."

"He's not that callous, or shallow," Meghan said.

"Oh please. He's a man, I'm a man. I know how men think. A woman who tempts and teases him every chance she gets, so she can try to kill him, but now—thanks to you—he knows she doesn't really want to kill him, and is actually attracted to him? That's the hottest of the hot! Irresistible! He'll be so stoked to have her, it'll be like nuclear fucking fusion!"

"Stop it," Meghan said. "If he takes the knife away, she won't go through with it."

"How can you be so sure?"

"You forget I'm in her head. I know exactly how she visualizes it—she'll feel for the knife as soon as she gets into the bed, but won't use it until the right moment. Mabel has convinced her not to bring out the knife until the moment of his climax, because a man is *lost* just then, he's at his weakest, most helpless."

"*Petit mort*, the little death," Derek said. "To be followed this time by the big death."

"No no no," she protested. "There won't be any death. Thomas, I'm warning you. You've got the facts now, the full information. Do not do it!"

"You're too late. You said yourself he's falling for her," Derek replied. "Has he tried to kiss her already?"

"Yes," she admitted.

"There you go, then."

"It was as a way of thanking me. He wanted to kiss *me*."

"He wanted to kiss *you*?"

"Out of gratitude. For helping with his daughter. He asked Sylvanne if he could embrace her, and kiss her, so that I could feel it."

"And did you?"

"Well, he held her head in his hands, and it was three light pecks, really. Here, here, and here." She touched her two cheeks and forehead. "Then she took his hand, and kissed his fingers. He pulled back as if she'd held them to the flame."

"But his kisses—did you feel them?"

"I think so."

"So what did it feel like, to be kissed by someone, when you're inside someone else's head?"

"It felt real. That's all I can say. It was as real as any kiss I've ever had. When he looked into her eyes I felt like he was looking straight into my eyes. Her eyes were the window to *my* soul, if that's not too weird."

"I think you have a crush," Derek said.

"Don't say it like that," she reproached him.

"I can't believe women sometimes," Derek laughed. "Here you are with the hots for the guy, and if he makes love to this woman you'll feel it, and you're telling him don't go for it."

"I'm telling him to be kind to her, and not to get himself killed."

"Sylvanne's doing everything short of a striptease to get the guy between the sheets," Derek asserted. "Let the dude have his fun, let him express his love to you, and who knows? Nothing's written in stone. Sylvanne might come around. She sounds like she's on the verge of coming around."

"I just want him to be careful," Meghan said softly. She had the sudden sensation of longing stirring inside her, like a tendril of new life erupting from an ancient seed. She wanted to nurture and encourage this feeling, to bring it to the light and examine it, but not here, standing before Derek in his shabby living room. "I really have to go."

"Keep me posted," Derek said.

"It's not a joke," she said. "It's real."

"Then I should be jealous of you, and of Thomas. You get to experience reality, I only hear about it second hand."

"I know. Sorry. I always leave here apologizing to you."

"Don't be sorry for hogging the reality, I have enough of my own, thank you. You're the one with too much."

33

Mabel was crossing the yard, escorted by a guardsman as usual to collect the supper, when she chanced upon Lord Thomas, who was tutoring three young pages in the martial techniques of the broadsword. He greeted her warmly as she was led by, and she asked if she might have a few moments of his time, to speak to him on a matter of great import. Thomas handed his sword to her startled guardsman, and bade him take charge of the lesson, while he led Mabel to a quiet room in the armoury, where weapons of all sorts were stacked against the walls. "Now my dear, what so heavily weighs upon your mind?" he asked her.

"Master, I must warn you, in confidence," Mabel told him solemnly, "that despite her warm and gracious behaviour toward you these last days, m'Lady still harbours ill will toward you."

Thomas smiled upon her. "I thank you for being so

forthcoming," he replied. "But you may spare me the details, for I already know them."

"How's that, sire?" she asked, greatly surprised.

"You procured for her a small knife, and the lady has hidden it in some convenient nook at her bedside. She intends to make an offer to me of her body, that I might use her as I wish, and then stab me as I lie with her upon the bed. Is that how the play is written? A bit of theatre requiring her to act two parts, lover and killer, while I play a single role: the willing dupe. The only wrinkle in the plot that remains unknown to me is whether she'll let me have my way with her first, so as to stab me as I lie defenceless, cloudy-headed and impoverished of strength after the act, or will she strike earlier than that, and thus maintain her honour?"

"You're a wizard, Sire," cried Mabel in astonishment.

"If I be a wizard, it's only for good, I hope. But tell me, why do you abandon loyalty to your Lady, and turn traitor at this hour?"

"I'm no traitor, Sir," Mabel protested. "It's for the Lady's good. Forgive me for speaking so directly, but the way I see it, if you were to succeed in joining with her, and if through this union you were to plant a seed inside her, then she might come to forget her other sorrows, for when the child is born, she'll be won over to it through maternal love. And as it grows, and takes on some of your own good looks, she'll likewise be won over to you."

"So it's your sincere wish that I join with her, and possess her?"

"It would be for the best, Sire."

"Your reasoning pretends an altruistic spirit, but wizardry apart, plain old gossip informs me you have ambitions for your own future."

Mabel blushed, but answered him assertively. "I want my freedom, Sir," she declared. "My life back home is over, and there is one who desires me here."

"Gwynn the poultryman, if I'm not mistaken."

She nodded.

"Good luck to you," Thomas wished her. "His first wife gave him three boys, and birthing the third is what killed her, so he's predisposed to gratitude toward womankind for that sacrifice. You'll benefit from it, and he'll be patient and tender in his treatment of you, not wanting to lose another. You speak of wanting freedom. Well I do warn you, trading the certitudes of service to your Lady for an independent life as wife of a freeman is no guaranteed improvement, especially when those three untamed young boys of his show every sign of growing up to be even bigger rascals than their old man. However, if you do succeed in domesticating father and sons, you'll have performed a great service to the community, and in expectation of that outcome I hereby promise that you shall have your freedom soon. Gwynn shall have his wife."

Mabel returned to her Lady's chambers with the supper and found Sylvanne looking out dreamily from the window.

"Ah, there you are. What kept you?"

"I was waylaid, Ma'am."

"Hmm. Look how early in the day the moon has chosen to show herself in the sky. Look how full and round she is."

Mabel came to the window and saw that it was true, the moon

hung round and swollen in the east while the autumn sun had yet to set over fields and forest. Below them, a peasant's fat cow had wandered into the bulrushes of the moat, the wooden bell around its neck making a lovely, earthy chime. To Mabel the serenity of the moment was marred only by the breeze that blew in through the unshuttered window. It was cool, and hinted of winter coming.

"This night feels right," Sylvanne said. "This is the very night we must strike, Mabel. Have them fetch hot water, for first I must bathe, then be anointed in something fragrant, then adorn myself as finely as that ancient Jewess who slew a general. Tonight I'll coax Thomas from his daughter's bedside, and induce him to return here with me."

"Good for you, Madame!"

"I must tell you something first, though. I've had a change of heart, a change of strategy. Rather than having you absent yourself, I want you here, in your bed. You be discreet, and make as to be asleep when we arrive," she instructed. "You'll hear us, and, peeking out from your anteroom, you'll ascertain the precise moment when he lies with me, and begins to lose himself in his attentions to me. Creep close, without a sound—raise the knife, bring it down!"

Sylvanne could not fail to notice the look of horror on Mabel's face. "Please Mabel, I need you," she pleaded. "You're stronger than I am. I don't trust myself to do it alone. I'll hold him tight, and you thrust the knife."

"Oh no, Ma'am," Mabel stammered. "Not me. You."

"You told me you'd do anything for me."

"But not that. Not murder. The man has been so kind to us and all—what if he howls in pain, or begs for mercy?"

"The same man murdered my husband. He deserves his head on a pike above the barbican gate," Sylvanne stated. But the words came out flat, neutral, and to Mabel's ears lacked conviction.

"Oh Madame. Is that truly how you feel?"

"It's not a question of how I feel, it's a question of justice. What matters is justice be done," Sylvanne said, her voice quavering.

"Forgive me for insufficient intensity of feeling, Ma'am," Mabel pleaded. "To kill a man needs passion stronger than I possess. If you feel it, *you* must do it."

Sylvanne shuddered deeply. "You're right, of course you're right. It's up to me, isn't it?" She was lost in thought a moment, then looked directly into Mabel's eyes. "I owe you an apology— I'm so frightened of failure that I tried to pass my own solemn duty into your blameless hands!"

"There, there, Madame," Mabel said soothingly. "Are you starting to have feelings for the Master and his young daughter? I shouldn't be surprised if you are."

"Don't talk of feelings, please," Sylvanne pleaded. "I'm bound by duty, and without fulfilling it what am I? I need to remember my duty. I need to trust myself. I need to believe that in the moment I will find the strength."

"That's more like it, Madame," Mabel said encouragingly. "You lure him to your bed, and lie with him upon it, and then, when he weakens after gaining his, his, when he takes rest afterward, he'll be sure to lie undefended. He'll be at your mercy, he will! That's the time to strike. That's the plan we hatched. Let's stick to that."

"That's the plan *you* hatched," Sylvanne responded. "But it's not you who must make a sacrifice." When she tried to picture how it would play out, to imagine the moment, her mind was overwhelmed by complexities of emotion. "Could I really be with him like that, arousing passion in him, persuading him to satisfy himself upon me, and not find myself susceptible to being..." She groped for the right word.

"Swept along, Madame?"

A new thought came to Sylvanne, and she eyed Mabel suspiciously. "It's funny, that you, an old virgin, are suddenly so full of advice about my comportment in bed," she said. "Not for the first time you express your preference that I let him have me before I strike. Why is that, Mabel? I'm frightened of the entire scenario, yet you fear only half—you're keen that I take him to bed, yet less enthused to see him dead. Perhaps I should worry about you, that you might call out and alert him, for as you've said yourself, the man's been so kind to us."

"Oh no, ma'am. I wouldn't. I would never alert him."

"I wonder if you already have."

After her bath Sylvanne arranged her hair up high upon her head, so as to show her lovely neck to its full effect. She anointed herself with perfume from a bottle that had belonged to Thomas' wife, a scent that pleased her greatly, with hints of leather and rose petal. She chose a kirtle of red velvet with white linen cuffs, and above its revealingly low bodice she arrayed a silver necklace of sapphires that had been an extravagant wedding present from

Gerald. When Mabel told her she looked stunning, she knew it wasn't sycophancy but the unadorned truth. Appraising herself in the looking glass she found that beauty gave her courage. She thought, in my raiment at least I have equalled that Biblical heroine Judith. Now if only I might equal her in action. But then doubts troubled her mind, for she knew the two circumstances were not identical. She thought, fair Judith had as motivation the rescue of an entire besieged city at risk of slaughter, while I, by comparison, seek merely to kill a widowed man who struggles to preserve his daughter. She did her best to drive from her mind such unhelpful small treasons, and focus on two simple thoughts. Tonight is to be the night. Do your duty.

Soon after dark the summons came as usual, and she was escorted to Daphne's bedroom. She arrived fully prepared to enliven the evening, to play sultry temptress and spark the heart of Lord Thomas, but on entering the room, she saw that the mood was sombre, and muted, with the candles dimmed. Daphne slept in the bed, and Thomas brooded in a chair close to her.

"She relapses, I fear. How faintly she breathes," he said pensively. "Her skin succumbs to that sickly pallor I so dread."

"You study her in her sleep too intently to be objective," Sylvanne suggested. "Most of this afternoon she chattered to me freely, in high spirits. She even took a stroll along the parapet."

"I'm not sure it was wise to expose her to that icy breeze."

"She dressed snugly and enjoyed herself. You do worry so," she consoled him. She came to him, stood close to him, and lay her hand on his shoulder. He turned his head, and rubbed his cheek against the back of her hand for comfort. The door creaked, and she pulled her hand away. Mabel entered, carrying sheets and feather bedding.

"Mabel has kindly offered to sleep here tonight, to give you recess from your constant surveillance of the child, and let you enjoy your own bed for a change," Sylvanne told him.

"Very kind, but I'm not sure I should."

"Oh, please do. Please. For me."

He looked at her closely for the first time since she had entered. By candlelight she did indeed look beautiful, almost irresistibly beguiling. A glance at Mabel told him all he needed to know about what was in store for him this evening. Life is a paradox, he thought to himself—what I truly long for at this moment is company, that is, companionship. A shoulder to cry on, as Meghan expressed so recently, in my dreams. Instead, this stunning creature who may or may not despise me offers her body, without knowing that it will be fully mine for the simple price of disarming her in time. Well, she's too beautiful not to take advantage of what she's put on offer, and I'll enjoy it doubly, knowing as I do that Meghan will be present in her, and will take pleasure in it too. Perhaps I'll speak to Meghan in the lovemaking, and remind her that it's for her, and for the kindness and companionship she has shown across centuries. As for Sylvanne, well, it needs doing, that's the main part of it—the playacting needs to end, and then perhaps we may start all over again, this time without pretence and guile.

34

They passed the better part of an hour chatting amiably, while Mabel made a bed for herself on a divan in the corner, and kept to it discreetly. Daphne did not stir, but sleep seemed to benefit her, and a little colour gradually returned to her cheeks. Thomas felt relieved, and when he stood at one point to stretch his limbs, Sylvanne announced, "It's time for me to be abed. Will you accompany me to my door? I don't like to be unchaperoned with any one of these guardsmen of yours."

Thomas carried a single candle to light their way along the passage to her chambers. When they arrived he unlocked the door and bade her enter.

"I'll thank you to come in, and help me light the candles," Sylvanne said to him. "It's a task always left to Mabel, and now that she's absent, I'm almost afraid to be alone."

"Shall I stay on, keep you company awhile?"

"That would please me very much."

With the flame of his candle he lit another on a small table, then set his own on the mantle of the hearth. Sylvanne moved toward her bed, toying with a ribbon in her hair.

"What shall we do to pass the time?" Thomas asked.

"I yield to your suggestion."

"I don't know. Do you play chess? I have a lovely board with soapstone pieces. I could send for it."

"I've never been one for games of the mind," she replied.

"Haven't you?"

"No. I prefer action over thought. There's beauty in movement, in a gesture," she said, lifting her hand and turning it delicately in the air, like a songbird in flight. "The poets might try to capture it, but they always come up short."

"They rely on words," Thomas noted. "Words are not always true to thoughts."

"Aren't they?"

"What are your thoughts at this moment?" he asked her.

"I'm thinking how handsome you are." She pulled at a ribbon, and let her hair tumble and cascade freely down over her shoulders. "And you, what are you thinking?"

"I'm thinking I should make love to you."

Their eyes locked. Thomas thought he could hear his own heart beating.

"Then let action win out over thought," she said.

They came together and their lips met. Although tempered at first by an underlying wariness, his desire was real, and from the lusty way she met his kisses with her own, he was almost convinced her passion was sincere. He took her head in his hands and stared searchingly into her eyes. Once again he thought he saw Meghan there, and desired to reach her, and felt the heat of his lust stoked and redoubled by a feeling like love. He began to undress her, slowly, worshipfully. Sylvanne compliantly let his hands strip her dress from her shoulders, let his fingers and his palms explore the smoothness of her breasts. He bade her sit on the bed, and knelt before her, pulling her dress down around her calves and ankles, then lifting her feet to slip them free. As he rose she wrapped her arms around him and desperately pulled him to her, falling back upon the bed sheets.

"What's your hurry?" he teased. "We have all night."

"I want it done."

"So it shall be."

He reared up from her, standing before her as he shed his own clothes. She covered her body with a sheet. As he made himself naked she saw that he was aroused. "Come warm this cold bed," she whispered. He climbed into bed beside her, and as before she clutched at him urgently, and fell back upon the pillows, pulling him on top of her. He rained kisses down upon her face, her neck, her breasts. For a moment he felt disoriented, and it came to him suddenly that she smelled of his wife's perfume. This maddened him—it fed his arousal and made him an animal, a dog rising to the scent.

"Let me," he demanded.

"I will."

"Then let me."

"Now who's impatient?"

"Let me now," he said forcefully.

He was so much stronger. The weight of his body trapped her beneath him, and he reached down with both hands to take hold of her thighs when a knife blade suddenly glinted golden in the candlelight. A sharp flicker of pain grazed his side—he saw her raise the knife again and instinctively caught her hand by the wrist, adeptly twisting her arm over the side of the bed. His two strong hands quickly stripped her of the knife. It fell, clattering harmlessly against the stone floor.

"I couldn't do it," she wailed. "I've spared you!" He was still on top of her, he still controlled her. He was so much stronger that his actions could be assured, yet almost gentle. He moved her to the middle of the bed and straddled her, pinning her arms while he looked down at the ragged rise and fall of her breasts, her flushed, reddened face distorted by humiliation.

"The knife came out earlier than I expected," he said, catching his breath. "Why didn't you wait?"

"I couldn't stand to make a gift of myself to you," she hissed at him. "I couldn't stand to give you something you haven't earned."

He was strong enough to imprison both her wrists with one hand, and with his free hand he checked his side where the knife had grazed him. There was a trace of blood, but she had barely broken the skin. "You came ever so close to doing me damage, my dear," he muttered. "An inch or two deeper and I'd have been slit open just the way a pig is bled. A more confident slice and I would surely now be dying—and you, trapped beneath me, would be drowning in a torrent of red. But though it stings, this scratch is nothing—I suffer worse on any given day of training for the jousts."

"I spared you, don't you see that?" She began to softly sob. "I could have plunged it deep enough to finish you."

"Is that your story, now that you failed?" he demanded. Yet he wanted to believe her, and looked for evidence of her sincerity in her anguished face. She refused to meet his gaze. "Why do you hide from me?"

"Leave me alone," she whimpered.

"You just tried to kill me, yet you pretend I should be grateful to you that you didn't."

"Leave me alone."

"I'm trying to understand what transpired."

"Go ask your Meghan."

"I will. She's told me already how turbulent and troubled your emotions are—that you're torn between a widow's pledge to a dead husband, and something else. A new life, perhaps—the potential for a future of happiness with a new man."

She lifted her eyes to him. Her look of surprise told him what he'd said was true.

"If you know everything, why do you toy with me?" Sylvanne cried. "Why did you come here if you knew there would be a knife?"

"Your maid told me it would come out later."

"That was her idea—and she almost persuaded my vacillating mind. My maid is a traitor."

"Not a traitor. She wants to see you happy."

"If she wants me happy, it's so she may abandon me in good conscience."

"That's very perceptive. I admire the sharpness of your thoughts. Do you know what would make me happy?"

"To be alive."

"Yes, that, of course. I'm happy to be intact. But what would make me even more happy would be to make love to you. Not to your surface thoughts, but to a deeper soul within. I speak of Meghan, of course. Hold still, damn you." She had turned her head away, and now he forced her again to look into his eyes. He looked searchingly into hers. "I'm going to call you Meghan. I'm going to say I love you. I love you, Meghan. I want to make love to you now, in gratitude."

He loosened his grip, and lay beside her, as if expecting his words to be enough to turn her into a willing partner. But Sylvanne would not be compliant, or yielding. She raised her mouth to his shoulder and bit him savagely, her teeth deeply puncturing his skin. He cried out in pain and shoved her roughly away from him. "Damn you to hell," he howled. "Your mouth has proved more dangerous than the knife!"

He climbed off the bed. Sylvanne pulled the sheet up to cover her nakedness. He knelt by the bedside and poured water from a bucket into a basin on the floor, then dampened a cloth and dabbed at the scrape on his side where the knife had barely broken the skin. Then he attended to the more serious bite wound on his shoulder, where her teeth had done real damage.

"Likely this mangled flesh is better left alone," he said,

examining the gash in the faint candlelight. "I'll put a shirt over it, and let it dry on its own."

He came back to where she lay curled upon the bed. Sylvanne turned her head away again so as not to look at him. "I'll say one more thing, to Meghan, if I may," he pronounced. "Dear Meghan, before the knife came out, in those candle-lit moments while Sylvanne so beguilingly playacted the temptress, I felt you watching. I felt your presence in a new way, as vibrations from some secret place. But then the blade glinted like a candle's flame, and suddenly what might have been beautiful turned ugly, and violent. Still, I did my best to reach you, to give myself to you."

He took Sylvanne's chin in his hand and forced her to look at him. "I need to meet your eyes. Meghan, I want to say I love you."

"Your love is too strange," Sylvanne muttered.

"So it might seem to you," he answered her. "Please understand that in a way I feel love for you too. Love in the form of admiration. Beyond your undeniable beauty, the depth of your loyalty to your husband is a testament to your fine character. I'll leave you now."

35

When ten-year-olds decide they don't like life, they can be extremely good at keeping to that philosophy, at least in the short term. But soon enough their natural inclination for joy and laughter wins out, and what they long for is some tiny scrap of evidence that life is good and sweet, so that they can officially change their minds about it. For Betsy that little scrap was indeed truly *scrap*, a gift made up of bits and pieces of abandoned and salvaged old bicycles, disassembled, redesigned, and cobbled back together into an eccentric unicycle.

She discovered it leaning ready-to-ride against the handrail of the stairs of her back deck when she went out to the garden one day after breakfast. She had just started to examine it closely, running her fingers over the scorched grey metal spots where it had been so recently welded, when she heard Derek call out to her.

"You like it?"

"My mom told me this would happen," she replied curtly. "She said, he's a man, men never apologize with words, they try to buy their way back into your good books."

"I didn't buy it, I built it with my own hands."

"That's because you're cheap."

"But do you like it? It's three-quarter sized, I made it petite, just for you. It could be the only one like it in existence."

Betsy stepped down to the second of the deck steps, and tried to mount the unicycle from there. "Go around the other side of the railing," Derek advised. "You've gotta get yourself right above it, and feel for that point of perfect balance, then you'll be on it in no time. You'll be pedalling it around on the trampoline like a crazy little circus freak!"

"I can't do it," Betsy complained. With the wheel slipping forward and backward under her, she couldn't find the courage to let go of the deck rail.

"Maybe I should come over and help you," Derek suggested. "I did manage to get up on it this morning, but it's easier over here—my yard is mostly hard-packed dirt, not like your squishy soft lawn. We should really take it out on the pavement."

Meghan came out onto her deck. She told Derek there was someone at his front door and he should go answer it.

"I'm not expecting anyone, it's probably Johos or something. Forget it," he said.

"What's Johos?" Betsy asked.

"Jehovah's Witnesses," Meghan replied. "Derek, it's not anyone like that, I think it's important that you go answer your door."

Catching an odd note of insistence in her voice, Derek gave her a puzzled look. Meghan, first making sure Betsy was preoccupied with her new toy, made a discreet gesture with her eyes that could only mean 'meet me over there.'

Betsy looked up from the unicycle. "I've decided to forgive him," she said happily.

"Good. You stay here, and for God's sake put your helmet on before you try to ride that thing." She headed back into the house. "You hear me? Stay in the back yard."

Derek opened his front door, and Meghan brushed quickly past him, striding to his living room. "I need to talk to Thomas," she said brusquely.

"I figured as much," Derek replied. "How'd it go? Did Tom and Sylvanne—"

"Terrible. I shouldn't have let you put him up to it."

"What happened? She didn't kill him, did she?"

"No. He—"

"That's all right then. No harm no foul, right?"

"There was harm. There was terrible harm. He tried to take her against her will, and he would have done it, except she bit him—and you know what? Good for her, I say. Good for Sylvanne! First time you've heard me say that!"

"Calm down, calm down," Derek urged her. "Where were they, when all this happened?"

"In her bed."

"And did he drag her there, or did she invite him?"

"She invited him. I know what you're thinking. She enticed him, yes, that's right, and then she pulled out the knife, and slashed at him. But did she really try to kill him? I'm not sure. She swung the knife, but it was half-hearted, like she wanted to fail. Like a criminal who wants to get caught. *Stop me before I do something evil.*"

"I thought you were in her mind. You're supposed to know exactly what she's thinking."

"I am. I was. Sometimes people don't know what they want. There she was, she had him exactly where she wanted him, like a lamb led to slaughter—and he'd totally dropped his guard, he was just crazed! Obsessed with having her! Worry about a little thing like a knife in the back? Forget it! He was like, I must take you, *right now!*"

"Then she stabbed him?"

"She grazed him."

"But drew blood?"

"Yes."

"Ouch. Must've hurt like hell. Probably made him furious. No wonder he tried to force her."

"The worst of it is he kept saying it was for *me*, he was trying to please *me*. But it didn't please me at all. I felt only her resistance, that she didn't want it, that she wasn't ready for it." She sighed deeply. "Poor thing. She had to listen to him mooning yet again over some bizarre futuristic woman she doesn't even believe in. That's what's preventing her from loving him—he keeps telling her he's in love with me! She put up such a brave fight—she really ripped a chunk out of his shoulder when she bit him!" Meghan nearly laughed at the thought of it, then turned sombre again. "I feel so sorry for her, so guilty for what I put her through."

"Don't make her sound innocent," Derek countered. "She took the lead. Bringing him to bed was her idea."

"Yes, but—"

"Up to a point, it all went according to her plan, right?"

Meghan shook her head. "The plan was, they would have sex, and it was going to be consensual—not consensual exactly, but she would *allow* him. But really that was Mabel's plan—Sylvanne just couldn't think of anything better, so she went along, because it did mirror Judith's story, which her husband had instructed her to follow."

"Blame the husband, then. I don't think we should blame Thomas for any of this," Derek said.

"I'm not blaming him, but I do need to talk to him."

"Fine. But keep in mind that he's a man of his time—and a man of his time would find it ludicrous to think he needs a woman's consent to have sex with her."

"Can you just let me speak?"

Derek made an exaggerated gesture of zipping his mouth shut. Meghan gathered her thoughts.

"Thomas," she began. "I beg you to leave Sylvanne alone. Promise me you won't force yourself on her, ever again. Can you do that, please?"

Derek couldn't help himself. "Maybe he liked it that she bit him. Maybe he thought, 'What a hellcat! A tigress!'"

"Stop it. A hellcat is a caged animal, frightened and cornered.

That's why she fought—because there was no escape, nowhere to hide."

"Ask him if I'm right. Thomas, am I right?"

"It's impossible to talk to you," she sighed.

"No, just the opposite. It's easier than ever. Haven't you noticed? I've gotten on board. I'm taking it seriously. I'm treating Thomas as real. You're driving, I'm riding shotgun. There's no map. So the best I can do is throw some ideas out there. For example let me say this: Way to go Thomas, thanks for fucking up and falling off your pedestal, from saint to sinner in fair Meghan's eyes. I like you better this way, a bit rough around the edges."

"You're making fun of me."

"No I'm not," Derek insisted. "I'm teasing him, not you—the guy obviously has massive feelings for you, and was trying to show it, the only way he knew how."

"Massive feelings—your words." Her mind was a jumble of high emotions, none of which she wanted to share with Derek. "May I say one last thing to Thomas?"

"Of course."

Meghan composed herself, then began to speak, slowly and forcefully. "Thank you for trying to reach me. Remember, when I'm inside Sylvanne, I'm privy to her thoughts, and a prisoner of her feelings. She was alone with her thoughts all night after you left. She's a very proud woman. There were moments when she hated herself for failing, for falling short in her duty. She could have finished you off with a single stroke of the blade, fast and deep. Why didn't she? Without that duty fulfilled, what is she? Oftentimes I feel there's so much guilt bottled up in her—guilt that she failed in her primary duty to her husband, to give him children, and failed even to truly love him as a wife should. Now that he's dead it's like she still wants to make it up to him, and wants to finally fulfill her duty to him—it's come down to one mighty act of revenge, and yet she still can't do it, she doesn't want to do it, she wishes someone would talk her out of it. She's lost. She wants to be rescued."

"Is that how she feels, or is that you?" Derek asked.

"I'm speaking for her. I'm trying to make sense of feelings she can't articulate."

Derek thought a moment before he spoke. "You know what's funny about this?"

"Nothing."

"Hear me out. Thomas is in my head, right? That means I can talk to him anytime I like, just by thinking. Whereas if you have anything to say to him you have to come over and visit me. So in a way I'm in the driver's seat, not you. He talks to you, but he listens to me."

Meghan looked at him coldly. "I'm still not sure if you're just fooling with me, or what you're up to."

"Well you're going to have to trust me to do the right thing," Derek said. "While you're here, I'm going to share my advice for our man Thomas. So Thomas, listen up, bud. There's a clear path you need to follow here: you need to woo this Lady Sylvanne! You owe it to her. You killed her husband. Sorry, but you did. And now she's all alone in the world, thanks to you. And yet she has some feelings for you. Give the woman a lifeline! Take care of her! You need to win her heart, like a chivalrous knight of old. And luckily for you, you just happen to be one, right?" To Meghan he said, "You'd like it if he did that, wouldn't you?"

"Of course I would."

"And if they get together, you'll still get your wish, of getting with Thomas."

"Now you're making it sound too devious," Meghan objected. "I'm asking him to be kind to her, simply because she deserves it. I don't want any ulterior motive attached to it. It's for her, not me."

"Then how about this? Thomas! No more talking to Meghan, or even about Meghan, when you're with Sylvanne. You hear me, pal? Looking into her eyes and telling her you see someone else in there—that's a total non-starter. That's pretty much guaranteed to turn her off, my man. If you want to win the poor girl's heart, do not even say the word Meghan. You hear me?"

"I think that would be good, actually," Meghan said. "Yes. She's just so weary of him constantly talking *at her*, rather than to her. So I agree—give her a break, Thomas. No talking to *me*. Talk to *her*."

"See? Once in a while I have a good idea," Derek said.

"Once, anyway."

"Here's another one. Thinking only of you and Thomas, of course—there's another way to get you two unrequited lovebirds together."

"Don't."

"No really. Come on. If you and I were to hook up, even for a casual thing, it wouldn't be casual for Thomas, or for you. The two of you tried to get together through Sylvanne, and it didn't work out, because Sylvanne wasn't part of the coalition of the willing. Well I am! Hell, I'm volunteering right now. Sign me up!"

"It wouldn't feel the same," Meghan objected.

"Don't reject it outright. Why don't we ask Thomas what he thinks about it? You sleep on it, then let me know what he has to say. Let him have the last word."

36

Mabel never returned to Sylvanne's room in the morning. The meal was brought by a young guardsman, who placed a plate and cup inside the door, and lingered there, leering at her, until she screamed at him to get out. Then she was alone again, lying in a fetal curl on the bed, obsessing over every pain and emanation from her body.

She must have slept most of the day, for when she awoke again the sun was streaming into her bedroom as it did in mid-afternoon. She opened her eyes to see Daphne standing beside her bed, peering down at her.

"You haven't been to visit me today. Are you unwell?" the young girl asked her.

"It doesn't matter," Sylvanne answered flatly.

"It does to me. You're my friend. Truly my only one."

"Then you have none. My friendship was a falsehood. It was an act, meant to gain me favour with your father."

"That's a lie," Daphne cried.

"I'm not a monster. I do like you. You're an innocent in this, and I feel sorry for you. But my sympathy doesn't change the facts."

"I need your friendship," the young girl pleaded, moving close and touching Sylvanne's sleeve. Sylvanne pulled her arm away and sat up in the bed.

"You can't have it. Leave me alone just now. Go. Please. Get out."

Daphne seemed rooted to the spot. Sylvanne slid her feet over the side of the bed and stood up. Daphne came to her, wanting to embrace her, but Sylvanne shoved her away so roughly that the young girl stumbled and fell to the floor.

"Now look what I've done," Sylvanne murmured. "Please just go. Today it seems I *am* a monster."

"You break my heart!" Daphne cried. She pulled herself to her feet, her face streaming tears, just as her father appeared in the doorway.

"What are you doing out of your bed? You're not well enough to be wandering alone," he scolded her.

"I wanted to see Sylvanne," she whimpered.

"Perhaps she doesn't wish to see you just now."

"She doesn't want to see me *ever!*" she wailed. She pushed her way past her father out the door. As the sound of her sobs faded with her retreating footsteps, Thomas glared at Sylvanne, the anger in his eyes tempered by self-blame for the whole sad fiasco.

She stood before him defiantly. He brought his temper under control, and reminded himself why he had come. "I don't want us to be enemies anymore," he said softly. "Last night I slept fitfully, and in my sleep, communication came from Meghan. I have something of great import to tell you, Sylvanne. Meghan has made me promise—she has made me swear to you that what I attempted to do to you last night will not be repeated. You have nothing more to fear from me. I came to apologize, you see—it was your beauty that truly beguiled me, and I made you suffer for it. From today forward, after these few moments, I will do my best to leave Meghan aside, and speak only to you, and you alone. But for one last time I need to speak to her now. May I?"

Sylvanne made no move. He came toward her until he could see her in profile, the afternoon light illuminating the soft curve of her neck. "My heart has changed, and it's thanks to Meghan. For one last time, I ask that you listen, so that she might hear. Let me say it and be done."

His manner was humble and respectful, his face unguarded and honest. Despite herself, Sylvanne felt a softening of her heart. With the slightest nod of her head, she bade him continue.

"Meghan, when we meet in dreams, I perceive you through the eyes and mind of Derek. I feel what he feels, and suffer his joys and longings, his pleasures and disappointments—just exactly as you must experience the life of this lovely young lady I so nearly wronged. But there's a difference in our circumstances: this poor woman wrestles with demons, and hates me at least by half, while Derek feels only love. He feels love for you in many forms, most especially love at its most lusty. He desires you. He wants you in his bed. I know the effect you have upon him, for I share it fully, and surpass it, even. When he suggested that you make love to him as a way to reach me, it seemed as if you brushed the idea aside. But if you are willing to let me have the last word, then let me speak from the heart.

"If you were to make love to him, I'm certain you would reach my own heart and soul. Dear Meghan, in Sylvanne's eyes I've glimpsed your presence as a ray of pure light that peeks out from behind her torn loyalty. I ask you to likewise search for me in Derek's eyes—he'll be only too happy to let you. I wager that for you, his eyes will open wide as the hungry throat of a newly-hatched songbird.

"I know your opinion of Derek is not highly favourable, Meghan, but truly, he is not a wicked man. He's neither spiteful nor malevolent, merely a drunkard and a reveller in strange substances unknown to me, whose properties play tricks upon the mind. His vices are weaknesses that harm only himself. Leave aside his vices, and consider his virtues. Most importantly, consider this: if there's an earthly garden of tender adoration where you and I might join together as one, it's through Derek that we will reach it."

He fell silent. Sylvanne lifted her eyes to look at him. "Are you finished?" she said.

"Yes."

"Truly finished? Henceforth you'll no longer speak of this Meghan?"

"I must put forward a single caveat. If Daphne's health were to worsen, so that I again feared for her life, then I would need to consult her."

"But otherwise, you'll only speak to me, from now forward?"

"I will do my best. You must trust me. In time you'll see the proof of my sincerity."

"It's not your sincerity I doubt. It's your sanity."

"I'm not surprised. Henceforth there'll be no more chatter about a woman I've met only in dreams. Meghan says you'll find that a relief."

"She's the sole reason you've spoken to me at all. What motive will bring you to me now?"

"A good question. I'm not sure. I suppose I'm used to you. Isn't that strange? I've told you I admire you, in many ways. You're a woman of fine character. I don't like the thought of ceasing to talk with you. I like being in your presence. You're something of a habit. A good one."

"Or maybe you wish to soften my heart, in order to win me, and thus win your Meghan too."

"You're clever to think of that, for that was exactly Derek's idea. But Meghan disallowed that plan. She forbade it. She's on your side now. The women have banded together. And I suppose the men have too."

37

Anne had opened her office window, hoping to catch a breeze on this muggy afternoon, and now noise from the street intruded. Grinding truck gears and the roar of transit buses combined with the stifling heat to give Meghan a nasty headache. Anne fetched her a glass of water and she drank the whole thing down in one go, finishing off with a gasp of satisfaction. "Whew, that's better, I hope it helps—I'm not thinking straight," she complained.

"Don't worry about it," Anne replied. "Often the best sessions happen when people aren't a hundred percent. Things pop up from the subconscious that surprise you. Now catch me up. What's been happening to you?"

Meghan dutifully described it to her—how Sylvanne had lured Thomas to her bed, and swiped at him with the knife, and how he had subdued her, and then so nearly taken her. "I've been feeling so guilty about it, because Derek encouraged him to go through with it, and I did nothing to dissuade him."

"Derek, your neighbour?"

"That's right."

"He's now talking to Thomas?"

"He says so. I'm still not a hundred percent sure he's sincere. He claims he's on board now, that he's my sidekick, or I'm his, but I'm not sure he really believes me even yet. Not that it matters—he doesn't have to talk to Thomas directly anyway, Thomas knows his thoughts."

"And what does Derek think?"

"He thinks the best way for Thomas to woo Sylvanne would be to stop mentioning me. Every time Thomas speaks to me through her, she thinks he's off his rocker, and you can't fall in love with a man if you think he's insane. So that means I'm the romance killer in the equation. He's better off totally leaving me out of it."

"And why is it so important that they have a romance?"

"I'd just like them to," Meghan said. She could feel herself turning red, because the real answer, the vital truth, was more selfish.

"You say Derek encouraged Thomas to have sex with her against her will?"

"Not exactly against her will, but he encouraged him to go for it, thinking she might get caught up in it. Of course he couldn't have known how it would play out."

"You say in hindsight you should have dissuaded him, but at the time you didn't. Why?

Meghan hesitated. "I did want Thomas to make love to me," she admitted. "And the first part, the prelude—the undressing, the first touches—it definitely was everything I hoped it would be." Becoming self-conscious, she cut herself short.

Anne waited for her to continue. "This is a place you should feel safe," she said gently. "I'm not here to judge you. The worst thing you can do is censor yourself. Try to tell me exactly what you're thinking, as the thoughts come to you."

Meghan took a deep breath. "I guess I was going to say that I really wanted him. When she brought him to her bed I was totally ready for her to yield to him, I was *hoping* she would yield to him, but then the knife came out, and everything changed. He pressed ahead, but Sylvanne wasn't yielding anymore. I was left feeling her fury, her disappointment, her hatred, of him and of herself. But underneath all that, what I felt most was my own longing, my own desire not getting fulfilled."

"It's not a rare occurrence for two people to feel a desire that can never be fulfilled," Anne said. "For example when one or both are already married to someone else. Literature is full of couples like that, and if the lovers do link up the results are usually disastrous."

"Thomas and I are both single, at least," Meghan said, managing a faint smile.

"Still, you're experiencing a kind of fixation on someone you can't have, not unlike, say, a woman who falls for a married man. In that case the best thing is to get over the fixation and move on."

"But there's another option we haven't tried yet," Meghan said tentatively. "It was Derek's idea, but Thomas gave it the seal of approval last night. He said if I were to make love to Derek, he'd feel it. He said we could reach each other that way."

"Derek. The same man you describe as an obnoxious boor."

"He's not always so bad. He's helped me out reading medical books. He's very good with Betsy. I know it sounds strange."

"And Derek is agreeable?"

"He suggested it. I was ambivalent about it when he said it, but now that Thomas is eager, I'm leaning that way."

"And what are you planning on saying when you see Derek next?"

"I don't know," Meghan lied, for she had already made up her mind. She lowered her head, afraid to meet Anne's eyes.

"Do you ever face up to the fact you will never be able to truly meet Thomas?" Anne asked. "If he existed at all, it was far away in time, in the distant past. For now, he exists, and always will, only when you dream."

"You make him sound like a figment," Meghan objected. "He's more than that. He's proven that."

"Has he?"

"He thanked me for my medical advice. He told me all about Derek's visit to his mother, something I couldn't have known."

"He told you about it in your dreams. People do occasionally dream things that turn out to be true."

"He's more than a dream."

Meghan's face was set in hard defiance. Anne looked at her and thought for a moment. "I'm going to suggest something," she said finally. "I'm going to give you a prescription for a specific sleeping pill. One of its side effects is that you will not have dreams, or rather if you do, you won't be troubled by them, because you won't remember them." She went to her desk and scribbled a prescription on a pad, then handed it to Meghan.

"You're telling me to get over him."

"Let me put it this way—for an attractive, newly single woman like yourself, there are plenty of potential partners around with advantages over Thomas, or Derek."

"I thought I was your special case, that you'd want to see this all the way through, not cut it short with medication," Meghan protested.

"As a doctor it's my duty to act in your best interest. If I see that you're starting to engage in behaviours that are self-destructive or inappropriate, then I need to intervene."

Meghan looked at the prescription in her hands. The writing was a typical doctor's scrawl, indecipherable to her. "I don't think I'm ready for this," she said. She folded the paper in half, then half again, then wrapped it like a cast around her index finger. "I don't want to suppress it. Just the opposite, really—I feel what's happening to me is something organic, something alive, and I want to respect it, and let it live. Cutting it off now would be like cutting down a strange tree that's about to flower. I want to see what the flowers look like."

"Well, it is your call," Anne replied. "I'm still very interested in what's happening with you, and I do want you to come back again next week. But you know my opinion."

"When Jan told me about you, she said you were into the occult, that you studied witches."

"I did. I do. But not because I believe in their world-view, in fact just the opposite. I study them as a rationalist, because I don't believe the things they do, and I'm interested in what makes them believe it. But that doesn't mean I'm not sympathetic to them. In fact I envy them the certainty of belief."

"You don't believe them—that means you probably don't believe me."

"Here's how I operate," Anne said. "I act like I believe everyone I see, because they need that to open up to me. On a certain level, I try to stay with them—if it's real to them, it's real to me. I also try to think of them as a best friend would, look out for them, and offer them the best possible advice I can give. And I've given you my advice."

"Okay," Meghan said. "I think I need to go kill a bottle of Chardonnay with Jan, my *other* best friend. I need it. Job sucks, house sucks, divorce sucks, relationship with Betsy sucks—the only thing I look forward to is my time with Thomas," she mused. "Whatever it is, I'm grateful for it. It's teaching me a lot. If I take some drug to cut myself off from it, I'll never know how it's meant to end. I've got a part to play, and I want to follow it through to the bitter end." She paused a moment. "You think I'm on the verge of doing something self-destructive, but I'd be doing it for love, and all love has an element of self-destruction, don't you think? Giving yourself completely to another, you lose something of yourself."

"I call love self-altering," Anne replied. "In love we alter ourselves to please the loved one. But in your case this loved one is not physically present, yet to reach him you're willing to offer yourself to a man you don't even like. And that I would call self-destructive."

"Enemies with Benefits," Meghan muttered to herself.

"Pardon?"

"Nothing. I'll look for Thomas first. He told me he could see me in Sylvanne's eyes, a ray of light through dark shutters. Unless I see the same glimmer in Derek's eyes, unless I'm certain Thomas is there, and feel a connection to him, I won't be able to go through with it."

"You felt so guilty when Sylvanne suffered," Anne reminded her. "What about Derek? He won't be raped or violated as Sylvanne almost was, but in a similar way he will be used, even if he enters into it willingly."

"Derek I don't worry about," Meghan said. "He's a hedonist. On that level he's going to love it."

38

Derek was checking ashtrays for a cigarette butt long enough to smoke. He found one on the kitchen counter; out the window he caught a glimpse of Betsy on the steps of her deck next door. He went out to see her.

She was dressed nicely, for a party or family gathering, he thought. She'd tucked the hem of her skirt into her waistband, and was balancing on the unicycle, riding it back and forth a foot or two, but still keeping hold of the deck railing. "You're getting it," he said. "Next step is letting go. What's with the duds? What's the occasion?"

"Church."

"Is it Sunday?"

"According to those who follow the Christian calendar, yes," she replied, feeling very clever.

"Aha. You believe in God and all that, do you?"

"God created the world. If he didn't, who did?"

"Well it wasn't me, I'd have done a better job. You would've too. Just think what the world would be like if you could invent it from scratch."

"There'd be no pollution, everywhere would be a park, and there'd be unicorns."

"Perfect," he replied. "I didn't even know you went to church."

"My mom says it's important I learn the Bible so I'll get all the referrals to it in books and art when I'm older."

"Good thinking. Planning for tomorrow today, that's your mother. Only problem is no one's going to look at books and art by the time you're twenty, it'll all just be tweets about pop stars."

Meghan came out. "C'mon Betsy, we're late. We gotta go."

"You're late. I was ready."

"Whatever. *We* are late."

"No, not we, because you don't even go to church." Betsy said. She turned to Derek and added, "She just drops me at Sunday school and goes shopping."

"Grocery shopping, not fun shopping," Meghan clarified. "C'mon, move your butt."

Ten minutes later Derek was surprised to find Meghan at his door. "What's up? What happened to shopping?" he asked.

"Shopping I can do with Betsy. This is the only hour I'll get all day to do something for myself, so I figured I'd take a break from being Supermom. Can I come in?"

"Of course, of course."

He led the way to his living room. Once there she didn't sit down, so he didn't either. She said, "I need to look into your eyes."

He let her do it. Her gaze unsettled him. It was unwavering, piercing, probing. "Come closer," she said. She continued to stare deeply and directly at him. They stood toe to toe, their faces mere inches apart. He had an urge to wrap his arms around her.

"Is this like a staring contest?"

"Shhh."

After a moment Meghan said doubtfully, "I *think* I see him. Thomas, I know you're in there, but it's like you're sitting in the back row of the theatre. I wish you'd come down front, where I can be sure it's you."

"Tell me—why exactly are you so in my face?" Derek asked.

"Thomas has taken your advice. He's promised to stop talking to me when he talks to her. And he had something else to say. Before I tell you, don't get any ideas that it's going to happen."

Derek lowered himself down and settled comfortably onto the couch, stretching out his jeans-clad legs. He said, "I think I like where this is going."

"I wanted to connect with him, through Sylvanne. He wants to connect with me. Through you."

Derek looked at her blankly for a moment, then suddenly crowed, "Jackpot!" His grin stretched nearly to his earlobes. "Thank you Thomas! Well then, what are we waiting for?" He patted the couch beside him. "Come on—let's give his Lordship the ride of his life!"

"I told you not to get ideas."

"Hey, it's Tom's idea now."

"His idea is different than yours."

"How so? I wasn't there, I didn't get to hear him declaim. Spell it out for me."

"The difference is the difference between falling in love and, well, what you have in mind."

"I see. He's all about the mind, I'm all about the body. Which is perfect—if he wants you to use my body to connect with his mind, I am one hundred percent totally okay with that."

"I knew you would be. I told my therapist you would be."

"Oh yeah? What's her take?"

"It turns out that even though I'm paying her, she doesn't actually believe Thomas is real, and tried to give me drugs to stop me from dreaming. You're about the only person who does believe me. You do believe me, right?"

"Of course I do."

"So that's one point in your favour."

"I'll try to think of some more."

"Believe it or not, Thomas gave me some more. He sang your praises. He's in your head, don't forget, so he knows all about you. He likes you—he told me to overlook your many faults and focus on your virtues. He says the only harm you do is to yourself. You're not wicked, just weak."

"Not wicked, just weak. That's good—a nice epitaph. I'll put it on my tombstone," Derek smiled.

"Wouldn't you like something more positive to sum up your life?"

"Thomas likes me, even if you don't."

"I want to like you," she said. "I was thinking about you this morning. I was reading the paper, and there was a story about a doctor who had a tragedy a lot like yours, did you see it?"

"No."

"He lost his wife and two sons, in a plane crash. And it changed his life—he gave up a very lucrative medical practice, and moved to Africa, and now he devotes himself to helping the poor there. So in a way, a terrible tragedy changed him, and made him a better man. More good."

"And you're comparing that to me?" Derek asked. "You try it sometime. See how easy it is."

"I'm not saying that," she protested.

He stood up from the couch. "Come here. I want to hug you."

"Why?"

"For a million reasons. For Thomas, for me, for everything bad that's ever happened to anyone."

She came to him, stood before him and held out her hands. He took them and pulled her to him. Tentatively, she laid her head on his shoulder. They held each other close, feeling each other's warmth, saying nothing for a long time. It was Derek who broke the silence. "Maybe that doctor was bad before, and suffering turned him good. I was good, and it turned me bad. Not bad really, but it made me stop caring about things like good and bad."

She pulled back to look at his face. "You're not all bad. You were very nice to Betsy."

"Until I wasn't."

"But then you were again."

"You're a very peculiar woman, Meghan," he said. "I don't even know your last name."

"It doesn't matter. It's my husband's anyway, my soon-to-be ex-husband's. I have to figure out what to do about that."

"Do you think we could ever have a normal conversation?" he asked. "Think we could just talk to each other, once in a while?"

"Yes. That's exactly what I'm trying to tell you. I'm not going to get together with you just to please him, but I'm open to getting together with you, if we can find a way of connecting, just we two."

"Only it's not just we two," said Derek. "It's like a ménage-a-trois where one guy promises just to watch."

"Don't even try to describe it," she said. "Let's not overthink it right now."

"Usually men say that to women."

"I know."

"Or maybe it's more like, we've got Thomas wooing Sylvanne, and now I need to woo you, is that it?"

"Let's say I'm open to you," she replied. "But you've got to be open to yourself, to find the best in yourself, and give it to me. That's what I want to give someone, and that's what I expect in return. Not all this diversion, and clutter, and jokey sarcasm, and substance abuse."

"You don't know what I was like before. Maybe I was like this already."

"I don't think you were," she said.

He didn't argue. He turned away and sat back down on the couch, looking slightly disoriented. "Let me look at you," she said, lowering herself to sit beside him. He turned toward her and their eyes met, and he felt an odd tremor in his body, warm like a breeze. Her gaze seemed to pass right through him.

"You're seeing him, aren't you?" he said.

"I think so."

"What would you like to tell him?"

"I want to tell him to go away. Right now I want to get to know Derek. Or I'd like to, except I have to get Betsy from Sunday school in about seven minutes."

"That's too bad," he smiled. "I was going to tell you to put your feet up, make yourself a cup of tea, or roll one up and spark it, for that matter—I was going to zip upstairs and shower and shave, and come back down all smooth-faced, baby fresh, and we'd pick it up from there. I clean up real good. No harsh chemicals—Ivory soap."

"Clean is always good." She looked up into his broad, smiling face and, unexpectedly, felt a shock of recognition. That hint of a flinty glare in his eyes—was it Derek, or Thomas? Or was it the light of two hearts? She kissed her finger and touched it to Derek's lips.

"I'll see you soon," she whispered. She glanced at her watch. "Why do I always have to be somewhere else?"

39

A thousand glittering ripples danced across the lake in the afternoon sun. Thomas, at the water's edge, turned and tramped across the lush grass of a meadow that bordered the shore, and climbed a small hill to higher ground, where a blanket had been spread. Sylvanne sat upon it, encircled by her gown, her knees drawn up and held tightly in her arms. She watched Thomas approach with a mixture of emotions. The despondency she had felt on the night he came to her bed had seen its jagged edges softened by his actions since. He'd been as good as his word—the man had bestowed nothing but kindness upon her.

The biggest change was that he had ceased to hold her hostage, and now allowed her to move freely around and about the castle. Thus liberated, she in turn had pleased him greatly by restoring her good relations with his daughter Daphne. The girl had led her on a wide-ranging tour of her favourite hidden corners of "my palace," as she liked to call it, and they had passed the previous two afternoons out of doors, nestled in a secretive nook along the castle's outer wall, where they could sit upon a grassy bank and watch swans skim across the glassy surface of the moat. Thomas had visited them there on the second day, and seeing how soothed Sylvanne looked by the tranquil movement of the water, he proposed an outing for the next day to another, more spectacular waterscape. "We'll make the journey on horses, just we two," he'd said, which had stoked the adolescent ire of Daphne. She had beseeched her father to allow her to come along, but he would not be moved. "After your last adventure on horseback, I think it best you continue to rest. Besides, I have no milder horse than Mathilde to give you," he'd said.

"I think you have another motive," Daphne had responded petulantly. "You want Lady Sylvanne to yourself."

If so, then his wish had now come true, for here they sat, alone together under a vast blue canopy of sky, with a fine view of a pretty lake and the surrounding countryside of fields and groves. "I wanted you to see this place and be dazzled by its beauty," he said. "I can hardly believe my good fortune at possessing such a lake, set like a jewel entirely within my own lands. I used to bring my beloved wife here on a summer's day—we both believed that Daphne was conceived on a smooth stone along the far shore, a secluded yet sun-drenched secret spot, which we christened the Altar of our Love." He stopped abruptly, worried that perhaps he'd overstepped propriety by sharing such an intimate detail. He glanced at Sylvanne to gauge her mood, and decided that she seemed unoffended, and contented enough.

"I'm grateful to know this place," she said. He waited for her to say more, but she sat on the warm blanket and was silent.

"What is your opinion of me?" he said suddenly.

She brought a hand up to shield her eyes from the sun's brightness and looked at him. "I've let myself be brought here without a chaperone," she said. "So I must trust you, I suppose."

"That's a start," he said. "A good one."

"You haven't mentioned that other woman for two full days," Sylvanne said. "Is it because she directed you not to, or has she vacated your dreams?"

"You know as well as I that she desires to be kept out of it."

"Yet I'm curious about her," Sylvanne replied. "If you're to be believed, then I feel myself inhabited by a phantom."

"Leaving her aside has made me appreciate your own unique virtues."

"What care you about my attributes? It seems you already love another," Sylvanne said mockingly.

"But she's *inside* you, that's the otherworldly truth of it. If I love her, perhaps it means I love you too." He fell silent for a moment. "I only speak of this because you brought it up."

"A Lady acts rightly who seeks to understand the workings of a man's mind, especially one who appears to woo her, yet speaks so lovingly of another."

"Yes, yes. I suppose," he said irritably. Something was eating at him—a feeling like a loss of status, or stature—as if yielding to Meghan's wish that he be gentle and kindly had served to make him appear weak in Sylvanne's eyes. He was not used to being mocked and teased. He rose from the blanket and stood over her.

"Don't spoil the moment. My intentions in bringing you here were pure, and it seems they sully. Let us untether our horses and depart this place."

"No, please," Sylvanne responded. She too rose, and stood beside him, unnaturally close. "It truly is magical here, perhaps the loveliest place I've seen in my life. I'm sorry if I offended you by speaking my mind. Under this open sky I felt we were equals, in a way men and women seldom are."

"Equals? Is that what you aspire to be?"

"It's what I felt, for a moment, that's all."

Her face was a mirror reflecting the beauty that surrounded them. He felt an urge to kiss her, and pulled her to him. She didn't resist. Her lips were soft and yielding for a moment, then suddenly she pulled herself away, for what had come unbidden to her mind was the equine face of her late husband.

"Are you testing me?" Thomas asked her. "If so, you can see there is no compulsion. No coercion. Nothing will be done without your consent."

"You urge me to trust you, and I do," she replied. "But if I were you, I should still be on guard, and take care when it comes to trusting me. You don't know what thoughts and ideas still invade my mind."

"Then you must tell me."

"I still feel loyalty to my husband, and yet I can't bring myself to do you the harm he wished. I begin to think God has put me here for some other reason."

"Were you happy with your husband?"

"Yes. Sometimes."

291

"Do you think you could be that happy again?"

"Yes."

"Then perhaps that's what God wants for you."

40

"How do you like my new look?" Derek called over the fence. He had cleaned himself up. It was the first time Meghan had seen him in a shirt with a collar. His face was free of stubble, and his hair still damp, combed back off his forehead. "I don't know how Thomas combs his hair," he said.

"He lets if fall forward, in bangs. Actually I like this better."

"Me too. Hey, would you like a cup of coffee? I'm inviting you over, like neighbours used to do before people had iPhones but no time."

In his living room he said, "You'll notice I cleaned up around here."

"You straightened it," she corrected him. "It's tidier, but I wouldn't say cleaner."

"What I really need is a maid. A servant. I'd love to just snap my fingers and say, 'Get us some drinks, would you?' 'Make it so,' like Jean-Luc Picard."

She followed him into the kitchen. "I have some bad news," she said. "Betsy has decided to run a temperature, so I had to keep her home from school. So yet again I can't stay long."

"Depends how you define long. She should be fine for a couple of hours. A lot can be accomplished in a couple of hours."

"By her or us?"

"By her, of course. We're just going to fritter it away, getting to know each other."

While he made coffee she vented about her daughter. "She lost her iPad, and her dad immediately bought her a new one, over my objections. He's trying to buy her approval, I suppose— we're not even legally separated and already he's the classic Disney Dad. Every time he shows up he's got some expensive new bauble under his arm. She's in bed with her iPad as we speak. I had to sneak away. I suspect she's actually a bit jealous of us. She wants you all to herself."

"I could come over and keep vigil at her bedside."

"Not necessary. She'll be fine."

"I don't think I have a cup that's not chipped."

"You know, I've never actually sat in a neighbour's house and had a cup of coffee like this," Meghan smiled. "My mom used to, all the time, when I was a kid. She was the classic stay-at-home small-town mom—her kitchen was her kingdom, and her girl-friends would just drop by unannounced. Her life was so much more casual—now everything's timed to the minute. I'm already feeling guilty about leaving Betsy. Not to mention the work I have. No matter where I am, I feel like I need to be somewhere else."

"I don't have that problem. I've pretty much retreated from that life."

"But what have you replaced it with?" she asked.

"What do you mean?"

"I don't know. Are you happy?"

"Let me put it this way. I see lots of people who are really unhappy, and I'm glad I'm not them."

"But are *you* happy?"

"Sometimes. Are you?"

"Not often, lately."

"Should we even be aiming for happy all the time? It takes such effort. Look Meghan, for whatever reason, fate has thrown us together, and I find you very attractive. I've let you know that. I told you I'm along for the ride—if you want to use me to reach Thomas, to fulfill some kind of romantic quest you've got going, well, I'm happy to be part of the expedition. Whatever your motivations, I'm into it. I can help you out."

His cell phone rang in the living room. He went to retrieve it, and held it out to her when he came back. "I think you can guess who."

"How does she have your number?"

"The day she cut her hand, I gave it to her. After I'd bandaged her up. Just in case."

Meghan took the phone. "Yes my love."

"What are you doing over there?" her daughter asked peevishly.

"None of your business, actually."

"You're supposed to be taking care of me."

"I do take care of you, 24/7. I was just on my coffee break."

"Come home."

"I'm coming. Give me a minute!"

She snapped the phone shut and handed it to Derek. "Someone's jealous," she said.

"Tell her it's platonic."

"Is it?"

"Platonic with the potential to be more," he amended. "I need to start working on my wooing." His lip curled into a slight grin. "How's Thomas doing with his?"

"Good, actually. I think he's winning her over. But every time she gets ready to let herself be won, she remembers her husband, and what he made her promise. Whether it's her personality, or the times she lives in, she thinks differently from me. It's almost like she lacks free will. She can't accept she has a choice. But he's become such a gentleman—he's so patient with her. You're being patient with me too."

"What else can I do? Unlike your Thomas, who had to learn to behave himself, I live in the age of consent."

"I think I'm ready to give it."

"Great. Good." He smiled broadly "Let's do it."

"Not now!" she laughed. "Not with Betsy waiting for me. It would be all tense, and furtive."

"Furtive is good," he laughed. "Furtive is like sneaky, and illicit, and generally makes things more intense."

"You're not a mom, obviously. Sneaky and illicit are fine when you're a kid hiding something from the parents, but when you're a parent hiding from the kids, it crosses over to being just plain sordid and weird."

"I think you should stop talking and kiss me now."

"All right. I will."

"Then do it."

She leaned forward and kissed him experimentally. His lips met hers hungrily, but a feeling startled her, and made her push him back so she could see his eyes. Thomas was there, she was certain.

"It's like there's two of you," she said.

"Is that good or bad?"

"It's good. It's okay."

His phone rang again. He checked the number without answering. "The brat," he smiled.

"I'm going, I'm going," Meghan sighed. "Tell her I'm on my way."

41

Thomas and Sylvanne went riding again together the very next afternoon. This time they gave the horses a thorough workout. Sylvanne rode like a man, with her skirt hoisted daringly high, so that her calves showed bare and white in the sun. At a place where a country creek widened into a kidney-shaped pond, they stopped to let their mounts rest and drink, and Thomas was moved to remark, "In horsemanship, I can truly say we are as equals."

Sylvanne smiled and said, "Oh really? Today I thought myself your better. But perhaps it was my mount that surpassed yours."

"Then we should switch horses," he suggested.

"No no. We must find another way of taking each other's measure," she said playfully.

"It seems we do so every time we speak."

On the way back to the castle they took a detour, slowing their horses to a walk to pass through the town. Sylvanne shifted to the more demure side-saddle style so that her legs remained fully covered by her kirtle. A confusion of streets no wider than alleys led them to an open square in the midst of the clutter of houses, a gathering place that had been decorated with garlands of flowers for a wedding celebration. A quartet of wayfaring musicians played a lively jig for the couples dancing on the hard-trodden earth, while children and dogs ran about underfoot. Women could be seen preparing the food for a feast, while their men folk availed themselves of the free ale that attracted all types of classes and characters, from the upright to the downright unsavoury. A couple of well-oiled locals noticed Sylvanne and Thomas approach, and boldly stepped in front of them.

"It's the lovely Lady Sylvanne," exclaimed one. "First time I've laid eyes on you since we drug you home from the siege. You're looking much better fed and prettier now than ever, I'm quite sure."

"You're drunk," Sylvanne replied haughtily.

"Course I am, I've every right to be, it's a wedding feast after all. What better occasion? Love is in the air, booze in the belly!"

The second man chimed in. "M'Lord, do us the honour of coming down off your steed and making a toast. Give your blessing to the happy couple."

"I would, but the Lady is not to be left alone among you rabble. I need to squire her home," Thomas replied. He thought a moment. "Bring the lovebirds out, I'll bestow the blessing here and now."

"Yes Sir!"

The two hurried off, wending their way through the milling crowd until they disappeared into a clotted-walled hall just off the square. A moment later they emerged with Mabel and Gwynn in tow. Sylvanne fixed Thomas with an inquisitive look, which he shrugged off with a smile, saying, "Honestly, I had no idea the happy couple would be these two." The new bride and her groom stopped in the shadow of the horses. Mabel, robed in a loose, sky-blue half-sleeved gown of linen, kept her head lowered, apparently too troubled by fear or shame to meet Sylvanne's eyes.

"Poultryman!" Thomas greeted Gwynn. "I see you've wasted no time."

"No Sir. I thank you, Sir, for setting this one free," said Gwynn merrily, giving Mabel a squeeze. "She'll be a boon to me and my boys." He looked around for his three brats, and pointed them out on the fringe of the crowd, pulling the tail of a snarling dog.

"Next time you deliver chickens, I'll make you a gift of one of my prized fighting cocks," proclaimed Thomas. "He'll be a tonic to your bloodlines, if he doesn't slay your hens in mating with them. For now I'll simply offer my congratulations, and wish you all the best in the future."

"Thank you Sir. Same to you, though it seems you've chosen a tougher lady to tame."

"Yes, well. You're lucky. Sweet Mabel here has accepted her new circumstances and made the best of them. I pray this one will do the same someday," he said, gesturing to Sylvanne, who did her best to hold herself erect and aloof upon her mount. The sight of Mabel, who had deserted her, raised her blood, and now to hear herself discussed like a chattel by Lord and freeman brought her emotions positively to a boil.

"If she's right and I've been wrong, why is she afraid to look upon me?" she said caustically.

"Now now, don't sour the poor woman's happiness on her wedding day," Thomas reproached her. "Come. Can you not say a few kind words to her?"

"I will try," said Sylvanne, but her tone remained harsh. "Mabel, I hope your husband proves as faithful to you as mine was to me."

Suddenly Gwynn spoke up animatedly. "More faithful than that, I should hope!" he cackled. Mabel slapped him soundly across the chest, and scolded him to button his mouth.

"What do you mean by that?" Sylvanne demanded, but the poultryman lowered his eyes. "Mabel, what does he mean by that?"

"Nothing m'Lady."

"You must have told him something."

"Nothing, m'Lady," Mabel protested, but her face had turned red and she still could not meet her mistress's eyes.

"This is hardly the time or place—" Thomas started to say, but Sylvanne cut him short, addressing Mabel sharply.

"I want you to come see me tomorrow, and I'll get to the bottom of this," she insisted. "Tomorrow, do you hear me?"

"Give the woman a full day to recover from her wedding night, at least," Thomas interjected. "Mabel, don't come tomorrow, make it the next day."

"Yes sir," Mabel replied glumly. "May I go now?"

"Of course, of course!" Thomas crowed, too merrily, in an effort to lift the sudden pall. "Back to your celebrations! Again I wish the both of you all the best, long lives and many children!"

As the wedding couple turned and retreated, he glanced at Sylvanne's face, still simmering with anger. "I freed you from your prison, yet you seek new ways to bring yourself suffering," he told her, but Sylvanne didn't seem to hear him. He turned his horse toward home, and her horse followed on its own, unguided by a rider whose thoughts were miles away.

42

"Where's the Find on this thing?"

"You don't know how to find Find?"

"I don't use this browser. Here it is. I'm fine. I'm fine at finding Find."

Derek's hard drive had crashed, so he'd invited himself over to use Meghan's computer. "It's actually for something we should do together," he'd said.

"Which is?"

"Research your Thomas of Gastoncoe. Trawl through the Domesday Book and any other medieval census we can get our hands on."

"You think I haven't done that?"

"I'm sure you have. I have too, actually. I'd just like to try some more."

"It's not just an excuse to get into my house?"

"Do I need an excuse?"

"No," she'd said. "Come on over."

She'd been working upstairs in her studio, and invited him to sit at the computer there. While he conducted his research she worked freehand at her drafting table, glancing over at him occasionally. She felt a delicious tension, knowing that they would soon be lovers. How could he not know it too? The last time they'd been together they'd kissed, and she'd told him she was ready. Now they sat in a hurricane's eye, pretending a kind of quiet domesticity, as if they were already lovers of long standing. She felt eager, yet patient—she wanted *him* to start the wheel in motion. He sat at the computer, muttering about Latinate surnames and the incompleteness of documents. She'd lost herself in a drawing when she heard him say, "I've found him." She looked up quickly to see Derek swivelling in his chair toward her, a big boyish grin on his face, his hair pushed down and falling over his forehead in bangs, the way Thomas wore it.

"Very funny," she smiled. He looked very handsome that way.

"Do I look like him like this?"

"A lot."

"Here's what I'm thinking," he said. "If you want to get to know me better, it's good we're here on your home turf. At my place there would be too many surprises—threadbare sheets and empty toilet rolls. And if you want to imagine that it's Thomas, come to you from across the centuries, you can take him to the same bed you've dreamed him in."

"You've got it all figured out, don't you," she said.

He came close to her. His skin really did smell of Ivory soap.

"Betsy's in school till when?"

"We have three hours."

"Perfect."

She took his hand and led him to her bedroom. The sheets were white linen. "Looks comfy," he said appreciatively. "Home field advantage was the right choice."

"Derek, don't say anything."

"That's gonna be diffi—"

"Shhh! Nothing."

She was wearing a tank top and jeans. She pushed him back on the bed, then slipped the top over her head, and peeled her jeans past her hips to the floor. She stepped out of them, clad only in black bra and panties.

"You're so lovely."

"I had a funny feeling this morning," she said. "I chose these specially—I just knew I'd be showing them off."

She smiled, but then the look in her eyes became so very serious, so possessed, that for a moment Derek felt uncertain, almost frightened. He pulled her to him on the bed and cloaked her face and shoulders with a rain of kisses, hiding himself in the concave privacy of her neck, to keep himself from looking into those fierce eyes. Him, Thomas, Meghan, Sylvanne, sanity, insanity, truth or hallucination, it didn't matter—he felt the urgent need of her body, and met it with his own. She was beautiful, possessed, and too impatient to unbutton his shirt, tearing at it blindly like a child shredding Christmas wrapping. He took hold of her wrists for a moment to slow her, whispering, "Let me help you." Then they were both naked on white linen in the sunlit morning.

"Are you ready?"

"Yes."

"Feel how wet I am."

"Yes."

Her unblinking eyes held his gaze as she guided him inside her. She was yielding, yet in charge, setting the rhythm, controlling him with her eyes, seeking something within him that made him feel jealousy in his want, and redoubled his desire. At the height of her orgasm she closed her eyes, and gave herself up to the helpless pleasure that comes in waves and ends in ripples. Derek came at the same time, and as the intensity of his surrender faded, his first thought was, She must realise I'm the one who gave her this. Not Thomas, me. She shifted her head so she could look at his face, and said, with less urgency than before, "The eyes—let me see. Let me see them."

"You don't need to find Thomas every second, do you?"

"No. I'm just curious to know that he's there."

"Is he?"

"I think so. Yes, I'm sure he is."

They were both still breathing raggedly, warm and damp with a cleansing, cathartic sweat. He lay on his back so that she would have to look at him in profile, without the soul-piercing contact of the eyes.

"I hope he liked it," Derek said. "I know I did."

"I did too."

"Maybe we should show him some more. I bet he'd like to see some tricks they didn't get back in the day."

"We already showed him how to put on a condom," she smiled. "What else did you have in mind?"

"Oral pleasure."

"Are you sure you're only thinking of him?"

"Of course. Him, and you. I'll do you first."

She sat up on an elbow. "Eye contact would be tricky."

"But not impossible."

"I think I'd rather be on top next. I'd like him to suck on my breasts. You, I mean. You too. But first let's rest a bit, let's snuggle and you hold me. I think I'm feeling him, even through your skin. You have nice skin, Derek."

43

Married life—all forty-eight hours of it—had profoundly changed Mabel. She was no longer a spinster, or a virgin, she was now fully a woman, and a wife. To her mind she had attained a status higher than Sylvanne, whose position in society was precarious, as a widow without protection of family. As Mabel bustled into her former Lady's presence she resolved to hold her head high and seize the initiative. After an exchange of pleasantries she got straight to the point. "Madame," she exclaimed, "I'll speak plainly. My husband let slip a hurtful remark that quite rightly alarmed you. But within it lies a truth that's been kept from you too long. Your Gerald was unfaithful. There, I've said it."

Sylvanne felt as if the floor were cracking open beneath her feet. As calmly as she could, she asked, "How do you know that for certain?"

"Everyone knew it, my dear. The man wanted an heir, and you had failed to deliver, so he looked elsewhere."

"Where, exactly? Don't spare me particulars."

"Alright, if I must." Mabel began to itemize. "There were milkmaids, the kitchen help, any number of pretty girls plucked from farm lanes in the countryside—Oh Madame, the man was quite notorious."

"To all but me, it seems. If you knew, why didn't you tell me?"

"Oh my poor dear," Mabel cried. "Don't you know how many times I was tempted to tell you, especially here in our new circumstances, as you plotted revenge on his behalf? But I held my tongue, as a loyal maidservant should. Instead you discovered it inadvertently, by chance. My Gwynn has many fine qualities, but a discreet tongue is not among them."

"I don't believe you," Sylvanne said softly.

"I think you do."

"Not so many days ago you took orders from me."

"Yes. And not so many years ago you sold me milk in the market. Now we're as equals again, and I feel brave enough to speak the truth freely."

The truth. Surrendering to it, Sylvanne felt her spirit break, and she began to cry. Mabel came to her and very tenderly embraced her. "There, there, my sweet Madame," she cooed softly.

"Oh Mabel, what am I to do?"

"My dear, there is a silver lining, if you wish to see it," Mabel gently suggested. "Take notice that your Gerald tried to make a child with so many other women, and yet always failed in it. What does that show us? That the fault lay with him, not you."

"My mother said the same," Sylvanne murmured. "That his family's bloodline was feeble, while mine was chock full of fit and fertile maidens."

"Of which you're still a shining example, my dear."

"I'm not a maiden anymore."

"Compared to me you are, and yet I'm not too old either," Mabel replied. A secretive smile pursed her lips a moment. "May I tell you something in confidence?" Without waiting for an answer she continued excitedly. "It's said that sometimes a woman knows she's with child from the moment of conception. Perhaps it's wishful thinking, but I'm blessed with that sensation since my wedding night." She let out a happy growl. "He certainly planted his seed deep!"

Sylvanne managed a smile. Seeing it, Mabel exclaimed, "That's more like it, my love! Look how much I have gained by the move to this new place, and you could do likewise. That's really what I've come to say, not to dwell on people and events dead and buried. I so love this new season of my life, and my place as wife! You cannot imagine how it thrills me to say that I cannot stay, that I've a husband who expects me home. Suddenly I have three sons to clothe and groom, and feed them thrice a day. The poor dears need a mother's tenderness, and the back of my hand to knock some sense into their witless little heads! They take after their father and I love them to death already!"

With that, Mabel prepared to take her leave. "Come by for a wee chat some afternoon," she said gaily. "I won't confuse you with directions—just ask the way to Gwynn the poultryman's— everyone knows it." In a daze, Sylvanne heard herself making a promise to visit. They hugged, and then Mabel was gone, taking her enthusiasm and good cheer with her.

Alone within the stone walls of her room, Sylvanne thought of Gerald, her mind groping randomly among jumbled recollections of married life, sifting through them for signs of his infidelity. She felt angry at herself, and humiliated, for not perceiving what had been known by all. She stalked the room, pride battered, fists clenched, muttering that she was a fool, such a fool, with mounting force and conviction, until she was nearly shouting. So caught up was she in self-disgust that she had failed to notice Thomas had entered. He was in a state of high excitement, like a boy bursting to tell a secret.

"I could hear you in the hall, and thought you must have company," he said. "Whatever troubles you, be gentle on yourself, my dear Lady." Sylvanne restrained her emotions as best she could. "I need to speak to you, I can't hold it inside another minute," he gushed. "Last night our Meghan and Derek at last made love, and as witness to it, I must say, it was incredible! It ranks among the most splendid experiences of my life—so impassioned as well as edifying! I learned all manner of positions and potentialities for pleasure that I'd never imagined, let alone attempted! If I may plead an exception and address the Lady Meghan—"

To his great and sudden surprise Sylvanne exploded at him. "Shut your mouth about Meghan!" she erupted. "You promised me you would never speak of her again!"

"I said I'd do my best. Yet it became fundamental I get this off my chest."

"I never want to hear that name again, do you hear me?"

"What is this?" he demanded, startled by her ferocity.

"Promise me you will never say that name again!" she cried.

"And if I do?"

Standing before him, her breast rising and falling in a deep ragged cadence, she looked ferocious and vulnerable at the same time. He thought of a hellcat, cornered. In a quiet, serious voice, she murmured, "It doesn't matter. I'm nothing to you. I'm nothing to anyone."

She was shivering, yet she stood proudly, bravely, with her head held high. He suddenly felt rise up in him a great pity for her and the circumstances he'd put her in.

"That's not true. You're something to Daphne. And to me."

"I begin to see that women to men are mere playthings, to be fed lies and toyed with, like a cat scratches a half-dead mouse."

"If I toyed with you, it was unintentional," he said. "I've never lied to you."

"Your stories might as well be lies, or fairy tales."

"Those fairy tales cured my daughter. You listened to them. For that I owe you my happiness. What can I give you in return? What can I do to make you happy?"

She shivered severely, and her shoulders shook. Closing her eyes, she brought her hands to her face in a gesture of prayer, the tips of her fingers touching the wetness of her eyes. The idea of happiness seemed impossible to her at that moment.

He watched her, then moved to her, and placed his hands softly on her shoulders to sooth their tremors. He almost expected her to push him away, to reject his empathy, but instead she leaned toward him, and let her forehead rest on his broad chest. He said softly, "You need the same thing I need, and that is to be loved."

44

"So you're having sex with a man you can't stand, because you're in love with another man trapped in his head," Jan said.

Meghan laughed into the phone. "Don't say it like that. I can stand him now—I'm even starting to like him. Quite a lot, actually."

"Then it must be very good sex."

"It's only been once, but it was great. Better than it ever was with Seth."

"You're making me jealous."

"I'm even—just a sec, someone's battering down my door."

Her doorbell had chimed, followed immediately by an insistent pounding. The bell chimed again. "I'm coming, I'm coming," she shouted. She opened the door to the sight of Derek's flushed, eager face, perched above a mass of messy, tousled red roses. With mock gallantry, he pronounced, "These are for my Lady fair."

"Huh. It's just like you," she smiled. Into the phone she said, "Gotta go. It's Derek, bearing gifts. I'll call in a bit."

"You better,"

"Promise."

She hung up, reaching out to take the flowers he laid gently in her encircling arms. "I feel a bit like Miss Universe," she said. "There's got to be at least four dozen here, that's a bit extravagant."

"Six dozen, in fact. Don't worry, I got them cut-rate."

"On closer inspection they look it," Meghan giggled.

"They're meant to make a huge, splashy first impression, not be scrutinized for every flawed bud or droopy petal. Can I come in or what?"

"Of course. I have some news for you—there's progress." They went to the living room and she laid the roses in a heap on the coffee table. "Sylvanne found out her husband had been cheating on her, not just once or twice, but by the truckload. It was just sinking in when Thomas came along, and he handled it just right. He dried her tears and told her very sweetly that what they both need is to be loved."

"*A human being's only really being, when he is being, loved,*" Derek sang. "He picked that up from me, I'm sure."

"Your advice for him to woo her was good. I really wish he'd marry her. Thomas, do you hear that? It's like Daphne said, you're in need of a wife. And Sylvanne needs someplace to anchor herself. She's too proud to beg, but she's allowing her heart to open, I can feel it."

"Great." Derek said. He gestured toward the roses on the table. "I'd tell you to put them in a vase, but you'd need a forty-five gallon drum."

"Is that all you have to say?"

"What? I'm happy, I'm happy for them. If they get together, great. I'm not as invested in them as you. You get to see them every night, but to me they're second hand. They're friends of friends."

"You're more than a friend to Thomas—he knows you better than I do." Her face suddenly broke into a wide grin. "He did say to say thank you for the performance yesterday. He found it—how'd he put it?—I think he called it passionate and edifying."

"Glad to hear we're giving him an erotic education," Derek smiled. "I think it's time for another lesson."

"Now? Not now."

"Where's Betsy?"

"She's just down the street. She took her unicycle to the skate-board park, it's made her a bit of a star there. The boys line up to try it out."

"Then it'll have to be a quickie."

"A super-duper quickie. Even then I don't think so."

"When did she go?"

"Ten minutes ago. I told her to be back in an hour."

"Fifty minutes—that's not a quickie, that's a slowie. A slowie with one ear cocked for the key in the door." He took her hand, and she felt herself carried to him by some force like a river's current. He put his arms around her and pulled her close, and felt her stretch pliantly against him. She planted kisses on his chest above the V of his collar, rubbing her nose at the base of his neck. "You smell good," she murmured. He sat back on the couch and she lowered herself onto his lap, straddling him. She stared deeply into his eyes.

"So we have time?" he said.

"No. We're keeping our clothes on."

"That's okay. A lot can be accomplished with clothes on." He undid the top two buttons of her blouse.

"That's far enough."

"Perfect for a peek. I love the view."

She put a finger under his chin and lifted his gaze from her breasts to her face. She looked deeply, searchingly into his eyes.

"Are you seeing him?"

"Uh huh. Him *and* you. Kiss me." Murmuring happily, he leaned forward and ran his tongue down to the little hollow at the base of her neck, and undid a third button on her blouse.

A child's voice called out, "What are you doing?"

Betsy stood in the hallway watching them, still wearing her bicycle helmet and a cyclist's day-glow safety vest. One of her knees was skinned and bloody. Meghan, mortified, jumped from Derek's lap, fumbling with her buttons.

"We're just wrestling a bit. Playing around," Derek said.

"I'm not stupid!" Betsy cried. She turned away and charged blindly down the hall to the front door. Meghan hurried after her, calling out for her to come back. She saw her race out the door and down the steps where her unicycle lay bent and broken on its side, saw her run across the sidewalk, darting between two parked cars into the street. "Betsy!" Meghan screamed. What happened

321

next she saw in slow motion, with her heart in her throat—Betsy running blindly into traffic, a white minivan whose driver stared too distractedly at his phone, a screech of brakes like the sound of murder. Meghan thought she would die, until suddenly she saw Betsy, unhurt, still running, down the sidewalk on the far side of the street, to the corner, then out of sight.

She flew down the steps and chased after her, the soles of her bare feet slapping against the unforgiving pavement. Suddenly Derek was at her shoulder, then past her, crossing the street first, and then waiting for her to catch up at the corner. Betsy had disappeared. They hurried to the next intersection. "You go that way, I'll go this," he told her.

She set off alone, muttering to herself that she should never have been so careless, that she would never again let love or lust turn her into such a sloppy fool, that she was first and foremost a mother, and a mother needs to keep it together, always and forever. All the while her eyes scanned for Betsy, but there was no sign of her. Suddenly she stopped, realizing that she was moving in the opposite direction from the skateboard park, which rested on the edge of a larger park with playgrounds and playing fields that was by far the most likely place for Betsy to run to, the only sliver of green neutrality in this whole monstrous urban world of parked cars and private property. She turned and headed back that way, the way Derek had gone.

The park was nearly deserted. Derek found Betsy sitting on the black strap of a playground swing, swaying limply, indifferently, one foot dangling down to scrape a toe at the sand. She glanced up and saw him coming, then kept her head lowered as he sat in the next swing.

"You didn't need to go running off," he said. "We were just kissing each other. You kind of snuck up on us."

Betsy said nothing.

"You need that knee cleaned up."

She bent to examine the scrape. Without looking at him she said, "I thought grown-ups did it at night, in a bed—not daytime, downstairs where everyone can see."

"That's not what we were doing."

"Why do people do it anyway? What's the big deal?"

He was relieved that she didn't sound angry, or hurt, but rather, annoyed. "You should be having this conversation with your mom, not me."

"We've had it already. She told me how making love makes babies. And how people like to do it even when they don't want babies."

"Yeah, that's right. The urge to do it is stronger than the real reason to do it. The urge to do it *becomes* the reason to do it."

"It's weird," she said, shuddering a little. "I think it's creepy."

"People do lots of weird things that don't make sense," he replied. "Look, Betsy—life's chock full of weird shit that'll knock you for a loop, but when it does, you need to remember there are people that love you and have your back. Your mother loves you."

"You love my mom."

"I like her a lot. I like you too."

"So what?"

"I don't know so what. I'll tell you something you probably don't know about me. I had a kid once, and if she was alive she'd be your age, maybe a year older. So sometimes when I tell you things, they're things I didn't get a chance to tell her."

Betsy was silent a moment. "Do I look like her?"

"No."

On tiptoes she spun slowly around on the swing, winding herself up, making the chains twist and tighten above her head. Then she lifted her feet and let the chains spin her a little dizzy, one way and then the other, until they settled her to equilibrium again.

"Are you going to move into our house?"

"What? Why would I do that? Separate bedrooms, separate bathrooms, separate music collections, and yet right next door? It's perfect as it is."

"Here she comes," Betsy said.

"Can I tell her we patched things up?"

"No."

When Meghan reached them she was out of breath, and leaned on one of Derek's chains for support. "I knew I'd find you here," she said.

"We haven't patched things up," Betsy told her.

"Do you know how happy I am to see you?" Meghan asked, and then her body trembled, and she began to cry. Derek made no move to comfort her, thinking it better to leave it to Betsy. Reluctantly, the girl got off her swing and put her arms around her mother from behind.

"I'm not supposed to be hugging you," she said. "I'm supposed to be mad at you."

"Be anything, darling," Meghan answered, wiping at her tears. She turned to face Betsy. "Just be what you want."

"Derek had a daughter," Betsy said.

"I know that."

"Everybody knows everything but me."

"That's how it is when you're ten," Derek said. "I know it hurts, but really, it's a blessing."

"No it isn't," she said adamantly. "I want to know everything."

45

As he did every morning, Thomas on waking and dressing went straightaway to Daphne's bedchamber. He found her in good health and high spirits, looking out from her window with her maidservant Beth so as to catch a glimpse of the young men in martial training in the courtyard below. The wound in her arm where the surgeon used to bleed her daily had healed so well it no longer required a dressing, and without it there was nothing to indicate she was anything but a vibrant young girl. "Don't you get any ideas about those boys," he chided her. "There's none worthy of you among that rabble. I'm going to find you a proper young nobleman, perhaps the son of a Duke or a Prince, or even a foreign King if you're lucky."

"But I want to marry for love, as you did with mother," Daphne protested.

"Your mother and I married to cement a negotiated union of two families, two bloodlines," Thomas corrected her. "We *found* love, after we were married, which is the greatest blessing God can give, and we were very grateful for it."

"I hope *I* find love," Daphne murmured.

"Don't start looking for it until I've presented you to your husband."

"Make sure he's handsome, then."

"Oh for certain he will be. Handsome, rich, strong, brave and true—I would accept nothing less for my one and only daughter. Now, not to change the subject entirely, on a matter related to marriage, I have something to discuss with you."

With a small gesture he dismissed the maidservant. When they were alone Daphne said, "This must be very serious, or else I'm grown up now. I don't think you've ever cleared the room to speak to me."

"Yes, well. What I have to say should be kept secret for now. You are growing up, and you've reached an age where for certain decisions in life I might seek your council, or approval, or help. I've been thinking about Lady Sylvanne—"

"You want to marry her!" Daphne shrieked. Thomas winced and glanced toward the door.

"Shush, you silly girl!"

"Do you or don't you?" She could barely contain herself.

"I do."

"Well then go ask her!" Daphne said excitedly.

"It's not so simple as that."

"Why not?"

"Well, first of all, I'm not sure exactly how the question is asked, when it's not arranged between families. And secondly, I don't want it to come as a shock to her, I want to give her a little time to consider the question before I ask. I only want to ask if I'm certain she'll say yes."

"Daddy. You have your pride, is that it?"

"I suppose that's what it is."

"I know she'll say yes."

"Well I want to be sure. And that's where you come in. I want you to find out what she thinks of the idea. Sound her out for me."

"I'll be like a spy," Daphne said gaily. "I'll be very subtle, and clever. I'll tease the answer from her!"

"You can be direct, if you wish. But don't try to convince her; let her express her own true wishes."

"I'll go to see her right now."

She invited Sylvanne for a stroll along the parapet, where far afield they could see peasants harvesting barley with scythes, and stooking the sheaves to dry. Daphne, fairly bursting with excitement, but thinking herself a very fine actress for her outward self-control, asked as casually as she could, "What do you think of love?"

"What do you mean?"

"What's your definition?"

"Love is something proven over time. True love behaves itself."

"Is it spontaneous, like a lightning bolt, or something cultivated?"

"Why do you ask these things?"

"My father wishes to marry you," Daphne blurted out.

"Does he?"

"Yes. What would you say to him?"

"I think he needs to ask me himself."

"I just know you'll say yes!" Daphne said excitedly.

"He needs to ask me himself," Sylvanne repeated.

Later in the afternoon, as the shadows grew long, Thomas made his way to Sylvanne's chamber. She had dressed herself in a lovely robe of lavender and had her hair pinned up off her shoulders to expose her graceful neck. He took it as a sign, confirming the breathless guarantee Daphne had given him, that he would not be disappointed.

They exchanged the briefest of pleasantries before she said, "I know why you've come."

The neutrality in her voice surprised him. He suddenly felt less confident, more self-conscious, a rare feeling for him.

"Well?" she prompted.

"Yes. Well. I think it best for all concerned, if, what I mean to say is, you're a fine woman, and beautiful, a prize for any man, and Daphne needs a mother, and I need a wife, and you need a husband—" He winced at the awkwardness and inelegance of his words. It was not coming out as he'd imagined it would. "My dear Lady, it comes down to this—there's too much sadness in the world, and not enough happiness. I see a way for two disparate souls to combine to make happiness."

"Are you in love with me?" she asked. He saw her lower lip tremble just a little.

"Yes. I believe I am. I want to be, don't you see? You've displayed such tremendous strength of character in all I've put you through. We began as enemies, and I admired you for putting up the good fight. As allies, I feel we could conquer the world. That's if you'll have me, of course."

"And what about this woman, this Meghan that you say dwells within me? Do you love her too?"

"I can't say for certain."

"Last night you told me you'd never yet lied to me," she said. "Does that still hold true?"

"Yes. I can't say that I truly love her, because that's something else. A dream."

"I will marry you, on two conditions," Sylvanne told him.

"I haven't even formally asked yet," he smiled.

"Wait until you hear the conditions, then you'll know to ask, or not."

"Continue then. You amaze me."

"First, you must promise truly that you will never speak the name Meghan to me, or speak to her through me, again."

He nodded.

"Second, you must do your utmost to find a method to drive her from my mind. I want my mind to myself, and I want you to myself."

She had delivered these conditions with a brave, stern countenance, but now her face softened into girlish vulnerability. "Is that too much to ask?" she said quietly.

He shook his head. "I will marry you," he answered, and knew for certain that he truly did want to.

"You haven't asked me," she smiled.

"Will you marry me?"

She went to him, cautiously. His arms encircled her trembling body and held her tightly to him a long time, until her ragged breathing calmed. "I had to make promises to win you," he said. "What will you promise me in return?"

She pulled back to look up into his broad, unguarded face, and said solemnly, "I promise to be a good and faithful wife, and to give you children and love them with you, as you love Daphne. And I promise to love Daphne as my own, as the eldest, as my mother loved me."

46

"Ever read *First Love*, by Turgenev?" Derek asked.

"No, but if *you* have, I'm impressed."

"Oh I'm well-read, if nothing else. It's about a teenage boy who falls for a beautiful, sophisticated girl next door, and they're always talking over the wall between their houses. Kind of like us."

Derek stood in his back yard, resting a hand on top of the fence, looking up at Meghan, who sat on the rail of her deck, close enough to him that she could easily reach out and touch his hand. "Betsy's home, so it's best we keep the fence between us," she said. "I wouldn't have thought you'd admit to reading romances."

"It's not that kind of romance. It's realistic—it ends tragically."

"Then it's not a *romance* romance."

"Oh really? So Romeo and Juliet doesn't count either?"

"I'm thinking of modern romances, the formulaic ones, where

the gruff, manly dude meets his match with the plucky gal, and they live happily ever after," she said.

"It happens, I suppose," he said. "But it's getting rarer. There's no shortage of plucky gals, but the gruff, manly dude is an endangered species."

"Thomas and Sylvanne are getting married," she said abruptly.

"Really? Wow. I thought you'd sound more excited. I can't believe you didn't tell me right off the bat."

"I know. I should be excited. She's a tough cookie, I must say. She extracted conditions."

"Which are?"

"Well, officially, he's never to talk to me, or even speak my name, ever again."

"That's not new."

"And secondly, she wants him to find a way for this to end—she wants me out of her head."

"Can you blame her?"

"No. I know I'm being ridiculous, but it hurts. The way he agreed to it so easily, I feel like I've been dumped."

"He didn't dump you, he just went with the flow—men agree to stuff all the time without having any intention of carrying through on it. Especially with women. Especially when it comes to romance."

"You've had experience with that?"

"Less than most, I'd say. I prefer to let the chips fall."

"So basically you're saying he lied to her."

"It's not lying, exactly, it's avoiding an argument. He agreed he should do something about it, but did he specify what?"

"No."

"There you go. No action taken. So in the meantime you'll still be in her head, he'll still be in my head, you'll still get to see each other."

"Or maybe he really does want me out of her head."

"If he wants you out of her head, it's easily done."

"What do you mean?"

"Your therapist suggested it. She gave you a prescription, remember? All you have to do is take some pills and you'll stop dreaming. End of story."

Meghan felt a chill run through her. "Oh God," she said.

"You told me about it, so he knows about it," said Derek. "The fact that he didn't suggest it to Sylvanne means he wants to carry on with the status quo, don't you think?"

"Or else he didn't think of it because it didn't register when he heard about it, or he's forgotten about it."

"Well now he knows. Thomas, my man, there's a readymade plan. It's up to you to accept or reject it."

She clenched her hands together tightly and brought them to her chest. A sudden pain had seized her, a premonition of heartbreak.

"What is it?" Derek asked.

"Nothing.

"Should I come over?"

"No. I told you Betsy's here."

"I'm offering comfort, not anything out of bounds."

"Thank you. But comfort would be more physical than I want her to see between us right now. We had a talk—it's all been a bit much for her with the separation, and her dad springing the idea of a new wife and baby on her. She wants me to herself right now. I don't think she'd like to see us hugging."

"That's cool. Wouldn't want her running into traffic again."

"No, definitely not." She relaxed a little, and reached down to put her hand on his, atop the fence. "Comfort can come from just holding hands," she said.

He didn't say anything.

"You're very patient," she said.

He shrugged. "You're not?"

"No. I'm just—I can't wait for the night. I want to see what he does."

47

Sylvanne wanted to be married as soon as possible, and Thomas, taking her at her word, decreed a mere two days from proposal to ceremony. The wedding would thus be a hurried, intimate, nearly private affair. Daphne appointed herself Mademoiselle In Charge Of The Bridal Gown, but there was no time to sort through rolls of fabric or consult with dressmakers. Here Sylvanne's practicality came to the fore, and the former farm girl settled for what was at hand, a kirtle of pale green silk she found in Daphne's mother's wardrobe, which she then transformed by adorning the neckline and bodice with embroidered pink flowers from one of her own dresses. "Would it trouble your father if I wore this?" she asked Daphne, and the girl said not to worry, for in the first place she had never seen her mother wear the dress, and secondly, even if her father knew of it, he would never recognize it with the lovely floral addition.

Well pleased at having so effortlessly fixed on the bride's attire, the two of them retired to Daphne's room for a far more thorny undertaking—to choose a dress acceptable to a twelve-year-old girl. Sylvanne passed the better part of the afternoon helping Daphne into all sorts of gowns and kirtles, some the girl's own, some her mother's, and some Sylvanne's, but no matter how she tucked and reshaped them to suggest how they could be altered to fit to perfection, none met with Daphne's wholehearted approval. Among an ever-more frantic scattering of dresses they were found by Mabel, who poked her head in for a surprise visit. "I heard the wonderful news and just couldn't stay away," she gushed.

"This is fortuitous—we're in need of a third opinion to break the tie," Sylvanne told her.

"No no, Madame, any such major decision must be unanimous," Mabel insisted. Daphne modeled several of the leading candidates, while Sylvanne pinned them to improve their lines, but still the girl stubbornly refused to make up her mind. "Such a parade of lovely fabric overwhelms my head and makes it ache," Mabel said gruffly. "This is turning more arduous than I expected. Daphne, run down to the kitchen and get us some dandelion tea, there's a good girl. Have them put a bit of brandy in it."

"I'll get one of the maidservants to go," Daphne replied.

"No, I'd rather you did. I need to have a wee chat with Madame, alone. We'll be done by the time you get back."

"Fine—exile me from my own room," the girl said peevishly. She departed in a sulk.

Sylvanne said to Mabel, "I was wondering why you came and lingered, when I'm sure your husband and boys expect you home."

"Yes, well, I've something quite important to say, or at least I've been told it's important, although I don't thoroughly grasp its meaning," she announced. Sylvanne looked at her questioningly. Mabel continued, "I'm feeling a little like an actor in some troupe of travelling minstrels, for my lines have been fed me, and I repeat them without fully comprehending them."

"And who gave you these lines?"

"Your fiancé, Madame—your soon-to-be husband. He made a promise never to speak to a certain woman again, and determines to keep it, yet he feels there is one more message this woman needs to hear."

"She doesn't," Sylvanne said sharply.

"Please, Madame. Hear me out before you decide what your husband is up to, and whether he should be scolded or praised."

Sylvanne made an effort to rein in her sudden temper. "Alright then. Proceed. Declaim."

"Very well." After clearing her throat experimentally, as if tuning a musical instrument, and cupping her hands together over her chest in preparation, Mabel at last began to speak. "To the Lady who Dwells Within. That's who this is addressed to. Ahem. Dear Lady, who listens to me now—Lord Thomas has a favour to ask of you. Last night he dreamt that the man Derek spoke to you of a medicine, a potion of some kind, that your physician—he's not sure of her title, but she's a counsellor of sorts, and of late she suggested this potion to you, so that you would sleep without dreams." Here Mabel paused, to gauge Sylvanne's reaction.

"Continue," Sylvanne bade her.

"Lord Thomas would be most pleased, then, if you did indeed possess such a potion, that you should take it, so as to be affected by it, so as to be absent from Lady Sylvanne's mind on her wedding night, so that her first night of Holy and sanctified marriage might truly be a private joining between husband and wife. Furthermore, he asks that you consume this dream-stifling potion regularly, from now forward, so that he may concentrate his full devotion toward his new wife, whom he intends to love fully and completely. Are you alright, Madame?"

Sylvanne eyes had moistened. "Yes, yes," she answered. "I'm well pleased."

"Thank God for that," Mabel sighed with relief. "I wasn't sure whether you still took his peculiar ideas as nonsense, like you once did, or whether you've come to accept them as real."

"I must have accepted them," Sylvanne mused. "For the words you have relayed feel to me like a sweet gift. A wedding gift." Suddenly she felt so exhilarated she couldn't stand still.

"What is it, Madame?"

"I feel an urge to fly to him, to throw my arms around his neck, and thank him with kisses."

"Then do so!" Mabel cheered. "Run off to your lucky man, and I'll head homeward to mine."

The two of them met Daphne in the hall. "I'll be right back," Sylvanne called out in passing.

"What about your dandelion tea?" asked the startled girl.

"You drink mine for me," Mabel told her. "Your soon-to-be mother needs to kiss her husband-to-be."

Sylvanne found him in a nearby courtyard, reciting history to a half dozen boys. Without a word she took him by the hand and steered him to a shaded alcove, and told him, "Mabel has delivered your message. I thank you for the gesture, which pleases me very much." A little furtively she looked about to make sure no one was watching, then stood on tiptoes to kiss him on the lips, and afterward let him hold her close.

"I'm glad," he replied. "It's a token of my intentions. I want you to feel cherished."

"But what of Daphne's health?" she asked suddenly. "I thought of that later—that's the one risk we take in severing your connection to this woman's counsel."

"I've weighed the danger," he replied. "My feeling is that Daphne is cured—she's fitter now than she's ever been in her life. That Lady's dictums as to hygienic treatment healed the girl's arm, while such things as oranges and onion and garlic improved her physical health, and I will be forever in her debt for prescribing them. But I also give much credit to you, for the company you've kept with her, and the cheer you've brought to a lonely girl whose very heart and spirit were broken by her mother's passing."

"You give me too much credit," Sylvanne protested. She pressed herself close against him, her head on his shoulder. "The fates are strange animals," she murmured. "They brought me here for what seemed a dark purpose, and now they bestow happiness upon me. I pray their work is done, and they leave us from here to build joy upon joy."

48

Derek left a message on Meghan's phone, but she didn't return it. The next day he left another, and again she didn't respond. He saw Betsy across the fence and asked her what was up—she told him her mom was super busy with work and kind of depressed. On day three with still no contact he wanted answers, and was about to walk next door to take matters in hand when Meghan showed up on his doorstep.

He decided to keep it light. "Hey neighbour," he welcomed her. "I've been worried about you, not to mention dying to hear the latest—how'd the wedding go?"

"I don't know," she answered.

"What do you mean you don't know?"

"I'm taking sleeping pills to stop me dreaming."

"Uh-oh."

"Yep. Thomas asked me to. Because three's a crowd. He didn't want me there on the wedding night. He wants me to go away and leave them alone."

"Wow. First impression, though, he's probably right."

"I know he's probably right," she said. "They need to get on with their lives, and have a healthy, normal, loving marriage, a happily-ever-after. He's the grown-up who saw it and called it. It still hurts, though. Remember I told you it felt like I'd been dumped? Now I *really* feel like I've been dumped."

"Half dumped," Derek said. "I didn't dump you. Though I was beginning to think you'd dumped me."

"No, I didn't. I haven't. I just needed time. I got very angry, for a bit. I was mad at both of you—you and him. For conspiring against me."

"Not against you. For Sylvanne."

"I know that. I've calmed down. I'm on her side too. But I still need time."

"Of course you do. Your heart is half broken," he said. "Which is better than fully broken. It's like the glass half full—we can fill it back up. We can mend the heart."

"You're very sweet," she said. "I missed you."

"What would you like to do?" he asked gently.

"I'd like to lie down with you on your couch, just lie on your chest, and kind of be held, and comforted. No hanky panky, just tenderness. I'm feeling tender."

Derek led her by the hand and they lay down. It soothed her to curl herself against the contours of his body. He played with a few stray strands of her hair at her temple, and noted that she was making no effort to look into his eyes.

"Here's the deal," he said. "You taking those pills means he's got his privacy now, but it doesn't mean we do. He's still in me, taking this all in, right?"

"Yep," she replied. "It's unfair."

"So what should our strategy be? How do we proceed, knowing he's there?"

"I want to start pretending he's not. If I'm not dreaming him anymore it means I won't see him, and he'll become like an ex-lover, or ex-friend, or some guy I once had a crush on—he'll fade from my mind. He'll diminish, and then maybe, when I look in your eyes, I won't distinguish what's him and what's you—maybe I'll just start thinking it's all you."

"A lot of maybes," Derek said. "You know what I think? I think we should just relax. Thomas or no Thomas, in the end we're like any other couple trying to figure out if it's worth it—it's going to come down to how compatible we are, how lovable we find each other, and whether our neuroses clash or mesh. Right now it feels very good to lie here with your head on my chest. I wish we could just stay like this forever, but before too long we'll need to get up and carry on. When we do, let's just hold hands and keep walking forward. As long as we're holding hands we'll be fine."

She didn't say anything for a long time. He felt her breathing get slower, and synchronize to his own. With her head on his chest he couldn't see her eyes, and he thought she might be falling asleep. He liked the idea of them curling up and napping together—it would bring on a sense of warmth, of trust and healing. But suddenly she sat up and said, "You know what? If we're really talking about a future together, just aimlessly wandering into it holding hands isn't going to cut it."

"The plan is to get to know each other."

Meghan chose her words carefully. "Some things I know about you make it difficult to really imagine it could work out."

"Like what?"

"Like the way you drink, and smoke. You know what I'm going to do? I'm going to take a page from Sylvanne. I was so impressed with the way she just laid out her conditions. I'm going to lay down mine. First and foremost, no substance abuse."

"Well of course no substance abuse. No one likes abuse," Derek answered. "But there's also substance *use*—substances in small doses can actually be good. A glass of wine with dinner, an occasional puff of weed after a stressful day—that's substance use. It's moderate, and medicinal."

"Don't try to weasel out of it."

"I'm not weaseling, I'm negotiating."

"Okay, I'll be more specific. No drinking to get drunk, and no drugging just to get stoned. No partying your face off, in other words. No drugs harder than pot—"

"I don't do anything harder than pot anyway."

"—and no pot around Betsy, or me for that matter. It's the smoke I hate. I'd love it if you quit smoking."

"You drive a hard bargain, Miss Meghan."

"Not really. I'm already compromising on the pot. You can still sneak off and do it sometimes. Medicinally. Although what you have to be stressed about, I don't know. You don't even have a job."

"I don't need a job. I own this place, and I have money making money, not a lot, but enough to keep me out of the rat race."

"Must be nice," she said.

He brought his legs up to give her more space on the couch. She leaned back and rested her chin between his knees, looking at the playful smile on his broad face.

"I feel like quitting smoking, just to show you I can," he said.

"It's more the booze, really."

"No no, if I'm going to do it, do it right. Do it big. Booze, drugs, cigarettes—I'll tackle the whole shebang. Besides which, if we're going to hold hands and walk into the future, then Betsy will be there too, and she might want to hold my hand sometimes, and you'll have my other hand, and then, how would I smoke?"

"Exactly," she laughed. "It's not possible."

"So it's necessary I quit smoking, whether you want me to or not."

She kissed his knee happily, then made a face. "Your jeans don't taste very good," she said. "They're quite dirty, now that I look at them."

"I'll wash them more often. You see? I'm agreeing to conditions before you even express them. I must really like you."

49

Of all his vices Derek found nicotine the hardest to wean himself from, but after two weeks he could think about a cigarette without his teeth clenching with the craving of it. He hired a cleaning service and two meticulous women came to scrub his house from top to bottom for three days straight, and he arranged for one of them to come back every Thursday afternoon to keep it ship-shape. He stocked his kitchen properly, and started to cook, not just for himself, but for Meghan and Betsy. Sometimes they came over to his house to eat, but usually he carried the meal over to their place. Very quickly this became a routine, and after a month, with Meghan's approval, he built a gate in the fence between their back yards to speed the passage from kitchen to kitchen. One night at dinner he joked that they should just knock a hole in the shared wall between their town-houses and have one big place together. Betsy was very excited by that idea, and thought it would be the coolest thing in the world to show off to her friends that the two homes, so normal from the street, shared an amazing secret. "Let's do it!" she cried.

"I hate to be the party pooper," Meghan told her. "But it's a bit too rash and permanent at this stage."

"Maybe someday though," Derek said. "Then we could tear down the fence and have one big back yard, too."

"Yes! Awesome!" Betsy yelped. "We could even play proper badminton."

Meghan smiled. "Why do I always feel outnumbered by you two?"

"We operate on the same wavelength," Derek said.

On the sixth-week anniversary of his smoke-free sobriety he showed up on Meghan's back deck on a Friday afternoon and came in the kitchen without knocking. He had a handful of documents. "I need to you fill these out and sign them," he said.

For a moment she felt wariness, and, almost, dread. "What are they?"

"Character references. I have to get a criminal record check, too. I went out and got a job. Not a paying job, but a volunteer gig."

"Really?"

"Yeah. I went down to the Boys and Girls Club on Spruce Street to see what I could do to help out. I'm actually thinking of going back to school and getting my CYC."

"CYC?"

"Child and Youth Care. It's a certificate you need."

"I'm shocked," she said. "In a good way."

"Yeah, well. Being around Betsy so much has reminded me I like kids, and I'm good with kids. Working with them wouldn't pay real well but it's good for the soul. I'm lucky I'm set up financially, more or less, so I can do it for love."

The way he said the word love sent a tingle through Meghan. "Let me hug you," she said, and stood on tiptoes while he held her that way, so that she was nearly floating on air above the kitchen floor.

"I used to think hiding from the rat race and puttering around the property was the perfect way to live, but now I see that sitting on my ass for days and years was bad for me," he told her. "It allowed me to slip. Sobering up isn't just about quitting drinking, it's having a cascade effect."

"I'm so glad for you," she murmured. She pulled back to look into his face. "Funny, isn't it? You cleaned up, and now I wish I could."

"Sleeping pills still messing you up?"

"More and more."

"They're meant to be temporary. Time's up. Time to stop."

"I want to. They're horrible. I feel like a zombie—I never wake up refreshed or revived, or energized. Just, drugged. Sleep without dreams is like, half a life."

"I'm staying over, right? Don't take one tonight, and let's see what happens."

"Actually there's been a change in plan. Betsy's not going to her Dad's after all—she didn't want to, and I can't force her. So she's home."

"Oh." He shrugged good-naturedly. "You want to wait till I'm around to go off your meds?"

"I think so."

Suddenly they heard Betsy shout from the living room. "It's all right, you can stay, Derek!"

"Have you been eavesdropping?" Meghan called to her.

"Not on purpose." She came into the kitchen. "I know he stays here when I'm not here, so what's the difference?" she said.

"Nothing, I guess, if you can handle it."

"I can handle it."

After dinner and dishes they watched *Shrek Forever After* on DVD. In the early going Betsy had to explain a lot of back story to Derek, because he had never seen the first three installments of the series, and later Derek had to explain to Betsy what a metaphysical paradox was. Then it was her bedtime, occasioning a collision of wills between firm mother and feisty daughter that Derek stayed out of. When Meghan finally came downstairs from Betsy's bedroom she wore that look of triumphant exhaustion that every parent knows. She slid next to him on the couch and said, "So, a night of firsts. First night you get to stay over while the kid is home, and first night I go without the sleeping potion."

"How are you feeling about that?"

"A bit scared. But hopeful. I'd just love to have a regular old dream."

"What if you see our friend?"

"I don't know. I'll tell him he's been replaced."

"Maybe you should have a plan—try to talk to him, tell him you don't want to be there anymore. Supposedly we can control our dreams, if we consciously will ourselves to."

"I thought about that. I've looked into it online. There's a lot of BS out there. I'll just see what happens, try to stay with it, assert myself if I can. Not that I expect I'll really be able to. You dream what you dream."

"Yeah. But tell yourself you're in charge. Try to be comfortable with yourself."

"I'm comfortable with you. Especially since you told me about your new plans. All the boxes are getting checked off—you're smart, you're funny, you're good with Betsy, handy around the house." She smiled, and snuggled closer. "You're also handy in the bedroom. And now it seems like you're shedding that aimlessness that I considered to be your last major liability."

"Hurray for me."

"Exactly, Hurray for you."

In the morning she woke up and nudged him awake. Her smile reminded him of what needed to be asked.

"Well?"

"I saw them. Faintly, and from a new place, not inside Sylvanne's mind, but outside, more like an-out-of-body experience. Sylvanne is going to have a baby. She's thrilled, Thomas is thrilled, and I was happy for them too. Daphne looks great. I saw it all in a glance, and that's all I needed. It was like I was waving goodbye, being carried somewhere else. And I had another dream—you and Betsy in bright sunshine, you were trying to ride unicycles on a sandy beach and got all bogged down. But you were laughing about it, and then there was something about an orange juice maker, the old fashioned kind where you pull a big lever to squish the orange."

"I have one of those, somewhere."

"It was mounted on your handlebars. You were making glasses and glasses of it and passing them around."

"Unicycles don't have handlebars."

"Yours did. Hey, I dreamt about you!"

"And then you woke up, and here I was."

"Kiss me."

And he did.

ACKNOWLEDGEMENTS

Here's to The Editorial Department, a sunny bunch down in Tucson, Arizona. Morgana Gallaway designed this book, and Kelly Leslie did the cover. Karinya Funsett-Topping and especially the indomitable Jane Ryder helped me straighten up the mess and reminded me which kind of endings make for happier readers.